HIT OR MISSUS

Also by this author:

Freezer Burn (A Peri Minneopa Mystery)
The Hot Mess (A Peri Minneopa Mystery)
A More Deadly Union (A Peri Minneopa Mystery)
Clean Sweep (A Peri Minneopa Short Story)

What Would Erma Do? Confessions of a First Time Humor Columnist
Are You There, Erma? It's Me Gayle
Raising the Perfect Family and Other Tall Tales
You're From Where?
Holly Jolly Holidays

Murder on the Hoof
From the Horse's Mouth: One Lucky Memoir

HIT OR MISSUS

by

Gayle Carline

This is a work of fiction. All characters, organizations, places, and events portrayed in this novel are either products of the author's imagination or are used fictitiously.

Cover art by Joe Felipe of Market Me (www.marketme.us).

ISBN: 1-943654-19-0

ISBN-13: 978-1-943654-19-2

Published in the USA by Dancing Corgi Press

To my husband, Dale, for putting up with my shenanigans.

CHAPTER 1

In the end, it was a good thing Mr. Mustard didn't like coffee any more than he liked baths.

"I'm sorry, Mister," Dottie Peters told the large, orange tabby. "But you were stinky."

The elderly woman wrapped a thick towel around her wet, struggling cat and lifted him to the rim of the bathtub. She rested a moment, then hugged the bundle to her chest and rose. Steadying her body against the wall, she finally stood erect, more or less, while the cat fussed in her arms.

"Oof, hold still."

Dottie put her nose to the towel and inhaled the warm, primal scent of feline, mixed with baby shampoo. She moved the morning's newspaper from the old leather recliner and sat down, still gripping her entrapped cat. After fumbling with the remote until the TV clicked to life, she leaned back into the overstuffed chair and began massaging her furry hostage. The morning news show burbled with happy tones, but Dottie didn't smile.

"Bob used to sit here," she said as she rubbed. It had been two weeks and a day since her husband's heart attack, and in his absence, the cat had become her confidant. "He used to have his coffee here in the morning and watch The Price Is Right, remember?"

Mr. Mustard howled.

"I know, Sweetie." Dottie rubbed at the tears stinging her eyes. "If coffee didn't give me heartburn, I'd turn the channel, but I can't watch The Price Is Right without a cup of coffee. It just wouldn't be the same."

Mr. Mustard gave one last growl and disentangled himself from his terrycloth prison, leaping from his mistress's lap. He marched out of the room without glancing back, his tail twitching.

"Fine, Grumpy." She turned back to the TV and watched a young woman point out the latest traffic snarl, happy she didn't have to navigate southern California freeways. Everything she needed was less than six blocks away from her small bungalow. Bob usually drove their little beige sedan anywhere she needed to go.

"Suppose I'll have to do all the driving now," she said to no one, tears pooling again before they tumbled to her cheeks.

She and Bob were no spring chickens—she knew that. Still, the sight of him slipping from his chair like a bag of potatoes from a shelf, kept replaying in her mind. Death was inevitable, but did it have to be such a damned surprise?

She rose and shuffled into the kitchen. "I think I'll have a little coffee anyway—for Bob. I can always take some Tums later."

The yellow paint on the walls of the small kitchen had faded, and there were grease spots over the stove that could have been wiped away, if Dottie's eyesight was better. An oak table stood in the corner with two matching chairs. Only one of them had a cushion, for Bob. Dottie always joked she brought her own padding to any chair she sat in.

She stretched up to the cabinet above the sink and retrieved a small tin of coffee, decorated in a gay autumnal theme, an orange bow still on the lid. After filling the coffee pot, she made sure it gurgled and sputtered before she walked back into her bedroom.

While the coffee brewed, she changed into a housedress, a shapeless swath of blue cotton with small pink roses decorating the collar. She returned to the kitchen and filled a green mug halfway with dark, aromatic liquid, then went back to the recliner.

A cooking show blared on the TV, the celebrity hostess showing the viewer how to make grilled shrimp escabeche for a family of four.

"Whose child would eat that?" Dottie switched the channel to watch the game show. She sipped her coffee, and puckered.

"This tastes different than I remember." She took another drink and watched Drew Carey invite a screeching young woman on stage. Dottie sighed. Different host, different coffee, nothing stayed the same.

She picked up the paper from the table next to the chair and read it while she drank. "Damned vultures. Think just because Bob is gone, I'll sell out."

Her pale brow wrinkled as she pushed her glasses back up on her nose.

An adhesive note was stuck to the paper. She pulled it off and looked at the message scribbled in bold black. DECIDE NOW, with a phone number, screamed at her.

"Pushy SOB." She wadded the note in her gnarled fingers.

A feline voice trilled from the hallway and Mr. Mustard trotted into the room, his tail high and vibrating. Dottie smiled and tossed the note across the floor. The cat ran to the paper and batted it with his forepaws, before picking it up in his mouth and carrying it back to his mistress. He leapt to the recliner's arm in one graceful bound and dropped his toy on Dottie's lap.

She threw it again, and, once again, the tabby gave chase. Retrieving scraps of paper was the cat's favorite activity. Bob often joked they couldn't teach the cat to use the scratching post, but he could fetch like a damned dog.

Dottie looked up at the TV. Drew Carey appeared fuzzy, so she took off her glasses and cleaned them on her dress. It didn't help.

A moment later, she clasped her right hand over her breast, just as Bob had done two weeks ago. As she reached out for the telephone, she lost her balance and fell to her knees. She managed to dial '9' before losing consciousness.

Mr. Mustard returned to the recliner and sniffed the coffee, splashed across the carpet. Sneezing, he walked out to find a warm spot for a nap, taking the crumpled paper with him.

CHAPTER 2

"Peri, you see my other sock?"

"In the kitchen, under a chair."

"And my tie—"

"On the printer in my office." She rolled over on her side and pushed herself from the bed. "Okay. I'm up."

Skip walked over and kissed her forehead. "Stay in bed, Doll. It's only six."

She stretched her long legs out before putting her feet on the cool wood floor. "And yet, we've already had such a lovely chat." Yawning, she shuffled toward the bathroom. "I should run before my meeting, anyway."

Ten minutes later, Peri followed the smell of coffee to the kitchen and found Skip sitting at the table, reading the paper. He looked handsome in his creamy button-down shirt and chocolate slacks. A Placentia Police Department detective badge lay on the table, along with his gun.

"I thought you had to leave early." She dug around in the refrigerator, moving last night's takeout boxes to get to the cranberry juice.

"I've got enough time to read the sports page. What's on your agenda for the day?"

"New client at ten. Don Keller."

"Don Keller? The developer?"

Peri closed the refrigerator, a small bottle of juice in her hand. "That's him."

"Why does he want to see you?"

"Oh, I don't know, because I'm a private investigator and he has something to investigate?" She frowned. "What's wrong with him coming to see me?"

Skip put the paper down. "Nothing. It's just that, he's kind of high-end."

"So was Mrs. Cheavers, but she came slumming to my part of town." She swallowed a handful of vitamins with her juice. "Of course, her husband shot me, which only proves you can never judge people."

Skip rose and picked up his badge and gun. "Well, if this is another cheating spouse case, maybe you should ask Keller if his wife is packing before you take it." He pulled Peri to him for a kiss, then took a step back to look at her.

"Shouldn't you get some new running clothes?"

Peri looked down at her gray t-shirt and black spandex shorts. She grabbed the shirt and held it out toward Skip. "Property of the PPD. Don't you like it?"

"It's just looking kinda old and sad."

She laughed. "Since when do I care how I look when I'm running? As a matter of fact, why do you care?"

"You got a great body, Doll—"

She patted his cheek. "For a fifty-year old."

"Well you don't look more than thirty-five. But those shorts are all stretched out, and I'm pretty sure that's my shirt."

"Again, who cares? I'm running a couple of miles, after which I'll be a sweaty mess anyway."

"I just think you could look a little nicer—"

Skip's cell phone interrupted them. Peri wrapped a scrunchy around her thick, blonde ponytail and stuck it through an Angels baseball cap.

"That was Dispatch," Skip said. "They got a call from your neighbors. It's Mrs. Peters."

"Uh-oh. Is she?"

He nodded. "It's gonna be pretty gruesome over there. I guess no one noticed they hadn't seen her in awhile."

She winced. "Eew. Poor Dottie. Bob died of a heart attack just a few weeks ago, and now she goes."

"Sometimes it happens like that."

"Can I come with you to Dottie's?"

"I thought you were going running."

Peri leaned into Skip, tilting her face to meet his. "I was, but I'd rather visit the scene."

"You have that meeting at ten."

"It's not even seven. I just want to peek in, Skipper."

He grimaced. "Dressed like that?"

"Oh, dear God, what is it with you and my clothes this morning? Did you get up on the fashionista side of the bed?"

"Now, Peri—"

She threw the juice bottle into the recycle bin, causing the other plastic bottles to spring up and scatter on the floor. "Never mind. I'm going running."

"We on for dinner tonight?"

Peri turned to face her boyfriend. "I don't know—I gotta get my tiara out of the dry cleaners." Her final word hit at the same time as the slamming door. "Later."

Who does he think he is? Peri's mind raced as her legs pumped along the sidewalk in her Placentia neighborhood. Normally, she started out at a slow trot, stretching, and increasing her speed. Today, her anger spilled into her muscles.

Stevie Ray Vaughn played a scathing riff into her ears, louder than usual, but she didn't adjust the volume. Instead, she let the shrill music goad her into running faster, the cool October air waking her lungs. Small, Spanish-style bungalows flew past her vision as she loped down the street. Even in this working-class neighborhood, the tiny front yards were well manicured. She caught glimpses of flower beds with a variety of color, from tall birds of paradise to the lower night-blooming jasmine. The occasional whiff of the jasmine smelled delicious, and Peri noted how much she loved the tiny, tempting wafts of scent, even if she hated the same smell in a perfume bottle.

She moved to the pavement, where she liked to run whenever possible, as the asphalt was kinder to her knees, even if it meant keeping an eye on the traffic. All the way, she griped soundlessly at her boyfriend.

Skip Carlton, thinks he's all that, just because he's a detective on the Placentia force... a good-looking, single detective... how dare he complain about my running clothes? It's because of that stupid article in the Register last week.

The Orange County Register had published an interview with Skip as part of Chief Fletcher's desire to raise the dial on the PPD's friendly meter. Peri couldn't wait for the article to be published; after she read it, she couldn't wait to burn it. The female reporter made it sound less like a career profile and more like a resume for a dating service.

"Placentia's most eligible detective?" she'd read aloud. "Because we're not married, you're eligible?"

Skip acted perplexed. "I don't get it. All she asked was, if I was married."

"And you said?"

"No."

Damn his police training, she thought, remembering the conversation. *Never offer more information than you're asked. Now he thinks he's hot stuff, giving me fashion tips—about what to sweat in? What a horse's ass.*

Peri rounded the corner near Morse Elementary School and headed back toward her home. She could hear a vague cacophony of sound and glanced over at the campus. Children of various sizes and shades littered the grass, running and jumping and standing and falling. It seemed early for the school day – this was probably the day care shift. Adults, teachers perhaps, hustled in and out of the low, brick buildings.

A ball jumped against the metal fence surrounding the playground, and a small boy ran up to get it, red-faced. His mouth moved, but Peri couldn't hear him over the music pounding through her head. She decided to make a little detour and run by Dottie's house, just in case there was something to see.

In addition to being her neighbor, Dottie had been one of her clients when Peri owned her housecleaning business. She gave a discount to every elderly client, but she especially liked the Peters and knocked a few dollars more off their bill.

Two police cars, the coroner's van, and Skip's dark SUV were still parked in front of the house. Peri slowed down to a trot and crossed the street. She saw two shadows just inside the screen door. The smaller shadow, a female, leaned into the tall, male frame, who bent over her.

Peri stopped short of the yellow tape as soon as she recognized the tall shadow. Skip looked cozy with someone.

Part of Skip's job entailed comforting people, so she had no reason to be jealous. Still, something tugged at the bottom of her stomach, like sour milk. She wavered, briefly, and glanced down at her t-shirt, which was dark with perspiration. Was that a hole next to the 'D'? Maybe this wasn't her best look, even if she did want to snoop around Dottie's house.

Peri made a U-turn and headed for home. She trotted easily for a block before stopping. The hell with appearances, she wanted to see inside that house.

Sorry, Skip. Looking good will have to wait.

By the time she returned to Dottie's, she saw a familiar brunette walking toward the Coroner's van. In addition to being the assistant coroner, Blanche Debussy had been Peri's best friend since high school.

Peri slowed to a walk and met Blanche at the van. "I heard about Dottie. How bad was it?"

"She was definitely on the compost side of the street." The petite woman put her glasses in their case and looked up at her friend. "How are you?"

"Good, considering Skip and I started off with a fight this morning."

"How many rounds?"

"Fifteen. No decision." Peri laughed. "He got on my case today about my running clothes. I mean, really." She looked down at her outfit, gesturing. "What else do you run in?"

"Looks like what I wear."

"Exactly. I guess now that he's the PPD's most eligible bachelor, he needs me to dress like arm candy."

"What a horse's ass." Blanche's husky voice made every opinion sound like fact.

Peri looked up and saw Skip at the front door. She smiled and waved. "Yeah, but he's my horse's ass."

CHAPTER 3

Skip had smelled the decay as soon as he stepped onto the front porch. *Too bad Peri's not here,* he thought, *she could probably determine TOD from that super-sniffer of hers.*

He still felt vaguely uncomfortable about their conversation this morning. Peri's reaction surprised him. Granted, her trip through menopause had resulted in some enormous burrs under her saddle, but he didn't expect her to be so combative, when he was trying to be complimentary.

Officer Ella Mason held the door for him. In her mid-thirties, Ella had been on the PPD for five years, beginning as the property room clerk. She had worked her way into the field, keeping her uniform sharp and her mind sharper. Skip noticed she held the back of her hand to her washed-out face. He smiled a little, remembering his first murder scene.

"First D.B., Ella?"

She nodded, and turned to face the rose garden before taking a deep breath.

"She's been here a few days, sir. No sign of foul play."

Skip walked through the door into the small bungalow. He saw a petite brunette kneeling by the body, which was already showing the signs of decay. Covering his nose with a handkerchief, he knelt down beside her.

"Hey, Blanche, how's it going?"

She paused from her work and looked over her glasses at him. "Hey, Skip. Peri with you?"

"Why would she be?"

Blanche's look became a stare. "Because she lives two blocks away, she used to clean the Peters' house, and she wouldn't pass up a chance to look at the scene."

"She was going to come, but—" Skip couldn't admit their argument. "She's got a meeting this morning."

"Meeting, huh." Blanche scribbled in her notebook, then stood up. "Well, offhand, it looks like a heart attack, which only means there aren't any signs of anything else. I don't know if she was under a doctor's care. Pretty coincidental that Bob had a heart attack less than a month ago."

Skip stood and looked at the scene. The coffee cup lay on the carpet, a dark patch in a splatter from the chair. "Yeah, that's what Peri said. I suppose two heart attacks in two elderly people isn't that odd." He paused, thinking. "But a blood panel would be a good idea, even if she has a note from her doctor. I'd like to rule out poisons, overdose, that sort of thing."

"You bet."

"Maybe it's a coincidence, but we should cover our bases." Skip walked through the small house, to the single bathroom. He opened the mirrored medicine cabinet over the sink, checked under the counter and opened all the drawers.

"I don't see any prescriptions," he told Blanche as he returned to the living room.

He saw Officer Mason standing in the doorway. She appeared to be talking on a cell phone, her face flushed and body tense. He walked toward her; as he approached, she pushed a button and stuffed the phone into her pants pocket.

"Everything okay, Ella?"

She looked at him, opened her mouth, and burst into tears.

Crying women were not Skip's forte. He tried to be comforting, but he really wanted to tell them to snap out of it. Peri understood. Sure, she cried sometimes, but mostly when she was physically injured, and usually she acted like she wanted to tell herself to snap out of it. Bracing himself, he stepped in closer to the young officer. Her hair smelled like a piña colada.

"Something you want to talk about?"

"Sorry, sir," Ella replied, taking several breaths to calm her sniffles. "Personal matter."

"Need some time?"

"No, sir." She straightened and looked him in the eye, her face puffy.

Skip stepped back. He and Ella stood and stared at one another while a clock in the living room ticked through the awkward silence. Ella blinked first.

"It's my son. He's in the principal's office again. I can't keep him out of trouble."

"Do you need to go take care of it?"

"No, not this time." She shook her head. "I've been jumping down to the school every time they call. Jorge treats it like another day off. I told him this time he'd have to tough it out in the office until my shift ends."

"Can't his dad help out?"

"We don't see much of him."

"That's too bad." Skip didn't know what else to tell her.

"It's just hard for Jorge. He lives with me and my mom and my sister, and I think he feels like there are too many moms in his life and not enough dads."

"I understand. Maybe if he was on a sports team, or maybe he could be in that Big Brother program."

She looked up at Skip with a smile that told him his suggestions were nice but not new, or helpful. "We'll work it out, Detective."

"All right, then," Skip said, patting her shoulder. "See if you can find a name around here of someone to notify. Talk to the neighbors."

He watched Ella turn for the door, wondering if he had just been as useless as he felt, but was interrupted by Blanche. "Why don't you call Peri? She used to clean their house."

"Yeah, I know." Skip opened the top drawer of the desk next to him and rifled through some papers. Most were stubs from bills, a few lists written in a shaky hand, but nothing said, *In Case of Emergency*.

"She probably knows where their contact information is."

Skip opened another drawer. "Yeah, I know."

Blanche held up her phone and smiled. "I got her on speed dial."

"Thanks, Beebs, I'll take care of it." He retrieved his phone from its holder and pressed Peri's number. His finger poised over the Send key, he hesitated. Peri's sarcasm was the worst part of her.

Man up, Carlton, he thought, and pressed the button.

"Hi, you've reached Peri Minneopa, Private Investigative Services…"

Skip waited for the end of the greeting, happy to have avoided any more arguments. He left a message, and then resumed his search of the house. More papers were in a pile on the small accent table next to the recliner. Skip leafed through them, documents in legalese, describing a parcel of land, title searches and name affidavits. It appeared the Peters had bought land out in Palm Desert. The documents were dated within the last year, but Skip wondered why they were lying out on the table. On a hunch, he dug his cell phone out again and pressed a number. It answered after one ring.

"Bonham here." Placentia's crime scene unit consisted of one officer, Jason Bonham, who tagged and bagged evidence before sending it to the Orange County forensics lab.

"Jason, can you bring your kit to the Peters' residence? ...Yeah, it looks like natural causes, but her husband died recently, too... I know, but I just don't like coincidences."

Skip hung up and walked back through the house. Blanche was watching the gurney with Dottie's body being wheeled out by two young men.

"Everything okay with you and Peri?" Her gaze remained on the black bag.

Women were like sharks, he thought, *when it came to relationships, they could smell a drop of trouble in a sea of love*. "Sure, fine."

Blanche walked toward the door. "I've got another call, but I'll get the autopsy and tox screen results to you as soon as I have them." She smiled and waved on her way to her car. "There's Peri now."

Skip watched Peri lope up the sidewalk, then slow to a walk. She took her iPod from its casing around her arm and pressed some buttons, then put it back and took her ear buds out, draping them around her neck. He studied the way she pulled her cap down and her ponytail back as she started up the path to the house.

She stopped by the coroner's van and talked to Blanche. Skip saw the way the two women smiled and grimaced and laughed in a way that made him feel like he was the main event. Peri glanced up at him and waved, confirming his suspicions.

He stood at the door, ready to hold it for her, but she paused again, at the clump of police officers, chatting and smiling. They smiled back.

He had to admit, even in sweaty running clothes, Peri was a good-looking gal. Craig Daniels, a recently divorced detective about their age, laughed at something she said, and Skip felt just a pinch of jealousy, mixed with the pride of being her – her what?

"Boyfriend" was so high school, "significant other" so dry. Forget "soul mates", that was just plain chick-flick. There was no term to describe them, but he was hers and she was his and they knew it, even if they had no rings or paper or even shared living quarters to prove the fact.

Peri bounded up the steps to the front door. "Hey, Skip, did I miss much?" She took a deep breath, followed by a shallower one. "Wow, it smells in here."

"Body's gone, but come on in. I was trying to find a number for someone to notify."

She gestured toward the hallway. "You can check Bob's nightstand, but I know they didn't have any children. They might have siblings—I think I remember a Christmas card from a brother."

A plaintive meow came from the hall as a large, orange tabby appeared. He trotted over to Peri, only looking at Skip to blink before leaning his body into her legs.

"Mr. Mustard, I forgot about you." She bent down to scratch his back. He arched his spine into her nails, his head cocked and eyes closed in kitty bliss. "This is Dottie and Bob's cat."

"He won't be able to stay here," Skip said. "I'll call Animal Control."

Peri continued to massage the cat, from face to rump. "Like, the pound?"

"I guess. Why?"

"Hmm, nothing. Well, actually, when I was little, I used to go to the shelter in Salinas with my mom. She was a rescuer."

"No wonder you don't do pets."

"It was nothing like that. I've told you about my folks. They were free spirits, but they weren't hoarders. Helen would take the adoptable pets home, spend some time socializing them, then unload them on gullible neighbors."

Skip laughed. "Gullible, huh? How'd your dad like your mom's hobby?"

"Erik didn't mind."

"I still can't believe you call your folks Erik and Helen."

Peri stood up and stretched her arms skyward. "Like I said, free spirits." She looked over at Mr. Mustard, who had strolled away to sharpen his claws on the leg of the sofa. "How long does he have, til, you know?"

"Til what? Oh, I think they keep them for a week before they put 'em to sleep."

"Really?"

"Yeah, I think." He watched Peri walk over and scratch the cat again. "Maybe less."

Mr. Mustard, having reached his fill of attention, nipped Peri's hand and ran back down the hallway.

She sighed and rubbed her forehead. "I know I'm going to hate this, but I'll take him home with me."

Skip looked at her. "The woman who can't keep goldfish alive? You know, you can't flush a cat, Doll."

"Ha ha. It's just temporary, until I can find a new home for him. Besides, I doubt if he'll let me forget to feed him. Fish don't meow."

The cat bounded back into the room, stopping at Peri to butt his head against her shin before dropping something at her feet. She reached down and picked it up.

"Mr. Mustard likes to play fetch." She opened the wadded paper and read. "'Decide now, five-five-five, oh-two-six-four. Think it's anything?"

Skip took the note from her. "I don't know, but we'll run it down. As soon as Jason gets here, I'm off. Want to get together later for lunch?"

"Sure, um, I've just got that meeting." Peri looked at her watch. "Crap, I'm running late. Can you drop the cat over at my place? His crate's in the hall closet, litter box in the bathroom, food should be on the second shelf in the pantry."

"Oh, Doll, I don't have time—"

"Come on, Skipper, please? I can't carry all that stuff back without a car." She reached up and kissed his nose. "I'll buy lunch."

Skip smiled. "Think you can afford me?"

She leaned into him and ran her hand down his shirt, her fingers massaging his chest. “I think I can make you forget about lunch altogether.”

CHAPTER 4

Peri usually didn't mind the steady 78-degree temperature maintained in her office, but today it wouldn't do. Meeting a wealthy client like Don Keller meant dressing for more success than usual, so she had worn her charcoal suit, which was tailored, professional, and too warm for autumn in southern California. Upon entering her office, she cranked the thermostat down to seventy.

Cold flooded the small space. Peri stood by the vent to push the air down the front of her sapphire blouse and up over her temples until she was sufficiently dry. The hormone regimen had taken care of most of her hot flashes, but stress and sudden activity could still trigger a round of profuse sweating. Comfortable at last, she returned the thermostat to its normal setting and put her suit jacket back on.

Keller was due in her office at ten. At ten thirty, Peri heard a loud male voice coming down the hall. She couldn't quite make out words, but no one else was talking, which meant the guy was either on a cell phone or a raving lunatic. Just at the point where she wanted to go outside and thump whoever was blabbering, her office door flew open and a man charged in. He let the door slam behind him and looked at Peri.

She rose and extended her hand. "Mr. Keller? I'm—"

"John, he's been telling us to wait a week for the past month." Keller ignored her and dragged the guest chair around until it was halfway toward the door, facing the wall to her right. He sat down, propping an ankle on the opposite knee and alternately glancing at the door, then out the window. A large silver Bluetooth earpiece was implanted in his right ear, effectively cutting her off from any conversation with him as he continued talking on the phone. "I know you like the guy, but we can't give him any more time. Get the paperwork started, I'll be in to sign it later."

Peri sat back and watched the scene, astonished, wondering why she wanted him as a client, apart from his deep pockets. From his navy wool suit to his shiny Oxford shoes, he oozed both money and power. The faint scent of high-end cologne drifted across the room, a combination of sandalwood and cigars that crawled up her sinuses and clung to the front of her skull. She hated cologne.

Mr. Keller continued to yammer, unconcerned about her presence. For a real estate developer, he wasn't very charming. *With the rich and mighty, always a little patience*, Peri thought, remembering last night's viewing of *The Philadelphia Story*.

She tried again. "Mr. Keller—"

He held a hand out to silence her as he prattled on with the unseen caller. Peri felt the warm glow of irritation creep up her chest. To hell with patience, she didn't want this client badly enough to be abused for the privilege.

She reached into her pink snakeskin tote and pulled out her iPod, selected a song, and plugged it into the docking station. The Who's "My Generation" began playing. Peri pointed the speakers toward Keller and pressed the volume controls until the walls vibrated with each stroke of Keith Moon's drumsticks.

At the first sound of music, Keller gave a disapproving look to the iPod, then scooted his chair closer to the door. By the time the volume reached critical mass, he was glaring at Peri and shouting over the noise.

"Just a minute, John," he said as he left the office.

Peri turned the music off. She hoped Keller wouldn't tell all his friends what a horrid witch she was, but he was so disrespectful, she almost didn't care. Besides, she had plenty of other clients who would rebut his claim. She took off her jacket and opened her laptop to work on some billing.

As her computer whirred to life, the door opened and Don Keller walked back in. He pulled the chair up to the desk and sat down, facing Peri. She was happily surprised, until he opened his mouth.

"Miss Minnowpia, are you ready to discuss business? I don't have a lot of time."

Despite her desire to throw something large and heavy at his head, she kept her expression as neutral as possible. "Neither do I, Mister Keller. If the appointment you made with me was inconvenient, then you need to reschedule. I have other clients to see after you, and I have no intention of making them pay for your lack of consideration."

She had no other clients to see, but her blood had gone from boiling to pure steam heat.

"And by the way, it's Minn-ee-OH-pa." She sat back and stared at the rich businessman, then looked down at her watch. "But you can call me Peri if it's easier. Now, what can I do for you?"

The hum of a vibrating cell phone interrupted them. Keller looked at his phone, and then at Peri. The moment hung between them like a heavy fog, the phone's low tone purring at intervals. At last, Keller reached down and turned his phone off.

"I need someone to investigate my wife."

Peri opened a file on her laptop. "I can do that for you, Mr. Keller. I'm assuming you suspect your wife of having an affair."

He smiled, revealing a row of perfect teeth, the front two slightly pronounced, all white as porcelain against his tan. Peri noted his wavy blonde hair, blue eyes and dark eyebrows, and wondered how much was good genes and how much was the work of professionals.

"Let's just say I wonder how she spends her days. Vicki Cheavers recommended you. She said you were very thorough and very discreet."

More discreet than she is, Peri thought. Her client told her philandering husband who she'd hired to track his movements, and the husband repaid Peri by trying to kill her.

Handing him several papers, she said, "This is my standard contract and statement of my rates. If it's agreeable, you can sign it and we'll get started."

She took the signed documents back from him and placed them in a folder. "So, what makes you so curious about your wife's whereabouts?"

"Little things. Some I can understand, but some of them—" He reached into his jacket and pulled out a small notebook, then opened it and skimmed through the pages. "Consistent tardiness for one."

"Is this something new?"

Keller tilted his head, as if thinking. "Yes and no. Nikki's always been scatterbrained. I mean, I love her, but she can be the definition of a dumb blonde sometimes. So she's been late to things before, but lately it's, I don't know, different."

"Can you pin down 'different' a little? Is she late to every event?"

"Maybe not every event, but more than she used to."

"How about her demeanor when she's late? Has that changed?"

Keller nodded. "Maybe that's it. You used to know Nikki was late. You'd hear high heels clicking, then she'd burst into the room. I swear the lights would get brighter, just from her energy."

"And now?" Peri typed on her computer as she spoke.

"She slinks in, doesn't announce herself. By the time I see her, I have no idea how long she's even been there."

"How long has this been going on?"

"I'm not certain, but maybe as long as six months. I guess I just wanted to think everything was normal." He reached into his pants pocket and pulled out a slip of paper. "Then there's this. I found it in our trash."

Peri took it from him. It was a receipt from the Titan bookstore, on the campus of California State University, Fullerton. Sunglasses and a t-shirt were purchased. "And what's the significance of this?"

"Nikki's a USC grad. She'd have no reason to be on the Fullerton campus, much less buy a shirt and sunglasses there."

"So you suspect her of buying these items for someone else?"

"I've never seen her wear them."

"Have you talked to her about any of this?"

He shook his head. "Odds are, she won't tell me the truth. Why should I tip my hand?"

Peri sat back and smiled. "Pre-nup?"

"I don't think we need to discuss that." He tore several pages out of his notebook and tossed them on the desk, then pulled several bills from his wallet and handed them to her.

"Thank you, Mr. Keller." She put the money and notes in the folder, and wrote a receipt. "How do you want me to get in touch with you?"

"Call my cell and leave a message, nothing too detailed. I'll call you back." He opened the door, and then turned, smiling. "Looks like your next client is running a little late."

Peri stared at him, smiling politely. "Some clients aren't very considerate, are they?"

She glanced at her watch as the door clicked shut. A little past eleven did not signal the lunch hour, but she hadn't eaten anything, apart from some cranberry juice. She had promised lunch with Skip, so she called him.

"Sorry, Doll, I can't get away before one," he told her.

Lunch plans cancelled, she stopped at a Chinese restaurant and picked up a quick bite to take home, where she could do a little research on Nikki Keller.

CHAPTER 5

Two steps into her kitchen, Peri's shins made contact with a soft but immovable object. She stuttered forward, trying to stay on both feet and hold onto the bag of Chinese food she'd just bought at Pick Up Stix. The object yowled as her foot came down on it and she fell to her knees, sending her chicken teriyaki bowl and egg rolls dashing across the floor and into the wall, where the container tops exploded.

"Ow-ow-ow." Pain pulsed from her hands to her elbows, her knees to her hips. She eased back onto her heels and rubbed her palms, looking at the chaos that was supposed to be her lunch, now splashed on the wall and floor.

Her new guest wandered over to the mess and sniffed. He picked up a piece of chicken and proceeded to shred and eat it.

"Damn cat, I forgot about you." Peri stood and limped to the paper towels.

Mr. Mustard sat and licked his paws while she picked up the food, then bolted away when she got out the spray bottle of cleanser.

Later, as she curled on the couch and ate a peanut butter sandwich while reading her notes, she felt a warm prickle on the back of her neck, as though she was being watched. She looked up to find two large, yellow eyes staring, unblinking, at her.

"Finding everything you need here?" She reached out and rubbed his ear. "Poor kitty, losing Bob and Dottie within a month. Don't worry, I'll find a good home for you. Someone who loves kitties."

Peri finished her sandwich and thought about Bob and Dottie. It wasn't unusual for elderly couples to die within weeks, or even days, of each other. Still, she thought it was curious.

She wadded up her napkin, and heard a strange, giggling sound. The cat at her side leaped to attention, staring at the paper ball in her hand. She held it up.

"You want this?"

The cat's tail vibrated. Peri threw the napkin across the room and watched him run after it, capture it, and return to her, the napkin in his mouth. She laughed and threw it again. The tabby gave chase, then dropped the napkin at her feet and waited. They spent a few minutes in this game, until the cat suddenly walked away and curled up in the window for a nap.

Peri thought about their game, and remembered the morning's events.

The paper Mr. Mustard gave me – "DECIDE NOW" – what was that phone number? She closed her eyes and visualized the note. It had been written in bold, dark print, making it easy to recall. Five-five-five, oh-six-two-four. She reached for the phone and dialed.

A woman answered, her voice low and words enunciated. "Keller and Patterson, how may I direct your call?"

"I'm sorry, I think I misdialed—is this 555-2624?"

"No, ma'am, it's oh-six-two-four."

Peri apologized once more and hung up. Why would Dottie have a note to call her client's office?

Forcing herself back to her own case, she logged on to her laptop and did a preliminary hunt for Nikki Simms Keller. A pass through the woman's internet presence was enough to give Peri indigestion. According to Classmates, Nikki Simms enjoyed life as a high school cheerleader before attending the University of Southern California as a communications major.

She checked Facebook next. Usually, people had their privacy settings so no one could read their information, but updates to the online social network sometimes reset preferences. Nikki's privacy settings were in the middle of the road, so Peri could see some of her information, such as her friends, her photos, and her notes.

Looking at her friends' photos, Peri saw one that looked familiar, Carol Hanlon. Carol was a woman she had once cleaned house for and was now in her Facebook friend list. She guessed Carol was Nikki's friend because they both belonged to the Alta Vista Country Club. Clicking on Carol's name, Peri was able to read some of Nikki's status updates.

"Party time tonight for all my Bettys," was the latest.

What are Bettys"? Peri searched the Internet, trying to figure out the meaning. Google was of no help; all of the pages were about businesses with 'Betty' in the name.

"No, I don't mean Betty's Baked Goods," she told her computer.

She printed basic information about her client's wife, including her previous addresses and criminal history. Peri glanced at them as she put them into a large purple folder with a number on the top. Apart from a few recent traffic citations, Nikki had no criminal history, and it didn't look like she had spent any significant time outside California.

The question of Dottie Peters and Don Keller's development firm tugged at the back of Peri's brain, so she decided to take a break and do a little digging in another direction. She was still wandering aimlessly through Dottie and Bob's histories when she heard a key in the back door, followed by the sound of the hinges, a simultaneous thump and cat's scream, and then Skip's growling expletives.

"Watch out for the cat," she said.

An orange streak flashed by her as the cat ran toward the bedroom. Skip walked in a few moments later with a bottle of beer.

"Thanks for the warning." He reached down and kissed her before collapsing into the couch.

"Rough day?"

"Not bad, except for Dottie. Death just leaves me feeling kinda… spent."

Peri put her laptop aside and wrapped her arms around him. "Sorry, Babe. Even when someone's older, it's hard." She kissed his neck. "And the older I get, the younger Dottie seemed."

They sat, entwined, for awhile, listening to the music from the stereo. Peri had put on Joe Sample, and the strains of smooth jazz piano floated through the room like a grownup lullaby.

She reached for his beer. "What's for dinner?"

He glanced at his watch. "It's pretty early. We could go for sushi."

Peri caught his wrist and checked the time. "Five on a Tuesday. Hmm, I guess Fish in a Bottle won't be that busy."

Their heads bent together towards the watch, his upper lip close enough to brush her lower one. In less than a second, they were kissing, losing themselves in the moment while they tried not to spill the beer.

"How hungry are you?" He nuzzled her neck. "Could we get something a little later?"

"Mmm, sounds tempting, but I could eat shoe leather right now. The damn cat spilled my lunch."

He kissed her again. "Here one day and he's already ruining our love life."

She stroked his cheek. "Well, feed me and we can get back to business."

CHAPTER 6

Under normal conditions, Peri liked to show up early in a client's neighborhood and park a few houses away to observe the comings and goings of the person she was tracking. The Kellers lived near the Alta Vista Country Club, their house backing up to the golf course. This small area around the country club was the high-end of Placentia; the homes were large, even if the lot sizes were small, and all of them maintained their million-dollar worth, regardless of the economy.

Mr. Keller had told Peri his wife was usually still asleep when he left at seven, but Peri didn't want to miss anything, so she pulled into the Alta Vista community a little past six in the morning. The Keller house was on a corner, which would not have made parking in an unobtrusive spot difficult, but her first pass through the quiet streets made her realize she couldn't park anywhere and remain unnoticed. A little blue Honda sedan would be considered nondescript in most neighborhoods, but not here. The curbs were littered with BMWs and Audis, and her econo-car would stand out like a sore thumb.

She passed a jogger as she drove around the block to the main drag out of the enclave, and tried not to watch the woman stare at her. In her rear view mirror, she saw the easy kick of tanned legs as the jogger tossed one more glance over her shoulder and continued on her route. This was not going to be easy.

The thoroughfare onto their street was not so ritzy. Block walls bordered the sidewalks, making the boulevard look stark. A few random cars were parked here, of the more economical variety. Peri found a spot on the side where she could blend in with the others and still see a corner of the Kellers' driveway. She might not be able to see details, but she could at least tell when a car was pulling into or out of the drive. Tucking down in the seat, she pulled her black ball cap over her brow, put her camera in her lap, and waited for movement.

A few minutes later, she saw the jogger again, running toward her at a healthy pace. Peri tried to push her tall frame further into the seat, but the woman didn't appear to notice her, allowing Peri to get a better look. The woman looked sleek in her fitted running clothes, black spandex capris and a turquoise, racer-back top. She wore a matching ball cap and Peri could see a long brunette ponytail swing like a pendulum as she ran.

She was definitely from the neighborhood. Peri had seen plenty of these women, and was always amazed at the 'something extra' they possessed. It wasn't that their skin was just tanned, it was golden and smooth, as if they had it buffed and polished every morning. And their hair wasn't simply blonde or brunette, it had an additional sheen of copper or silver or gold to make it burn brilliant in the sun. They wore makeup that never smudged and lipstick that never disappeared from their soft, unwrinkled lips.

Looking that good must be exhausting, even if I had the money. Peri licked her lips. They were dry, as usual, so she applied some balm.

By seven o'clock, she watched Keller drive out in his Mercedes SUV, a sleek dark silver model that exuded luxury. She thought he glanced at her car, but wasn't sure. A few other residents drove past, but none paid any attention to her. A flickering light in her rear view mirror distracted her, so she looked up.

It was a police car.

Although she wasn't doing anything illegal, she had a sudden urge to hide her activities. Rumor had it, the police didn't really like private investigators and might try to make her job difficult.

She stashed her camera under the seat, and fumbled in her glove compartment as the officer approached, looking for her insurance card, registration, and a reason to be parked in a high-end neighborhood. There was a first-aid kit, a flashlight, two old tampons and a notebook. She took the notebook.

"You okay, ma'am?" The officer stood just behind her open, driver's side window. Peri recognized him at once, Officer Kenneth Chou.

"Yes, Officer. Is there a problem?"

"No, ma'am, we just had a report that a car had been stopped here for awhile."

"And you wanted to make sure I wasn't dead or something?"

The young, Asian policeman smiled. "Or something."

Peri held up her notebook. "I'm taking notes."

His smile remained, unchanged.

"I'm counting the number of cars in the morning, to see whether we need a traffic light at the intersection."

He continued to smile.

His stare was making her nervous, but she tried not to let it show. "There are a lot of new homes here, you know. Traffic has increased. We need to think about the children who walk to school this way."

A car rolled by them, so Peri wrote in the notebook. "See? There goes one more."

She wasn't certain if he believed her, but he suddenly spoke. "Aren't you Detective Carlton's friend? I don't know if you remember me, but I worked the Needles case."

"Yes… yes, of course… Officer Chou, isn't it? How have you been?"

"Good, thanks. You working a case?"

"Kind of." Peri didn't want to give away too much information. "I'm doing some research for a background check. Pulled over to write up some notes."

"Oh, sure. If another call comes in, I'll handle it."

"Thanks, Officer." Peri smiled at him. "I'll be going soon, anyway."

She watched him walk back to his car, talk on his radio and prepare to leave. As he pulled away from the curb, the jogger reappeared in Peri's side mirror. This time, she caught the glimpse of a tattoo on the woman's ankle, obscured by her sock. Again, she didn't look over at Peri as she passed, but Peri could have sworn she saw the woman smile.

The street grew quiet again and Peri settled back to wait. An hour later, she finally saw a metallic blue BMW whip out of the development, with a stunning blonde behind the wheel. This was Nikki Keller, in all her morning glory.

Peri rolled away from the curb, watching Nikki turn left onto Alta Vista Street before she drove forward to follow. Even though it was small, the little sports car was easy to tail from a safe distance, and Peri's Honda was able to get lost among the rest of the vehicles on the road.

She traipsed along as her client's wife ran mindless errands, to the dry cleaners and the local Bank of America, before stopping at the Brea Mall. Peri watched Mrs. Keller enter the Glen Ivy Day Spa. The spa offered everything from massages to pedicures. After waiting ten minutes, Peri entered.

The front desk sat at the entrance to a gift shop on the right and a lounge area to the left. A small door past the chairs probably led to the spas. The piped-in music was an inoffensive tune played by a trio of harp, flute and running water, and the scents of several flowers and herbs fought for control of Peri's nose. A young woman, exotic in an Asian-Hispanic-Polynesian way, looked up from her computer screen behind the desk and smiled at Peri as she approached.

The phone rang and the girl answered. "Just a moment," Peri heard her say, then watched her walk over to the gift shop.

It was an opportunity Peri couldn't resist. She quickly moved around to the side of the desk and scanned the appointments on the computer screen. Nikki Keller was here for a manicure and pedicure with Emma. The girl returned.

"Sorry about that," she said. "May I help you?"

"I was interested in your services. Do you have a brochure?"

The young girl handed Peri a small catalogue, done in soft neutrals and matte finish. Peri thanked her and left, returning to her car.

As she waited for Nikki to finish her manicure, Peri read the brochure. *Holy crap, fifty bucks to get your nails painted?* At some point, she might need to get chummy with Emma, but not until she had to, not at those prices.

Two hours later, Nikki's next stop was the Alta Vista Country Club. The club was a jewel in Placentia's crown, a yawning sea of greens that reached up to Rose Avenue, crossed Alta Vista and came to rest at Buena Vista Street.

Peri parked in a section far away from Nikki's sports car and checked her watch. Twelve thirty seemed too late for a golf game, but what did she know? A jaunty little tune began playing in her Bluetooth, so she tapped her earpiece and answered.

"You busy?" Blanche's voice was unmistakable.

"Working a case. I'm waiting outside the country club, thinking of going in. Why?"

"No reason. I got the day off and was bored. Thought I'd see if you wanted to come over."

Peri had an idea. "Want to join me for lunch at Alta Vista?"

"Oooh, can I be part of your operation?"

"Yeah, my very special ops team – of one. I'll go in and get us a table and nose around for info."

"I'm ten minutes away."

Removing her ball cap, she fluffed her hair away from her scalp, and then put on a pair of wire-rimmed glasses with clear lenses. She also slipped out of her gray zippered hoodie, before stepping out of the car.

Tall glass and wood doors stood at the end of a long colonnade of stone columns, which supported an oxidized metal roof. Square, window-paned lights hung inside, illuminating the way.

Peri watched herself walk toward the door in its glass reflection and stopped. When did her khakis get so wrinkled? And her blue polo shirt, the one she liked so much because it brought out the blue in her eyes, looked baggy and tired. Were these people going to believe she could afford to join their country club?

She took another step forward. *Dressed up or not, someone should be able to give me information.*

She hesitated. *But I might get more information if I was dressed like everyone else.*

Peri watched her hands smooth over her slacks in the reflection. Beyond her image, inside the clubhouse, she saw someone walking past. With a deep breath, Peri set her shoulders back, lifted her chin and reached for the brass handle.

Maybe Skip is right, I do need a little shopping trip. After I talk to some employees in this place.

The foyer was large and reflected the craftsman-style architecture of the exterior. Rich browns and caramels with slashes of burgundy were brightened by the light from the floor-to-ceiling windows that peeked from the rooms in the back. Peri heard the quiet murmur of a man's voice announcing scores, so she guessed one of the rooms was a bar.

An older woman was on the phone, checking a computer screen. "I see a foursome for tomorrow morning," she told the caller. "But nothing under Barber."

While she waited for the crisis to be resolved, Peri looked at the latest newsletter. Very glossy, high end printing with lots of pictures, it told of members and their accomplishments, as well as their absences. Peri recognized Don Keller's partner, John Patterson, in a small blurb about having knee surgery. The article wished him a speedy recovery, as the Heritage Golf Tournament and Banquet was coming up.

The woman turned toward Peri and smiled. "May I help you?"

"My boyfriend and I were thinking of joining the club, and I was wondering if you had any brochures."

The woman stood, almost as tall as Peri, and reached across the desk. She was elegant in her crisp, long-sleeved white shirt and navy slacks, her silver hair pulled back in a loose ponytail. A small pin on her shirt said 'Linda'. Holding out a blue folder with a business card, she told Peri, "This folder has all of our fees, and services. And this is the manager's card. You can call Jeff if you have any—"

At that moment, a collected burst of laughter from the bar interrupted them.

Peri smiled at her. "Sounds like a lively crew."

"Yes, that group of ladies meets here for lunch every week."

"Wow, so they're members—do they play golf here as well?"

"Oh, yes, they're a regular foursome."

Peri nodded and smiled. "How lovely, to have a group of friends to do things together." She picked up the folder. "Thank you so much, Linda. I have to discuss this with my boyfriend, but I hope to be in touch soon."

Another round of laughter could be heard from beyond the foyer. Peri looked up, tapped the folder against her palm, and hesitated. "You know, maybe I'll have lunch here, if it's okay. Give me time to read over this information and see if I have any questions."

"Absolutely," Linda told her. "Our restaurant is open to the public."

Peri turned toward the bar and felt her chest tighten. If she guessed right, Nikki's group of friends would be as casually perfect as darling Nikki. She smoothed her wrinkled khakis one more time, blew out the air she had trapped in her lungs, and walked toward the restaurant.

It felt like being back in high school.

CHAPTER 7

The room was a study in contrasts. The polished oak of the tables, chairs and bar could have darkened the space, but the pale walls and full-length windows stretching across the back of the room lifted it into the light. There were a few occupied tables, and a couple of servers strode from the kitchen to the diners and back again. A black man with gray on his temples and a roadmap of years on his face wiped the bar, occasionally glancing at the TV screen, where a baseball game was in progress.

A young, lithe woman in a simple uniform of white shirt, black slacks, met Peri at the door and led her to a table near the windows. Nikki and her friends were seated near the bar, all as coiffed and beautiful as she imagined. She gave them a relaxed glance as she walked past, and catalogued two brunettes and an ash blonde in addition to Nikki's golden curls. One of the brunettes looked up from her salad, and Peri could feel the intensity of her gaze as much as she could see it in her peripheral vision.

The hostess offered her the seat beside the window. This didn't give Peri more than a slight side view of Nikki's table, but she didn't want to appear suspicious, so she sat down. The same woman came by to take her order. She asked for a spinach salad and iced tea, then opened the brochure and began to read.

Twenty thousand dollars? Peri fluffed her hair and tried not to grimace as she read. *Plus annual dues? And monthly dues?* She turned the page. *Green fees? Isn't the golf course green enough?*

Laying the packet aside, she studied her surroundings. To her left, golfers dotted the grassy carpet outside. She thought they looked similar in the way they walked around the area, faces tilted to the ground, occasionally looking up, as if gauging the distance. They were all tanned, wearing standard issue polo shirts, dressy shorts, white socks and golf shoes. The men wore hats. The women had a mix of hats and visors, but it didn't matter. Their faces were all still golden from the sun.

"Hey, Girlfriend."

Peri looked up to see Blanche, casually gorgeous in a pair of tailored, knee-length tan shorts and a sheer lilac blouse, the lace of a white camisole peeking out. She got up to hug her friend and gestured to a chair.

"How nice to see you," Peri told her.

They motioned to the server, who came over and took Blanche's order, giving Peri another opportunity to glance at Nikki's table. They were lively and loud, which meant it should be easy listening.

The server brought their drinks.

"So, thinking about joining?" Blanche pointed to the brochure.

"Possibly." She noticed the volume of her own voice. As much as she enjoyed having her friend here for support, it dawned on Peri she would not be listening to Nikki's table if there was too much conversation at her own.

"You're a member, maybe you could explain what this means." She placed the brochure next to Blanche and leaned in. As Blanche looked at the paper, Peri whispered, "I need you to identify who is talking at that table behind me."

"Hmm." Her friend pointed. "Oh, those fees only count if you aren't a resident. Here, give me a pen and I'll circle the ones you'd pay."

As the server arrived with their salads, Peri heard her cell phone. Tunneling through her wallet, car keys, and assorted flotsam, her fingers closed around a familiar object, a small digital voice recorder. She often used it to take notes. While her hand was still buried, she turned the recorder on. Perhaps she could capture their conversation and listen to it later.

Pulling her phone out, she looked at the number. “Skip.”

“Did you guys kiss and make up?”

“You know we never stay mad for long.” She swirled the baby spinach leaves around to coat them with raspberry vinaigrette and picked up a fork full of leaf, mango, and candied walnut. A crumb of feta cheese clung to the leaf and completed the sweet-salty-umame trinity in her mouth. “We’ve had worse arguments.”

“Oh, yeah. I remember when you tried to live together.”

“I might have thrown a few objects,” Peri said.

“To get your point across?”

“Hairbrushes are good for punctuating sentences.”

They laughed, loudly, until Peri noticed she wasn’t hearing the women behind her. She looked at her friend and rolled her eyes in an attempt to point to the table she was watching. Blanche smiled and gave her a small nod.

“So what did Don say?” The question from the table was asked by a voice that sounded like a muted trumpet.

Peri looked at Blanche and pointed back to the brochure. “What about this?”

“Some people like to pay extra for that,” Blanche said as she picked up the pen and scribbled, *Susan Leske*.

“Oh, I don’t know.” This voice was high, almost childlike.

Peri took the pen and wrote *Nikki?* Blanche nodded, as the voice continued. “He was all, ‘Nikki, do you have to find the most expensive dress in the mall? Who is this Michael Course guy, anyway?’“

Several women joined her laughter.

“Course? Like golf course?” Peri noted this voice was lower, and the words had a bit of a slur to them. She wondered if this woman had lived in the South for awhile.

Lisa Silvan, Blanche wrote.

A soft, languid voice seemed to quiet the whole table. "Your husband needs a lesson in designers, that's all. Perhaps we could instruct him in the difference between Michael Kors and Alta Vista."

Laughter started again, although it didn't erupt as much as it bubbled.

"Oh, Kim, it doesn't matter." This was Nikki again. "Don doesn't really care. He just likes to tease me."

As Blanche scribbled another note in the sidelines, Peri heard Lisa say, "Clinton does the same to me. What are those shoes again? Choo-choo trains?' They tease us, but they love it when we look good."

"Which is why I'm so happily divorced," Susan said. "I have the Jimmy Choos and no one to get on my case about them."

The server came by Peri's table and offered more iced tea. She looked confused by the silence between the two women. Blanche put the brochure back in the folder. "I'm sure you can read all this when you get home."

"Thanks for the info," Peri told her. The server busied herself by taking their empty plates, so Peri turned to Blanche again. "How's the landscaping coming?" The question sounded so banal she felt like slapping herself, but it was the safest thing that popped into her head.

"It's a good thing Paul's on travel. Took us months to work out the design with the landscaper, and now every day is a brand new day for these guys. A new supervisor shows up, doesn't know what's been done, what's supposed to go next. Then I have to step in and undo the work…"

She said a lot more, but Peri's focus went back to the women behind her.

"Oh, Susan, how you tease," Nikki said.

"At least as long as those alimony checks keep coming," Susan added.

Lisa changed the subject. "Did you see this Sunday's LA Times?"

Peri heard Nikki say, "I so want that Kate Spade outfit in the magazine. Too cute."

"It was okay," Kim replied. "I wasn't crazy about the bag."

"I couldn't get past that hatchet piece on USC," Susan told them. "How dare they say our alma mater is egotistical."

"Bet the writer went to UCLA," said Kim.

"Kim, that's not exactly fair." Nikki's words were harsher than her delivery. "There are dozens of schools who envy USC."

"Shoot me now." Blanche's voice was a graveled murmur, but it was clear she had been listening, too. Peri choked down her laughter.

Lisa spoke. "So, what's our game for this week?"

Peri thought she saw unusual activity out of the corner of her eye. She resisted the impulse to turn and look, but got a brief impression of the women's arms reaching toward something in the center of the table. There was quiet chattering, none of it intelligible. She looked at her friend, her eyebrows raised in question. Blanche smiled back, so Peri knew she'd get the rundown later.

Peri heard the light pinging of glass upon glass. Someone was making a toast.

"Bettys rule," Nikki said.

Peri's phone began to vibrate again, so she turned to her bag and noticed the women all getting their purses out, too. They were preparing to pay, which meant she had to make her exit first. Her phone had stopped ringing, but she pretended to answer it anyway.

"Hey, you ready to go?" she said to no one. "Okay, I'm on my way."

She fished out a twenty and gave it to Blanche. "I need to pick up –," here she fumbled for a name, "Benny. This should cover my lunch."

"No problem, Kiddo. I'll see you later." Blanche held out the folder to her. "Don't forget this."

Peri picked up her tote and stood. As she walked toward the door, she heard Kim's voice again, although she couldn't make out the words. She did catch a comment about "ladies room" and saw money being taken out of bags, so she continued outside, to her car.

After reaching her car, Peri put her ball cap on again and assumed the air of the inconspicuous private eye. She read over Blanche's scribbles as she waited. According to her BFF, Kim Patterson was the longhaired brunette, Susan Leske had the darker complexion, and Lisa Silvan spoke with the southern lilt.

Blanche had written her notes next to the price list. Peri saw the numbers again and rubbed her neck. If she needed to follow Nikki Keller any deeper into that establishment, she may need Blanche's help as a member.

Peri finally saw Nikki walk out of the entrance, with two of the women at the table. Susan dug in her purse while Lisa turned to listen to Nikki. There was no sign of Kim. They all laughed and strolled to their cars, hugging as each one was dropped off.

Although they were of varying heights and hair color, the trio shared a common patina. Peri thought it was the glow of money, then scolded herself for judging.

They can't help it if they're rich.

She watched a blue Beemer and a silver Benz slip out. Nikki's convertible eventually reached the entrance, so Peri started her car and eased toward the driveway. She and a dark Range Rover with tinted windows arrived at the exit simultaneously, but the Range Rover paused and let her go first. Nikki made it across the intersection just as the light changed, making Peri wait. The light was mercifully short and Peri was able to see her target pull onto her home street.

Peri drove past the Keller enclave, planning to turn around at the next cul-de-sac, but the stream of luxury vehicles behind her made her travel further into the country club homes. Turning left got rid of some of the cars, but the Range Rover still tried to push her down the street, obviously trying to get home. Finally, it turned into a driveway and Peri could return to Nikki's house.

As she rounded the corner, Peri felt her car grab to the right, then heard the familiar thwop-thwop of a flat tire. She pulled over to the curb and got out.

The tire slumped against the pavement, giving her Honda a definite list to starboard. Peri looked up the street in time to see Nikki's car whip out, toward Alta Vista.

Damn.

There was nothing to be done, except change the tire. Peri opened the trunk and peered inside. It wasn't a pretty sight. In addition to two plastic bins of paper she needed to file, the trunk was littered with papers she needed to put into the bins, along with a pair of running shoes, an emergency roadside kit, and a small bag, which was stuffed with a few toiletries and clean underwear, in case she had to tail anyone for more than a day.

So far, she'd used the roadside kit more than the toiletry bag.

Peri thought briefly about changing the tire herself. It wasn't rocket science, after all. She moved the trunk contents to her back seat, then lifted the carpet to find the spare tire release and the jack kit.

It took her exactly five minutes and two fingernails to realize that, although she had the brains for the procedure, she lacked the brawn. She called the Auto Club and spent her waiting time throwing loose papers into the plastic bins.

After an hour wait, then thirty minutes more while the tire was changed, Peri was finally able to drive, although not in pursuit of Nikki Keller. Hungry again, she stopped on the way home to pick up skordalia chicken from Sophia's, the local Greek restaurant. She felt like everyone's eyes were on her car as she drove; the little blue Honda still sat at a tilt with its emergency donut where a real tire should have been. Car troubles sharpened her cranky edge, so she decided to spend the evening working out a schedule for tomorrow.

She pulled into her driveway and stopped. Ordinarily, she left the car parked next to the front door. Her one-car garage sat back, detached from the house, and as much as she loved her older neighborhood, walking to the garage at night to get her car out made the hair on the back of her neck stand up. But she wouldn't be going out tonight, so she went ahead and yanked the garage door open, drove the car in and locked it up.

Having learned from the previous afternoon's encounter with the cat, Peri entered her house slowly, looking down to keep from stepping on the large tabby. Mr. Mustard was nowhere near. She set the food on the counter and walked through the rooms, turning on lights.

"Here Kitty-Kitty," she called.

There was no response.

"Mr. Mustard, Kitty-kitty-kitty." Peri looked in all the corners of the living room. "Great, I've lost the cat."

As she moved toward her bedroom, she heard a soft, shuffling noise, followed by thumping. She slipped off her shoes and tiptoed to the door, hoping it was the cat and not an intruder.

The sight before her made her wish for the latter. Mr. Mustard had found an old spool of red and green curling ribbon, probably under her bed, and had wound it around every object in the room. It was knotted around all of the legs of her shaker-style furniture, and had actually pulled the nightstand away from the wall, knocking a candle onto the floor. Pillows were on the floor as well, and one of them showed definite signs of shredding.

The cat was busily pushing the now-empty spool through the maze he'd created. He looked at Peri, jumped straight up, and then ran out of the room.

Peri looked around, trying to decide whether to eat first, or clean first, and whether she might actually be able to flush a cat. Cleaning won. She armed herself with a pair of scissors and a trash bag, and went to work. Half an hour later, she finally sat down in the kitchen with her dinner and her notes.

She was enjoying a mouthful of the rich, lemony chicken when she felt a warm, furry body rubbing her shins.

"We gotta find you a new home, cat."

As she read through her scribbles about Nikki and her friends, a rhythmic beep-beep-beep interrupted her study. She picked up her phone, but it wasn't the source of the noise.

The next ten minutes were spent checking clocks, smoke alarms, kitchen gadgets and anything else that might be setting off a warning signal. Peri finally narrowed the sound to her pink snakeskin tote in the living room. She dumped the contents onto the floor and sorted through her portable life until she found her digital voice recorder. A tiny red light flashed with each beep.

"Oh, yeah, I forgot I turned you on." She picked up the small, silver rectangle and took it back to the kitchen.

After another bite of dinner, Peri turned on the recorder and listened. There was a fair amount of extraneous noise from the room, but she could clearly hear the women's voices. She worked her way slowly through the recording, identifying each voice and taking notes on what was said. The conversation was pretty benign, even boring, by Peri's standards.

Right after Lisa asked about the game plan, she heard the server ask about more tea and turned the volume up to listen to as much of the background voices as she could. All she got were disjointed words, "blonde", "one of us", "discourage", and "force". She replayed the section several times, trying to add one more word to make it all make sense, but the ambient noise overpowered.

At last, she gave up and let the recording continue to the end. She heard the scrape of the chair as she arose, and the fluctuation of sounds as she moved through the room. Closing her eyes, she pictured where she was at each rasp, rattle, and voice. Suddenly one voice became clear.

“There goes the mark,” Kim said in a whisper.

Peri’s pulse trotted a little faster, wondering if she was Kim’s “mark”. She listened to the last part a few more times, but was unable to hear anything else. Leaning back in her chair, she speared another piece of chicken and put it in her mouth. She chewed, thinking.

If I could somehow separate the different sounds like they do on those TV shows. Grabbing her cell phone, she called Jason Bonham. He probably wouldn’t be able to process her file, but he might be able to tell her what kind of software program would.

Mark or not, she was going to find out the game for the week.

CHAPTER 8

By 8 a.m. the following morning, Peri was waiting for her mechanic, Allen, at the auto shop on Valencia Avenue. It was a small, two-car bay with an office in the back, tucked in with other utilitarian businesses in a block of industrial buildings. She sipped her coffee and checked her watch as a green 1965 Shelby Mustang purred into the parking lot.

"Eight-oh-five, Dude," she said as Allen walked toward the rolling shop doors, keys in hand.

"Sorry." He held up his stainless travel mug. "Needed fuel."

She watched him take her tire out of the trunk and followed him. A tall, muscled man with a ruddy face, Allen carried the tire with as much effort as Peri used to carry her purse.

The inside of the garage bay smelled like motor oil and gasoline, with a sharp metallic finish. Allen rolled the tire around, looking for obvious holes, and then got it wet to search for bubbles. At last, he was rewarded with small gurgles on one of the treads.

Reaching down with a pair of needle-nose pliers, he pulled out a metal fragment. "Someone sabotaging your tire?"

"Why, what've you got?"

Allen smiled. "I'm just joking with you. It's a little metal shard of some kind. Probably fell off a construction truck." He pulled out a second fragment. "Of course, it would be a great way to stop a car without looking suspicious."

Peri stared at him. "What would?"

"Tire spikes."

"What, like one of those strips they stop car chases with? I think I'd remember running over one of those."

"Not exactly. These are more like, um…" He paused for a moment, moving his thumb and index finger an inch apart as an approximate measure. "Like one of those jacks kids play with, except that all of the edges are sharp."

"Never heard of those. Wouldn't you find the whole thing stuck in my tire?"

Allen shook his head. "As you drive, the spikes are driven into your tire while the rest of the metal is broken up. There's no way to tell it's a spike or accidental road shrapnel—at least, not without some serious lab equipment."

Peri thought about the voices on her recorder from yesterday. *Could one of those women really have access to that kind of hardware? How would they even know where to get them?*

She watched him remove two more fragments and toss them into a round pan, the metal hitting metal with a bright tinkling sound. As he worked, she remembered the Range Rover's emblem filling her rearview mirror.

Reaching into her tote, she pulled out a plastic bag. "I think I'd like to save those pieces, just for kicks."

* * *

An hour later, Peri drove back over to the Keller house, hoping she wasn't too late to catch Nikki at home. A grey Toyota parked in front, jarring the pristine scenery of luxury cars. Peri saw an older woman at the front door, slight but sinewy, in a pale cotton shirt and denim capri pants. A large bucket sat beside her on the porch.

The cleaning lady, Peri thought. She tried to drive by slowly, but not so slow as to attract attention. The woman dug into her pocket. Peri turned her car around in the cul-de-sac and came back in time to see the cleaning woman let herself in.

Nikki had already left, she reasoned, although the cleaning woman's appearance gave her an idea for closer surveillance. She drove back to her office to do more research. On her way, she decided to stop by and see if Skip was at the police station.

His black SUV was in the lot, so Peri parked and entered. Skip stood in the doorway to his office, leaning against the doorjamb with his arm stretching to the upper molding. Sharing the space with him was Officer Mason. Her chin tilted up, her eyes meeting his face, lids slightly lowered as if focused on his mouth.

As Peri processed the scene, Jason Bonham interrupted her thoughts.

"Hey, Miss Peri, how's that software working for you?"

Peri watched Skip's head turn toward her, just as her focus drifted down to the young CSU officer, who was sitting behind the front desk. In that split second, she saw the innocence in Skip's eyes, felt her stomach relax, and silently berated herself for her pettiness.

She turned back to Jason. "I downloaded it last night, but I haven't run the file through yet. Thanks for the information, though. I really appreciate it."

Skip smiled and nodded at her, so she walked toward his office. Ella moved away from the door.

"Hey, Doll, what's up?"

Peri reached up and kissed his cheek. "Not much. Thought I'd stop by and say hello."

"How's the cat?" He sat down and began to take papers out of his inbox.

"Still alive, Smarty. I haven't had time to find a home for him." Peri pulled up a chair and relaxed into it. She watched Skip pick up papers, glance over them, then throw some away and stack the rest on a corner of the desk.

"How about Blanche?"

"No good. Paul's allergic to cats. I was thinking of one of those cat rescue places."

"Mm-hmm."

Peri sat up, seeing Skip's attention to the paper in his hands. "Anything interesting?"

"Mm-hmm… What? Sorry." He continued to read. "This is the tox screen from Dottie Peters."

Muffled conversations could be heard in the hall, while Peri waited for his next word. Finally, her thin patience wore through.

"And?"

Skip looked up, his expression grim. "Listen, I have something to tell you." She tried to keep her impatience muzzled as he paused and fumbled for words. At last, he said, "The thing is, the chief likes you, but he'd like to see a lot less of you in the station."

"What?"

"You know how the police view P.I.s—they're usually a pretty scummy lot."

Peri felt the heat rise up in her core, her cheeks burning. "He didn't think I was scummy when I emptied his trash cans at night."

"I know, but that was when you had a cleaning service, not a detective business. Now he feels that, even if you are the honest, ethical gal he knows, he doesn't want to encourage other private dicks to think we have an open door policy."

She started to speak, but Skip held his palm toward her. "And he doesn't want any impression that there's any impropriety between a detective and his sleuthing girlfriend."

"So I'm, like, banned for life?"

"Not banned. Maybe try coming less often, maybe just to pick me up for lunch or something."

Peri scowled. "This so sucks." She looked at the report, still in Skip's hands. "Maybe you could soften the blow a little." She nodded toward the paper.

"Peri—"

"Come on, Skipper. Dottie was client of mine. I liked her. What did the tox screen show?"

He sighed. "All right. Turns out she had oleander in her system. Mimics a heart attack."

"Poisoned? But why? How?"

"I don't know, but I'm glad I had Jason come over and process her house."

"My God… Who'd want to poison Dottie? Bob died of a heart attack a couple of weeks earlier. Do you think he—"

Skip stood, interrupting her. "That's what I'm going to find out. Time to get a court order for an exhumation."

Peri followed him out of the office. "We on for dinner tonight?"

"Sure, Doll." He looked at his watch. "I should be done by six."

Peri returned to her office. Back at her desk, she dug her laptop out and powered it up. If she couldn't discover anything new about Nikki, she could at least enter her notes and hours worked, for billing purposes. It irked her to not be following that woman today, but it couldn't be helped.

She thought about Allen's conspiracy theory and Nikki Keller. At the country club, she hadn't struck Peri as much of an intellectual, but intelligence wasn't needed to sabotage a tire. She decided not to make any hasty decisions about Nikki's IQ.

This time, Peri focused on Nikki's acquaintances, starting with Facebook. She had many friends, men and women, and it took Peri several searches to narrow the results down to those in the north Orange County area. Finally, she had a list of five women and three men; she printed their profiles to add to her folder.

She recognized the women's pictures from the country club. Peri thought Kim looked a lot like the jogger on the street, but she wasn't sure. She wondered why Kim didn't exit the club with the rest of her friends. Perhaps, she mused, while she was watching Nikki, Kim was busy tossing a few sharp objects under her tires.

She considered this theory as she took out her notes and began to type them. She liked to have her notes in two places, written and on the computer, in case of disaster. As she flipped through the papers, Peri became aware of a whirring noise in her tote bag, so she excavated her cell phone and answered it.

"Miss Menopause?" Although not a blast, the voice was definitely from her past.

"Benny, please call me Peri."

"Oh. Yeah. Miss Peri. I'm out of jail."

Peri's former client, Benny Needles had been convicted of receiving stolen property. With no priors and a full, weeping confession, he had only spent 30 days behind bars. She heard he was now completing a few hours of community service.

"I know. How are you?"

"I'm good. I'm good."

"I was a little worried about you in jail. I'm glad you're out." Peri didn't think Benny's obsessive-compulsive constitution would hold up well in an Orange County Jail cell. In addition to his OCD, Benny was an incurable Dean Martin fan, and had stuffed his house with Dino memorabilia. He needed his things, just as he needed certain foods, and a certain schedule. Under stress, Benny either suffered anxiety attacks requiring hospitalization, or he reverted into "Dino mode." Neither of these was good for a stint in jail.

"It wasn't so bad," he told her. "Except I missed my house and my things. And they wouldn't let me wear my suits in jail. And their food didn't taste very good. But I taught all the guys in my block to sing 'That's Amore'."

"That's nice," Peri said. "What can I do for you?"

"I have to do community service, Miss Mmm—Peri. One hundred fifty hours. It's hard."

"What are you doing?"

"That's the thing… I was working as a janitor at Aunt Esmy's church, but I guess I don't keep things too clean, which was okay 'cause they never played any Dino music there. So then I went to work at the library, but the director didn't think the Dean Martin biography belonged at the front of the shelves. We kinda fought about that, so I wasn't invited back. I tried to help out at Bradford Square, but those people are so old and cranky."

"Geez, Benny, how many jobs have you had?"

"Ten."

Peri felt uneasy about the obvious next question. "How many hours do you have left?"

"Ninety. I was wondering if you had anything for me to do."

"Well, Benny, I think you have to be a non-profit or some kind of state agency to offer community service hours."

"I know, Miss Peri, I know. But I talked to my parole officer, Miss Catherine. She's real nice, even if she likes some guy named Oscar Mayer better than Dino."

"Oscar? You mean John Mayer?"

"Maybe. Doesn't matter cause he's just another flash in the pan."

Peri took a deep breath and blew it out. "What did Miss Catherine say?"

"She says if you fill out a form and have the police department sign it, it'll be okay if I work for you."

"Um, well, Benny, I can't really think of any—"

"Miss Peri, please." His voice rose. "I need these hours or they'll maybe send me back. I can't go back there. I can put papers in files, or dust or something. You used to clean for my mom. I could clean for you."

Peri nearly erupted in laughter, but held herself back. "I don't know—"

"I could run errands, do your shopping. Miss Peri, I gotta do something and it won't even cost you."

Not in money, but probably my sanity, Peri thought. *The cat's bad enough—do I have to foster Benny too?*

"Okay, Ben, we'll try it out," she told him, while Robbie the Robot appeared in her head, bellowing *Danger, Danger, Will Robinson*. "Bring the papers by and I'll fill them out."

"Thank you, Miss Peri. Miss Catherine will be so happy. She's hoping you won't complain as much as the other people."

"Good luck with that," Peri mumbled under her breath, then told him, "Come to my office tomorrow afternoon at two o'clock. I'll fill out the forms and give you something to do."

"At two? But Rio Bravo is on TV then, and I wanted to—"

"Don't push me, Benny. Be there at two tomorrow or the deal's off."

"Yes, ma'am."

Peri finished the call, sat back and rubbed her scalp, hard. What sin had she committed to deserve this?

CHAPTER 9

You may want to come up for air, soon," Peri told her boyfriend, who was breathless with laughter.

"Benny..." he heaved between guffaws."Working... for you..."

"Yeah, thanks for the sympathy. Oh, look, here comes the waiter. Should I ask him for a liter of oxygen?"

Skip and Peri sat at a corner booth of Antonia's, a pizza and pasta joint in a small strip mall near the post office.

"You'll have to excuse my friend," she told the waiter before placing their order for a large pizza and two more beers. "He's... not well."

Skip wiped his eyes as his laughter subsided. "Sorry, Doll, I just can't think of what that guy's gonna do for you."

"Drive me crazy, probably. Maybe I'll get lucky and Chief Fletcher won't sign off on it."

"Oh, I think the Chief will be happy to help out."

Peri scowled. "Help Benny, or me?"

"Maybe he can watch the cat."

"Now that's not a bad idea. I wonder if Benny would like a pet."

"Aunt Esmy might," he said with a smile. Benny's Aunt Esmy studied taxidermy and loved animals—especially dead ones on the side of the road.

"Maybe, but I'd be a little worried. I mean, she does *wait* for them to die of old age, right?"

"We can only hope."

The waiter delivered a large, loaded pizza, two plates, and two new beers.

Skip took a long drink. “How’s the case?”

She opened her mouth, then thought about how much she was going to tell him. If she even hinted at sinister conversations and possible sabotage, she’d find herself in the middle of the never-ending debate over her career choice.

“It’d go a lot better if I hadn’t gotten that flat tire. Cost me a day and a half of surveillance.” Peri helped herself to a slice. “By the way, did you investigate the note the cat brought me over at Dottie’s?”

“Not yet. I was waiting for it to be ruled a suspicious death before I started processing the evidence.”

“Oh.” She savored the smell of garlic and onions, before she sank her teeth into tomato sauce, cheese, and a cornucopia of vegetables.

“Oh, what?”

“Well…” She paused a moment, wondering how much trouble she was about to wade into. “I called the number on the note yesterday.” She took another bite while she let him absorb what she had said.

“You gonna make me dig the information out of you?”

“No, I was just trying to see how mad you were going to be before I told you. It was Keller and Patterson. Someone in their office wanted Dottie to decide about something.”

Skip reached over and took Peri’s chin in his hand. “Peri, look at me. This. Is. Not. Your. Case. Do you understand?”

She nodded and kissed his thumb. “Yes, Skipper.”

He didn’t look convinced. “Tell me what I just said.”

“This is not my case. I understand. I get it.” She smiled. “Trust me, between Benny and the cat and the case I’ve got now, I don’t need more work.”

As she reached for her glass, Peri got a whiff of inexpensive perfume, and felt a shadow darken her corner of the booth. She looked up to see Ella Mason, the police officer. But Ella wasn't on duty tonight. She was in a jersey dress, wrapped tight as sausage casing. The vibrant red and black pattern commanded attention, as did the deep neckline and short skirt. Ella's dark hair, usually tamed into a bun, flowed loose and curly around her shoulders. Her makeup accentuated large dark eyes and full lips.

"Detective Carlton," she said, smiling. "It's so nice to see you."

Skip smiled back, but Peri felt no need, as Ella hadn't even glanced in her direction.

"You look like you're ready for a night on the town," Skip told her.

"Just Back-to-School night," she replied.

Peri faked a yawn to disguise her raised eyebrows. *If this is how you dress for Back-to-School night, what do you wear on a date?*

"I just wanted to thank you for your suggestions about my son the other day. You're right, he should have a male figure in his life. Maybe I'll look into one of those Big Brother organizations for him."

"I hope it all works out." Skip said.

Ella stood by the table for another minute, grinning, until the silence became an abyss.

"Well, I'll see you at work tomorrow," she told Skip, finally, before swaying out the door on spiky heels, held onto her feet by thin gold straps.

Peri watched Skip watch her leave, and felt herself growling inside, like a dog preparing to bite.

Skip picked up a slice of pizza and looked at her. "You weren't very friendly, Doll. You didn't even say hello."

"Next time, you'll have to introduce me."

"Oh, I'm sorry. I thought you knew each other." Skip turned his attention to his meal.

"I guess I didn't recognize her in her street clothes," she told him, hoping he didn't notice the way she carefully avoided adding 'walker'.

"Yeah, that was quite a dress."

Damn, Skip, she thought, *I love you, but you are the most clueless man on the planet.* She stared at him, trying to listen to the filter on her brain, the one telling her to be agreeable.

That filter was in need of some maintenance.

"Really? *Quite* a dress? In its color or its brevity?"

His eyes widened. "I've never heard you sound so—"

"Catty? Snarky? Completely insightful and observant?"

He leaned toward her, a smirk playing around his mouth. "Sexy."

Startled, she laughed, then ran her fingers across the back of his hand. "Finish your dinner so we can head back to my place."

* * *

Later, after they had finished their second round of unruly, energetic sex, Peri thought about how she used to wonder when their lovemaking would wane, from ferocious to exuberant to perfunctory. She let her fingers trace Skip's neck, around to his ear, and realized they'd have to find something else to complain about; perfunctory sex didn't exist for them.

He kissed her nose and lay back onto the pillows, which allowed her to wrap her warm body around his. They were quiet for a few moments, just long enough for her to close her eyes and drift into a sleepy twilight.

"I've been thinking." His voice rumbled through to her ear, which lay against his chest.

She sighed. "Mmm?"

"Ella—Officer Mason—is having a pretty hard time with her son."

Peri's eyes popped open. "And?"

Skip's fingers rubbed her back. "Maybe I could have a talk with him or something. Show him around the station, take him to a ball game, I don't know."

"Why you?"

"There's no dad in the picture, no men in his life."

"So..." She felt her breath slow and shallow, while she listened to his heart rate against her body. "She's in a male-dominated field, when she's off duty, she dresses—well, she doesn't hide her light under a bushel, but there's no man in her son's life?"

"Maybe she's picky. Or protective of her son." He shifted around to prop himself on his elbow. "I've never seen you jealous before. What's up with you and Ella Mason?"

"Nothing, I barely know her. It's not jealousy. And I don't begrudge you trying to help a kid in need, Skipper. I just worry about you. I don't know this kid, but you could get sucked into a bad situation. And you could be opening a big fat can of worms by fraternizing with a lower-ranking officer."

"I know, I thought about that. I just hate to see a kid dig such a hole, especially someone in our department. I could maybe make a difference in his life and save his mom some heartache."

She reached up and kissed him. "I'm sure you could make quite a difference. Perhaps you could get some of the other guys to help. Tag team him."

"That's an idea." He settled back down to entwine his arms around her. "I wonder if he likes hockey. We could take him to a Ducks game."

Peri nuzzled his neck. She told herself it wasn't jealousy, but that oozy feeling sat in her stomach. Sure, Ella Mason had been overdressed and overdone tonight, but she had made an attempt at allure, something Peri hadn't done in awhile. Stretched-out exercise gear, sad, wrinkled khakis, faded polo shirts, what was sexy about that?

She felt his hand run down her back and encircle her waist, fingers pressing lightly into her skin. Was that extra padding he was massaging?

Glancing over at the clock, she wondered if midnight was too late to call Blanche. For the first time in a long time, she felt like she needed some advice, along with a shopping spree.

An hour later, Skip's breathing indicated he had retreated to sleep, arms draped across his chest. Peri turned from one side to the other, covers off and covers on, until she finally gave up and wandered into the kitchen, throwing a shirt on as she walked. Her grocery store had a sale on Ben & Jerry's ice cream, so she reached into the freezer and got a pint of pistachio out. She grabbed a spoon, then headed to her laptop, still in the living room.

Googling 'Bettys' hadn't done her much good earlier. She kept digging through the pages and found more businesses, Facebook and MySpace people, but nothing that made sense.

"Damned if I know," she said, her voice a soft mumble.

Tired of spinning her wheels, she turned to shopping. Macy's online store had collections, outfits already put together. She chose a couple of looks that she thought a fifty-year old might wear, clicked on 'Buy' and 'Express Shipping.'

A heavy object suddenly hit her shoulder, knocking her laptop from her legs. She pulled it to her chest to keep it from hitting the hardwood floor. Mr. Mustard slipped down from the back of the couch, where he had jumped, and sat next to her. He began cleaning his face in long, languid strokes, gazing at her without expression.

"Goddamn cat. We gotta get you a home."

CHAPTER 10

The six o'clock alarm stabbed Peri's temples as she flung her hand about, trying to stop the beeping. Skip was already up. She walked past him to the bathroom, then returned to stand in front of her closet, willing herself a new wardrobe. If she had to follow Nikki Keller into any highbrow places, she didn't own anything that would meet their standards.

"Up early Doll?"

"Surveillance."

He paused at the shower door, looking at her. "And you don't have a thing to wear, I suppose."

"Hmm, you could say that." She reached in and selected a pair of olive slacks and a beige top. *If I can't be stylish*, she thought, *I'll at least be invisible.*

Skip emerged from the bathroom as she pulled her cement-colored ball cap over her hair.

"See you tonight?"

He shook his head. "Teaching class tonight. How about tomorrow?"

"Sure."

Peri drove two blocks before she realized he didn't kiss her goodbye. Or was it her who didn't kiss him?

Once parked outside the Keller enclave, she didn't have time to think about her love life. Nikki was out early, her convertible flying low, around the corner and across Alta Vista Street, to the country club. Peri hung well back, staying outside the gates until she saw the little blonde dash into the building. She parked her Honda in between two grey sedans and waited.

I need to get in there and see what she's doing, Peri thought. *This waiting outside will not get me any information.*

She watched the maintenance workers move about the club. Sturdy Hispanic men in green work clothes and massive boots, they raked at gardens, carried trash barrels, and walked around with leaf blowers to clear the refuse out of the parking lot. A man drove a golf cart around the clubhouse and left the gate open.

"Too bad I'm not a cleaning woman anymore," Peri said. "Looks like the only way I'd get in here."

A black cat slunk from under the bushes. It stopped and glared at her, and then dashed away. With a few graceful leaps, it crossed the pavement and disappeared onto the golf course. As she watched it, Peri thought about Mr. Mustard and had an idea. She got out of the car and walked toward the open gate.

Nobody seemed to notice her as she slipped onto the grounds. She stayed on the path, taking slow steps and looking for Nikki. By the time she had reached the corner of the clubhouse, she spotted her target.

They were almost completely obscured by a grove of silver-barked trees, but Nikki appeared to be having an intimate conversation with a man, punctuated by lengthy kisses. Peri wished she could take out her camera and use the telephoto lens, but she had left it in the car, thinking it might look too obvious. She could possibly take a picture with her cell phone, but they were too far away.

A few golfers were just beginning to populate the greens. They gave Peri pleasant, if confused, smiles as they passed. She knew she didn't have much time before someone asked her where her clubs were and, by the way, what was she doing there. Continuing on the path, she kept the clandestine couple in her peripheral vision.

Finally, she saw them come up for air, and with one, last kiss, they parted. Peri turned to move back down the path, away from Nikki's advance, and ran into the golfer behind her. He was an older man, in crisp chinos and a striped jersey polo, pulling a wheeled cart full of golf clubs. She planted her feet and put her hands forward against his shoulders, to steady them both. The golf cart rattled, but stayed upright.

"I'm so sorry," she told him.

"No problem," he said, then looked her in the face. "Are you a new member?"

"Actually, no, I'm looking for my cat. I saw her jump over the fence here, and they said I could take a quick look for her. I get so worried about coyotes, you know."

"Oh, I hope you find her."

"Thank you, sir."

"I hate cats." He continued down the walkway. "They crap in the flower gardens."

Whatever, she thought, and looked around for Nikki's mysterious kisser. The cat-hating man had actually done her a favor; Mr. Kisser had just reached the path in front of her. Peri stepped forward with her best "help me" smile.

"Excuse me, but I'm looking for my cat. Did you see a little black kitty run past here?"

He was young, somewhere in his twenties, tanned and cute in that boy band way. His hair was dark, his eyes were hazel, and his teeth nearly blinded Peri when he opened his mouth to speak.

"I have seen a black cat around, but I haven't seen it today. Is it yours?"

"Yes, I live around the corner and he keeps getting out."

"I'd love to let you look around more, but we've reached our tee times and I can't let you out on the course. You might get hit by a ball."

"Oh, okay. Do you work here?"

He smiled again. "Yes, ma'am, I give lessons here."

"Oh, you're the golf pro?"

He stretched himself up a bit taller. "I have been certified by the Professional Golf Teachers Association of America."

"I'm sure you have." She smiled back. "You know, I've always wanted to learn to play golf. Where would I go, if I couldn't afford the greens fees here?"

"I'd try the Birch Hills Golf Course. It's public, and the instructor there is a friend of mine. Tell him Tyler Garvey sent you."

"Tyler Garvey," Peri repeated. "Thanks, I'll tell him."

She followed the path back to the side gate, but it was locked, so she turned around to find a door into the clubhouse. The walkway was deceiving; it looked as though it followed the curve of the building, but it took a turn away and wound up and around a putting green, before settling back to the exit. Peri didn't want to get caught on the path, but figured she'd be in more trouble if she traipsed across the well-manicured grass, so she kept moving along the paved trail. At the top of the slope, she stopped to look at the course.

It really was lovely, for a golf course. Rolls of emerald green carpet with outlined patches of beige, and rounds of lighter green, punctuated by flags. Off to the right was a pond. Peri thought she saw a fountain spray in the middle of it.

She was enjoying the view, when she heard the whooshing sound of an object cutting through air. A sharp pain at the back of her skull pushed her onto her knees and into darkness.

CHAPTER 11

John Patterson sat behind a large mahogany desk and extended his fleshy pink hand to Detective Skip Carlton. He offered the obligatory greeting. "John Patterson, Keller and Patterson Development, nice to meet you."

Skip nodded, his obligatory response.

"Please, sit down," Patterson said, gesturing to a buttery leather chair on the opposite side of his desk.

Skip looked at the large beefy man, but in his peripheral vision, he catalogued the room. Minimal décor, lots of chrome, glass, and leather. There were four golf trophies on the shelves, along with a few reference books.

"So, Detective, what can I do for you?" Patterson's voice was a soft tenor, in contrast to his large frame.

"I'm looking into the death of Dottie Peters, and we found a note with your phone number on it." Skip turned a page in his notebook. "We were just curious what business you had with her."

"Peters? I'm not certain. Let me have Tanya pull the file."

Skip's cop senses went to work on Patterson's answer. The voice was a half-step higher and noticeably forced. His pale eyes shifted up and left. Skip was used to people lying; as a matter of fact, he routinely assumed the people he interviewed were hiding something. No one's life is an open book.

Patterson picked up the phone. "Tanya, I need the file on Peters. The paper file." He turned back to Skip. "Was this a homicide?"

Skip kept eye contact with him. "We like to cover all the bases."

"Yes, of course."

Silence gave Skip the opportunity to watch the executive fiddle with pencils, check his Blackberry, and attempt to look like he was still in control. Skip always wanted to smile in these moments, but he resisted. At last, the secretary walked in with a folder.

"Normally we have this information on the computer," Patterson said as he looked at the papers. "But we had a major crash last week and we're still re-entering data."

Skip nodded and wrote. "Can you give me a brief description of your business with Mrs. Peters?"

"Yes, yes." The words blustered out. "It says here that we offered to buy a property she owned." Skip watched his eyes focusing on the paper, jerking from top to bottom. "Yes, I remember now – she and her husband have a parcel of land near Palm Desert. We're developing that area and thought we could use their property."

"But they weren't in the mood to sell it to you?"

"Well, at first, they were reluctant. Seems they've got a little trailer out there and like to go out when the wildflowers bloom, or something like that. But with the husband's recent death, we approached Mrs. Peters again."

"Thought you'd take advantage of his passing to get a piece of land from the widow?"

"Well, it wasn't as mercenary as all that." Patterson flashed a white, snake-oil smile. "We didn't actually need the parcel. It's just a neighborhood enhancement."

"Not necessity?"

"No, Detective. It's at the end of the development. We were going to put a park there, drought resistant, with benches, play area, so forth. It's good for community relations." He shrugged. "If we didn't get the land, we didn't have the park. But we still had the shopping center."

"The note made it sound a little more important than that."

Patterson smiled again, but Skip noticed a hardness in his eyes that did not match his upturned mouth. "Our assistants sometimes like to show their initiative by aggressively seeking land procurements."

Skip looked up from his notes. "That sounds like a nice way of saying you let the kids bully old people."

"Believe me, Detective, it's not sanctioned."

"But it sure is useful." Skip continued to write. "I'd like copies of everything in that folder, if it's alright."

"Certainly. I'll have Tanya do that." He bent over, behind his desk, and retrieved a crutch, then used it to raise himself out of his chair and slowly limp toward the door.

"Injury?"

"Nope, just a bad knee. Had it replaced a couple of weeks ago." He disappeared for a moment, then returned to the office. "She'll have that for you in about ten minutes."

Skip glanced over his shoulder to see Patterson standing at the door, as if waiting to make his farewell. Usually, in this situation, he would say his goodbyes and wait at the secretary's desk, but Patterson had a button he wanted to push, even if he didn't know why.

He eased further into the chair and wrote in his notebook instead. Most of his notes consisted of a list of things to do, his grocery list for the week, and ideas for Ella's son, but he managed to busy himself until the secretary handed the copied file to her boss. Only then did he unfold his lanky frame from the chair.

"Thank you, Mr. Patterson." Skip held his hand out for a handshake. "I'll call if I have any questions."

Patterson took his hand, smiling, but Skip saw the bead of sweat meandering down his right temple.

He left the office with a folder and an uneasy feeling about Keller and Patterson Development Company. As he walked to his car, the familiar vibration of his cell phone on his belt beckoned him. It was Blanche

"Skip, have you heard from Peri?"

"No, but I didn't think I would. She's working a case and I teach class tonight, so we were going to get together tomorrow, if possible."

"Oh, maybe her phone's on quiet."

* * *

Nestled in the well-groomed bushes outlining the Alta Vista Country Club, the faint strains of "Girls Just Wanna Have Fun" drifted toward the ears of the groundskeeper as he knelt beside a palm tree and adjusted a sprinkler head. He paused and listened, then stood and walked toward the music.

It stopped, so he waited for a moment and looked around the grass. Just when he thought he wouldn't find the hidden phone, a new song started. "Message in a Bottle" pounded, a little louder than Cyndi Lauper, and led him directly to the bushes against the fence.

He put his hand up to his mouth when he saw the tennis shoes. "Dios mio."

CHAPTER 12

Peri opened her eyes, then shut them again with a groan. "What happened?"

She heard Skip's voice, soft and grainy like a fading radio station. "We don't know, Doll. The maintenance guy found you. Lie still, the paramedics are going to check you out."

"I-I was on the golf course." She tried to sit up, but grabbed her head and sank back. "Then I was waking up. Can't tell you much more than that."

"Ma'am." Another voice intruded. "We're going to transfer you to a stretcher and take you to the hospital."

She opened her eyes, then winced at the sunlight and held her hands up for shade. "What are you, twelve?"

"No ma'am, I assure you I'm an adult, thoroughly trained to assess and treat injuries."

"Sorry. I'm used to arguing about whether I need to go to the hospital." She whimpered as they lifted her onto the cot for transport. "This time, I think I'll let you take me."

Placentia-Linda Hospital was a convenient five minutes from the golf course, so Peri did not have to endure a long ride. Once inside, a steady stream of nurses attended to her. One took her name and insurance information, a second took her temperature and pulse, then a third wheeled her down the hall to the X-ray lab.

Each one wanted to know her name, date of birth, and why she was there. At first, she thought they were too lazy to read the chart; it finally dawned on her that they were testing her mental faculties.

Eventually, they parked her gurney in a room slightly larger than her hall closet.

By the time the doctor entered, she was able to sit up with a more manageable headache. She watched him look over her chart. He was a short man, with gray hair and narrow features on a wide face. She smiled at him. He did not smile back.

At last he turned to Peri and began his examination. As he looked through the lighted scope into each eye, she tried to read his expression, but it he barely acknowledged her as more than a number with symptoms.

She decided to try a joke. "So, will I live?"

"Of course. That's a stupid question."

"I'm sorry, Doctor. I guess I'm not thinking correctly, since I got *hit over the head*."

He didn't respond to her sarcasm, except to put the x-rays on a display light. "It's not bad. You have a very mild concussion. You may have a headache."

"Ya think?"

"Dizziness is also common." He turned the light off and looked again at her chart. "The symptoms may last a few days, but not more."

"So, what should I do?"

"Are you dizzy now?"

"How should I know? I've been on my back for over an hour." Peri was beginning to dislike him.

"Well, you can take any over-the-counter pain reliever for the headache, and call your regular doctor if you feel dizzy for more than a day, or if the pain relievers don't work." He stared at her as if he were assessing her looks. "Do you live alone?"

She stared back, wondering whether to answer or slap him.

"You should have someone wake you every two hours," he continued. "To make certain you still know your name and address."

"I can do that."

A shadow crossed the doorway, and Skip entered the little room. "Ready to go?"

At the sight of the detective's badge, the doctor stepped back and looked from Peri to Skip. "I didn't know I was treating a suspect."

Peri frowned. "Gee, and I thought the gang tats would give me away."

She saw Skip's mouth twitch in a small grin as he took her arm to help her off the table. Her legs wobbled and her head pulsed, so she leaned against him for a moment, then stood and walked toward the door.

"Thanks for all the help," she told the doctor. "I'm sure they'll be able to wake me every two hours at the jail tonight."

"You're gonna get me in trouble." Skip's voice was quiet and low. "That doctor will probably report me for fraternizing with a criminal."

"That doctor needs to get laid," Peri said as they walked past the nurses' station. She heard boisterous laughter from the women at the counter.

Once outside, Skip helped her into his SUV. "My place tonight?"

"Sure." She squeezed his arm. "Wait, no, I gotta feed the cat."

"Wow, Doll—you're supposed to *forget* things when you get conked on the head, not remember them."

"Very funny. Should we go by and pick up my car?"

He slipped behind the wheel. "Why don't we just pick it up in the morning?"

"Why can't we pick it up now?"

"I just think it would be safer if you didn't drive for a few hours."

She buckled her seatbelt. "I'm fine. I have a little headache, that's all. I'll take some Motrin when we get home."

"Doll, humor me this once, okay?"

"I'm the one who got hit over the head. Why aren't I being humored?"

He started the car. "I want to make certain you're okay. Please don't argue with me. I want to get you home, safe and sound, where I can watch over you tonight."

"What about your class?"

"I already cancelled."

She grumbled. "All right. We can get my car in the morning."

As they drove back to Peri's bungalow, they talked about the attack.

"I was working my case and I needed to get onto the golf course. I discovered something, but it was impossible to get any evidence."

"Did you hear anything before—"

"Before total pain and instant darkness? No. I was, hmm, I think I was standing up on a little hill, looking at the course. I remember looking at the water, spraying up in the pond—wait—there was a sound. A whooshing, like someone teeing off." She looked at Skip. "Maybe it was a golf club."

"Maybe. You know, it's also possible you were hit by a stray ball."

"Did you find a ball nearby?"

"No, but Jason went over there to collect evidence as soon as we called. Maybe he'll be able to tell us something."

He said a lot more, but she didn't hear. She was thinking about this case, from the jogger who ran past before Officer Chou drove up, to the flat tire, to her current headache.

I'm not a paranoid person, she thought, *but I'm beginning to think someone doesn't want me to follow this Nikki Keller*.

They pulled in the driveway and parked. Peri eased out of the seat to unlock the front door and saw a something black on the step. She walked over to see what it might be, and cocked her head in wonder.

"I forgot to ask if you had anything in the house for dinner," Skip said. "Do you have any—"

The words died away as he joined her at the step and saw what she was staring at. He took his pen from his jacket and leaned down to poke the object around.

"It's a crow," he told her.

"Oh, poor thing. Did it hit my house and break its neck?"

She watched him examine the dead bird. "Not unless it decapitated itself with a sharp object."

An image of four women laughing at a country club instantly flooded Peri's mind. She pushed it away, while her right hand drifted up to her throat, as if to push her heart back into her chest. "I think I'm glad I humored you."

Skip stood up and pulled out his cell phone. "Hey, Jason, you busy? I need you to process a scene."

"A scene?" She shuddered. "Sounds so lurid when it's your own front steps."

He hung up and turned to her. "Jason's on his way. We're going to wait for him, and then you can pack a few things to stay at my place."

"Geez, I feel like I'm keeping your CSU-boy occupied full-time."

"It keeps him busy. By the way, I hope you understand, Craig Daniels will be working your case. Chief Fletcher thinks it would be too much of a conflict if I investigated."

Peri nodded. "That makes sense."

Jason arrived ten minutes later, slipped on his gloves and began processing the front steps.

Skip gave Peri a hug and kissed her forehead. "Let me clear the house before you go in, Doll."

She was aware of his holster pressing her chest and thought about him searching her house, gun drawn, possibly encountering an intruder. "Be careful," she said, trying not to choke.

After a few minutes that seemed longer, he finally came out and allowed her to enter. Once inside, she opened a can of food to meet Mr. Mustard's insistent demands. She felt disembodied, as if her hands prepared the cat's meal while her mind wandered through the events of the last couple of days.

Skip stroked her neck. "At least they didn't break in, whoever they were."

"Yeah, whoever." She moved away from him. "I'm gonna go pack a bag. Be right back."

Skip held her arm."Is there something else you'd like to tell me?"

She didn't look at him. Instead, she stared at her curio cabinet, studying all the moose figurines she collected. The array of antlered bric-a-brac, gathered from her early childhood, calmed her. "Give me a little time, Skipper. Then we'll talk."

She disappeared into her bedroom and came out a few minutes later with a small overnight duffel. On the way out the door, she stopped and rubbed the cat along his spine as he ate.

"See you tomorrow, Mr. Mustard."

The cat sat down and licked his paw, and then rubbed his face. If he was going to miss her, he didn't say.

CHAPTER 13

Back at Skip's, Peri went to the bedroom, stripped off her grass-stained clothes and put on a pink flannel lounge set decorated with martini glasses. She traipsed to the family room and curled up on the leather sofa. Skip handed her a mug of hot tea and sat down with her.

"Ready to talk?"

"Okay, but try not to overreact," she said, and told him about the lunch at the country club. "It might not mean anything, but when I combine the flat tire, the head wound, and a headless bird, I'm feeling a little paranoid."

"Is this the Keller case? What are you supposed to be doing for him?"

"The usual." She took a careful sip. "Suspicious husband, possibly cheating wife. He's right, too. I saw her this morning, making out with the golf pro behind a grove of trees."

"So write up the report and be done with him."

"It's not that easy. I may have seen them, but I don't have any physical proof. No pictures, no hotel receipts, nothing."

"Peri—"

"Oh, don't yell at me, I know I should've planned it out better. I was sick of sitting in the parking lot, wondering what she was doing on that golf course, but I couldn't think of how to nonchalantly take pictures."

"How did you get onto the course?"

She told him about the missing cat story and he nodded.

"Good one. But next time, maybe you'd better think it through." He stroked her hair. "How's the head?"

"Hurts. I should take something."

He stood up. "Wait here." Returning with a bottle of pills, he said, "Take a couple of these."

She shook two orange tablets into her palm. "I don't think they were trying to kill me. They'd have hit me harder."

"Maybe they just didn't count on your head being such a tough nut to crack."

"Ha ha," she said, and then swallowed her medication with a mouthful of herbal tea.

He sat down again and put his arms around her. "Until we find out who did all this, I don't want you to be alone."

"I appreciate that, but I don't think I can do my job with a police escort."

"Well, I've got an idea." He hugged her a little closer. "Just hear me out, Doll. You're supposed to hire Benny, right?"

She broke from his grasp. "Oh, man. I forgot, I was supposed to meet him at two today. Damn, he's gonna be mad. I stood him up and made him miss some movie on TV."

"At least now you have something for him to do."

She looked at him, her eyes widening, while the idea sunk in. "Wait a minute—you want me to lug Benny around while I finish this case? Have you lost your mind? I am not going to be stuck in a car with that man while I try to get my work done."

"I'm not saying it'd be pleasant. But I think there's someone who doesn't want you to tail Keller's wife. Either you need to decline the case, or protect yourself, and since you don't carry a gun—"

"I need to carry Benny." Peri sat back and rubbed her head. "I guess I'd better give him a call. Man, he really won't want to keep *my* hours."

She picked up the phone and dialed Benny's number. Skip rubbed her back as she apologized several times, then asked Benny to meet her at Skip's house at seven the next morning. Finally, her patience wore out.

"For God's sake, Ben, if I didn't have a headache before, I'd have one after talking to you. I'm sorry I was too unconscious to meet you today. I'm sorry you don't want to be at Skip's so early. If you want those community service hours, your butt will be in the driveway tomorrow, on time. I suggest you turn in early."

Skip took her mug. "I think you'd better turn in early, too. After all, you've got to wake up every two hours and tell me who you are."

She stretched up from the couch and laughed. "Good luck with that. You know how I get when you wake me from a sound sleep."

* * *

Skip was sitting at the kitchen table when she staggered through at six o'clock.

She reached over and kissed him. "How bad was I last night?"

"Including the time you called me a moron and the swing you took at me, not bad."

"I am so sorry."

"I been called worse." He swatted at her hip as she turned toward the coffee maker. "And you hit like a girl."

She laughed and walked back to the bedroom. "Gotta get ready for work. Don't want to be late for my carpool."

At 7:05, Peri looked outside to see a gleaming, black Coupe de Ville rolling into the driveway, fins sleek as a pair of sharks. She walked toward the front door, keys in hand and pink snakeskin tote over her shoulder. Skip stopped her.

"Whoa, there, Samantha Spade, you're not going outside without me."

They walked out the front door, Skip pulling it shut behind them. "I should fix this thing," he said. "The latch isn't lining up properly."

Benny Needles sat behind the wheel in Dino-casual wear, a V-neck sweater over a white collared shirt and grey slacks. He had lost a little weight since Peri last saw him, but he was still the same needy man, who wanted to be the King of Cool, if only he was six inches taller, fifty pounds lighter, and normal.

"Hi, Benny." She slid into the red leather interior. "First thing we're going to do is go get my car."

"You mean we're not using my car?" He sounded anxious.

"Your car is magnificent. But it's also easily identifiable, so we can't use it for surveillance." Peri saw his worried scowl, so she offered more. "We are parking your car at the Alta Vista Country Club. It's really ritzy—Dino would have probably played golf there if it had been around."

"No one will mess with it?"

"No. No one will mess with it."

She finally convinced him he could part with his automobile briefly, and they drove down Kraemer Boulevard to Alta Vista Street. The morning light had broken, although the low clouds prevented the sun from warming the air. Once at the country club, Benny pulled in and out of three different spaces before he found one to his liking.

One of us is not getting out of this alive, Peri thought. "Before we go driving, Ben, I want to look around the club."

"Why?"

"I need to find a vantage point to take some pictures."

"Pictures of what?"

"Of the case I'm working on." Peri sighed. "Just hang out with your car for a minute."

"Okay. No, wait—Detective Skip told me to stay with you." He said this as if he suddenly remembered his task.

"And you are," She reassured him. "I won't wander off."

She walked to each side of the clubhouse, looking for a place to get a view of the back side of the greens, where Nikki and her young lover might sneak away unseen, but she couldn't find one. To her right, a row of upscale houses bordered the golf course, their patios and gardens fenced with decorative wrought iron that didn't obscure the view. Peri was never sure whether this was to alert the homeowners of incoming shots, or because golfers all thought they were worth watching.

There was a smaller section of fence four houses down the street that didn't seem to belong to a home. Peri thought this might be some kind of easement. She turned around to motion Benny to walk with her and found him a foot away, his face pointed upwards, like a hunting dog awaiting a command.

"Dear God." She tried to whisper her surprise. "Don't sneak up on me like that."

"I need to stay with you."

"Fine. Let's go for a walk."

As they moved down the street, she wished she were alone. A woman dressed in casual wear, as she was, could be out for an energetic walk in the neighborhood. A woman in casual wear out for a walk with a chubby little man in vintage 50's apparel, however, would be more noticeable and harder to explain. But she had promised Skip she'd keep Benny with her, so off they went, following the sidewalk as it curled around the golf course.

"Sue Drive," Benny said. "That's a funny name for a street. I wonder how they named it that. Is it a lady? Or did somebody sue someone to name the street?"

"I don't know."

"I wonder how you'd find out. Maybe you could look at some old city hall meeting minutes." He hopped in front of her and turned to walk backward. "What's say, after this, we go to City Hall and look it up? I bet there's a lot of weird stuff in those old records."

"I'm sure there is, but that's not the way my day works. We probably won't have time for City Hall."

"But if we do, can we go?"

She sighed again, and pulled out her mother's pat answer. "We'll see."

When they got to the easement, she saw a large metal box, one that might house controls for power or phone lines, locked into the narrow area by a large gate. She studied the lock, and considered the climbable nature of the wrought iron. It was unfortunately not as ornate as the homes' fencing, being about six feet in height and mostly straight up, with few crossbars. The vertical bars were punctuated by arrows pointing skyward.

Peri considered the possible outcomes of trying to climb over. At five-feet-nine, she could probably heft her body over the fence, but not without a struggle, which would attract attention. Plus, she really didn't want to snag her clothes, or her skin, on those points. The view she needed was on the other end of this narrow aisle, if she could only find a way in.

She turned to Benny. "Dean Martin ever pick locks?"

"Of course. Matt Helm picked 'em all the time."

"I don't suppose those Matt Helm movies taught you how to pick them."

He laughed. "Don't be silly, Miss Peri." He reached into his pocket and took out a Swiss Army knife. "I learned how to do that in jail."

Peri stepped aside and used the back of her hand to lift her chin and close her gaping mouth, while her new employee proceeded to poke about the inside of the lock with one of the knife's many attachments. He closed his eyes and hummed a little tune as he adjusted the pin and tugged. Finally, she heard the click of victory and Benny handed her the open lock.

"I gotta say, Ben, I'm impressed."

His smile reminded her of when he was a boy and his mother would brag about him while Peri cleaned her house.

"Okay, you stay by the gate," she told him, and handed him her cell phone. "Act like you're busy, fiddling with the phone, texting or checking email or something. If someone comes, whistle."

"I can't whistle, Miss Peri."

"Well, then, cough, or sneeze."

"Which one?"

"I don't care. Sneeze. Loud, though. So I can hear you." She slipped in, past the power box, and crept to the gate at the opposite end.

There were a few well-placed shrubs, which weren't quite tall enough to hide her, but could offer some camouflage for her gray sweats and oatmeal cap. She knelt down, took out her camera and looked through the telephoto lens at the grounds. The grove of trees where Nikki and Tyler hooked up yesterday was easily visible from here. It was a perfect place to rendezvous; too far from the trail to be noticed, with the trees close enough together to hide anyone behind them, unless you were looking for them. Peri leaned back against the fence and waited.

Ten minutes later, she saw a small blonde walk along the cart path, then take a detour, up to the grove. A tall, tan form approached from the opposite direction soon afterward. Peri raised her camera and focused her telephoto lens. It was Nikki and her boy-toy. Peri kept her finger on the trigger and clicked a freeze-frame report of the meeting.

Tyler reached out to hug Nikki, who responded at first, then pushed him away. She appeared cross. Tyler questioned; Nikki whined; Tyler apologized; Nikki pouted; Tyler appealed; Nikki softened; Tyler caressed; Nikki embraced. They kissed, made up, and made out, all to Peri's adoring lens.

"Ah-Choo!"

Peri whipped around to see Benny in a rigid stance. She heard footsteps on the sidewalk, so she scooted around to the side by the power box and crawled behind it, just as a man's voice spoke.

"Good morning."

"G-g-g-ood morning, Mister Officer." Benny's voice was about three octaves above normal.

Shit, a police officer, she thought. *If Benny doesn't go into Dino mode, he's gonna have a freaking heart attack.*

"Someone called and said you'd been out here for awhile. I guess they were worried that you were lost or something."

Benny giggled like six-year old girl. "No, no. I-I-I was out for a walk, see? And, I started messing with my new phone, and I wasn't—um—sure of some of the buttons and then I got it stuck in some kind of mode and I forgot about walking and just kinda stood here playing with it."

Peri was surprised. It was a halfway decent explanation. She heard the officer laugh.

"Yeah, I've done that too."

"Hey, at least I wasn't driving." Benny's voice had returned to normal, and Peri detected some Dino-swagger to it.

"Good point. Well, I was just making sure you were okay. You have a nice day, sir."

"You, too, Officer. Thanks for checking up on me."

Peri listened for the footsteps to diminish. The sound of an engine meant the officer had returned to his patrol car. She watched the black and white sedan pass Benny, then turn around in a driveway and leave, before she exited, making certain to lock the gate behind her.

"Let's go," she said.

As they walked back to the parking lot, Peri thought about who might have called in that report about Benny. Maybe it was dumb luck that a squad car happened by, but she popped the memory card out of her camera and slipped it into her bra. Just in case, she told herself.

"Okay, Ben, how about following me back to my office?"

"But the detective—"

"Skip said to stay with me. If your car stays right behind mine, you'll stay with me. Anyway, it's less than a mile away. What could go wrong?"

CHAPTER 14

The five minute drive to her office stretched into ten more while Benny found a safe place to park the Caddy. Peri stood at the entrance to the building, alternately checking her watch and tapping her foot. At last, she saw him walking toward her, his steps small and quick.

Once at her office, Benny pushed ahead of Peri as she unlocked the door. "What do I do now?"

"Well…" She sat her tote down by the desk, reached in the bottom drawer and took out a soft white cloth. "How about dusting?"

He smiled. "Yes, ma'am."

While he busied himself, slapping the rag at the picture frames and sneezing, she tried not to notice that he wasn't really removing the dust, just rearranging it. Peri opened her laptop and fired it up to download her pictures. She was one report away from being clear of this case. Then maybe Benny wouldn't have to be her shadow. Maybe then she could relax.

Maybe she could even find time to get Mr. Mustard a new home.

"Hey Benny, how do you like cats?"

"Not so much, Miss Peri. They claw things."

"Oh, yeah, all your Dino stuff."

"Did I tell you I got tables from the set of Some Came Running?"

"Yes, you even showed them to me." Peri dug the memory card out of her bra and plugged it into the computer. File created, pictures downloaded, she pulled the card out and replaced it in her camera, then reconsidered. She had a new 3G card in the top drawer, so she put that in the camera. The old one still needed hiding, she felt, so she opened the back of the picture frame on her desk and pressed it into the upper corner, right behind Skip's face.

Still not satisfied, she compressed the pictures to a zip file and emailed it to her account.

You're only paranoid if people really aren't out to get you, she told herself. *Otherwise, you're cautious.*

"Okay, I'm done dusting. Now what?"

"There are some files I've been meaning to organize." She walked to the corner cabinet and pulled open the bottom drawer. "See this big folder lying sideways? It's really four cases. I have individual folders for them all, but these little notes and receipts in this folder need to be put into the right case file."

In the next instant, the sound of breaking glass and rushing wind and high-pitched ringing knocked them both to their knees. Peri looked up long enough to see the window burst into a million jagged pieces before she covered her head and felt sharp droplets on her arms.

Fearing he wouldn't answer, she called out, "Benny?"

His voice came back, high, but reassuring. "I'm scared, Miss Peri."

"Me, too, Ben." She crawled behind the desk and reached to the side for her tote. Her phone was at the bottom of the bag, as usual, and the shaking of her hand didn't help her reach for it. "Goddammit, where—there it is."

She dialed 9-1-1. "Get someone over to Kraemer and Chapman—shots fired."

The dispatcher was a calm, if perplexed, female voice. "Ma'am, the police department is on Kraemer and Chapman. Where are you directing us?"

"Founders Plaza." Peri tried not to scream or cry, but her voice shook. "Suite 102. Someone just shot my window out. Get Detective Carlton."

"Ma'am, try to be calm and stay on the line. I'll send someone over there."

Peri looked up to see Benny crawling for the door.

"Benny, get back. They may be waiting on the other side."

The little man ignored her and continued to go for the exit.

She reached up and grabbed his clothes. "Get back here, you bonehead. Do you want to walk into an ambush?"

"Miss Peri you're stretching my sweater."

"Get. Over. Here." She spat each word at him with such force, he turned and joined her behind the desk. "Sit tight, Benny. The police are coming."

She became aware of a voice asking, "Ma'am? Ma'am?" She realized she had dropped the phone, so she picked it back up.

"I'm here."

"Ma'am, the police are on their way. Which detective were you asking for?"

"Detective Carlton. I'm Peri Minneopa, his girlfriend."

"I'll see if I can contact him for you."

Peri listened to the woman talking to someone in the background. She remembered watching breaking news on the TV, seeing the dispatcher staying on the line with the caller. She assumed this woman would not hang up, but her arm felt so heavy and her heart bounced against her ribcage in an attempt to escape. Her hand, with the phone, drifted away from her ear.

All she could hear was Benny's raspy breaths, rapid as a panting dog. The rest was stillness. Waiting for the next shot. It was that place in the movie before the assassin claimed his victim; Peri chewed her index finger to keep from screaming.

Hearing the sounds of sirens at last, howling closer, she thought she'd feel better, but she shook harder than before.

"Thanks," she managed to tell the dispatcher. "I hear them coming."

Officer Chou was the first through the door. He took one look at the situation and called over his shoulder. "Looks like the shot came from the west side of the building, through the atrium." He knelt and motioned to Peri and Benny. "Crawl this way and we'll get you out of here."

Benny needed no urging and practically galloped on his knees to the officer. Peri followed, dragging her tote. Once outside, they were led away to the safety of the three squad cars that had responded.

"Would you like to sit down?" Officer Chou gestured to a back seat.

Peri looked at the seat and shook her head. Her body still quivered from the adrenaline. "No, sorry, thanks, can't sit right now."

Benny stepped away from the car, as if it might snatch and eat him. "Thank you, I don't care for black and white cars."

"Sir," Officer Chou addressed Benny. "Can you tell me what happened?"

He held out his sweater. "She stretched the hem out."

Officer Chou stared at him for a moment, and then turned to Peri.

"Maybe you could tell me what happened."

She looked at him, nodding, opened her mouth, then held up her hand. "Give me a second," she said and pinched her nose in an attempt to stop her sudden tears.

The next thing she knew, familiar arms were around her. She smelled Skip's lotion; he held her while she composed herself. After a few seconds, she straightened, nodded at Skip, and took a deep breath, before turning to Officer Chou.

"Here's what happened," she said and described the events while he took notes.

"Can you think of anyone who would want to hurt you?"

She looked at Skip, who nodded. "It may have something to do with the case I'm working on."

"Can you give me names?"

She thought this over. If she told him it had to do with Don Keller and his wife Nikki, and the police interviewed them, she could kiss that account goodbye. She needed to hand in that report first.

"Can I get a rain check on that?"

"Peri." Skip's voice was stern.

She dragged him away from the group and whispered in his ear. "I have the evidence now. All I have to do is hand in the report and collect the rest of my fee. Then I can give Officer Chou their names and not lose any sleep. Or money."

"Is this really the time to worry about the money?"

"Only if I want to pay the rent this month." She rubbed her forehead. "Not to mention the fact that I've already taken – and spent – the retainer fee. What if he wants it back because I didn't finish the case?"

Skip didn't look happy, but he turned to Officer Chou and said, "She needs a day to get her client's report turned in. I can bring her in tomorrow morning to make her full statement, if that's okay."

"I'd be happy to write everything up for you this evening," Peri added.

Chou nodded, then looked at Benny. "How about you, sir? Any enemies?"

Benny's eyes widened. "Enemies? You think someone wants to hurt me?"

"No, Ben," Peri said. "They're just asking—"

But the damage had begun. "Who would want to hurt me? Officer, you gotta find out. I can't live like this, always lookin' over my shoulder." He grabbed Skip's arm. "My house, I need to get home. What if they're trying to get my things?"

A tall, thin officer loped up and joined them, undoing his flak jacket as he came.

"Looks like it must have come from one of the walkways on the opposite side," he said. "There's no roof access, and no sign of any broken tiles."

Skip turned to the officer. "Are you sure it was a shooting?"

The young officer nodded. "Bullet stopped in the laptop. We'll send it to CSU, but it's pretty mangled."

Peri groaned. "My laptop. This case is getting freakin' expensive."

Officer Chou turned to Skip. "We'll call Bonham to process, if you'd like to get Peri home." He nodded toward Benny. "We can give him a ride."

Benny took another giant step away from the patrol car. "Oh, no, my car is here. I can drive myself home."

"I don't think that would be a good idea, Ben," Skip said. "We'd like the police to accompany you home, to make certain you're safe."

"But they could follow me. Like you said today, Miss Peri, 'If your car stays right behind mine, you'll stay with me.' We got here okay, right?"

Skip frowned at Peri. She returned her best Don't Be Mad smile.

"Here's the thing, Ben." Peri shifted her weight, studying the pavement, trying to find a way to avoid setting the little man into orbit. "The police would like to make certain you're safe."

"But the shooting's over."

The tall officer had not witnessed Benny's earlier tirade. "Not if they're hunting you."

It was a launch worthy of NASA. "Hunting me? Hunting me? I'm not some animal. Who would be trying to shoot me?"

"Calm down, Benny." Skip grabbed his shoulders, towering over him. "It's standard procedure when we think someone is a target. Quite frankly, I think Peri has more immediate enemies than anything you can dream up." He turned to the other officers. "I'll take Mr. Needles to his house and check it out, if I can have one of these cars follow me for backup."

Officer Chou motioned to the tall officer. "Go ahead. We'll be expecting you both in the station tomorrow to give your statements, yes?"

Benny looked aghast, but Peri patted his shoulder. "Tomorrow should be fine," she replied.

The trio got into Skip's SUV and headed out of the plaza, down Kraemer Boulevard, a squad car following in their wake. The morning sun had burned through the clouds at last, but it didn't warm them. They sat in silence until they reached Benny's house, behind the post office.

Although most people's homes suffered if left untouched for a month, Benny's recent incarceration had not had much of an effect on his bungalow. What paint still clung to the wood had long been bleached from its original salmon pink to a quiet blush. The weeds had died of neglect, allowing the gnomes to peek at passersby from the missing slats in the picket fence.

Peri and Benny sat in the SUV while the police did their job. Skip stood outside, keeping one eye on the landscape and the other on his cargo.

"How long are they going to be in there, Miss Peri?"

"I don't know." She regarded the state of his house. "Benny, I think we need to talk about this place."

"What are they doing? Are they moving my stuff? I hope they're not moving my stuff. They might break something. What if they break something?"

"They just want to check the doors and windows, make sure nobody broke in." She went back to her original topic. "You need to hire someone to fix your house a little. It needs paint, yard work, cleaning up."

"It's not so bad."

"Yes, it is, Ben. Your neighbors are going to turn you in to the Health Department. Or the police. Someone." Peri rubbed her temples. She wanted a drink, but it would exacerbate her headache. Maybe she could have an aspirin with her martini.

At last, the officers emerged. They both appeared to be wiping their hands, as if the state of the house made them feel unclean. After speaking with them, Skip leaned into the open car window on Peri's side.

"Looks good, Benny. You can stay here tonight, if you want, or go to a friend's or relative's house. We'll keep your car at the station overnight, so it'll be safe. An officer can come by and bring you past the squad room to give your statement, then you can drive home."

"Pick me up? In a squad car?"

"Yes."

"Does it have to be a squad car? I don't like squad cars."

"Benny." Skip's voice dropped an octave.

The little man changed the subject. "What time?"

"I don't know what time, Ben. Before noon."

Benny turned to Peri. "What time do you want me at work tomorrow?"

"You want to come back to work tomorrow?" She tried not to sound as incredulous as she felt.

"I gotta have my hours."

"I've got an idea," Skip said. "Let's all go to Peri's place right now. She's going to pack up a few things and stay at my house for awhile, but she can show you where the kitty supplies are, and you can get her mail and her paper and take care of the cat while she's away."

She brightened. "That's a good idea. Ben, I'll sign off eight hours a day if you'll take care of my house while I'm at Skip's. You can work the hours you want. Deal?"

"Deal."

Skip motioned to the two officers, then got back in the SUV and drove down Yorba Linda Boulevard to Peri's neighborhood off Bradford.

"Miss Peri, will this cat shed on my clothes?"

"Not if you don't let him sit on you."

Benny laughed, a high, little hiccupping squeak. "Why would I let a cat sit on me? Do you know where his butt has been?"

"You may have to get new furniture, Doll," Skip told her. "His butt's been everywhere."

CHAPTER 15

They pulled into Peri's driveway, and Skip made her and Benny stay in the car until the uniforms checked the house and back yard. Given the 'all clear', he opened the door and ushered her in, Benny following close behind.

Sunlight flowed through the windows and brightened the living room. A pale blue vase lay in fragments on the floor below the television; Mr. Mustard sat in the bookcase, a "So what?" expression in his eyes.

Peri stood, looking at the mess on the floor. She hoped the jagged ceramic edges hadn't scratched the wood.

"Broken dish, that's too bad," Benny said.

"Eh, my ex-mother-in-law gave it to me, so it wasn't sentimental." She knelt down and carefully picked up the pieces. Mr. Mustard took one graceful bound from his perch to the floor, then strolled to Peri and rotated himself sideways to rub his backbone against her arm.

"Ew, is he gonna do that to me?"

"Not if you don't let him." She brushed at the pottery dust left by the break. No evidence of scratches found, which was good.

"Go ahead and show Benny what he needs to do," Skip told her. "Then throw some stuff in a bag and let's get out of here."

"Who knew I'd have to pack for more than an overnighter? Come on, Ben." She led her unpaid laborer through the kitchen to the laundry alcove, where she showed him the cat food, the litter box and the cleaning supplies.

"I don't know if I can." He looked down at the clumps of kitty refuse Peri was scooping into a bag. "I have to clean it every day?"

"Yes, Benny. Every day. Who knows, I may only be gone for one day. I'll work all night long if that's what it takes to get this report finished." She opened the cabinet under the sink and pulled out a box. "Here are disposable gloves you can wear."

"That's a little better," he said, curling his nose.

Peri went to the drawer by the stove and retrieved a kerchief. "Here. If you don't like the smell, tie this around your face. You'll look like a bandit, but what the hell."

He looked at the red bandanna. "Dino never wore anything like that."

"What does that—never mind." She threw the cloth on the counter. "Wear it, don't wear it, I'm just offering. Quite frankly, I don't know how you can be so squeamish. I've seen the inside of your house, remember?"

"That's my mess, Miss Peri. They're my smells. They're not from some stupid animal who breaks things and scratches things and poops in gravel."

Peri thought perhaps she had offended Benny.

"Oh, wait," he said. "Maybe he wore one in Something Big. I'll have to go home and watch that movie again."

Bad feelings averted, she excused herself to pack. When she returned, Benny was sitting in the kitchen chair, staring at the big orange tabby, who was on the kitchen table, staring back at him. The little man's hands were folded in his lap, his shoulders collapsed forward, and his uni-brow furrowed, in worry or concentration, Peri couldn't tell. She watched them for a moment. They never moved or broke their gaze. Finally Benny turned away, rubbing his eyes with his two pudgy fists, as if erasing his face.

Skip joined them in the kitchen, tapping her on the shoulder. "Ready to go?"

"Yeah. How about you, Benny?"

"Cats can stare a long time," he said.

“Yes they can,” she replied. “Let’s get you home.”

After they dropped Benny off, Skip pointed the SUV north on Kraemer Boulevard toward his house. They zipped across Yorba Linda Boulevard and followed the straight, smooth pavement toward Bastanchury Road.

“Before we go to your house, can we swing by Best Buy?”

“For?”

“A new computer. I gotta get that report written.”

His foot hammered the brakes to a stop at the light. “What?”

“The sooner I get it written, the sooner I get my money, the—”

“Yes, you told me, but can’t you just use my computer?”

“I could, but I need to download files from my external drive, then remove them when I get my computer replaced, and I’d rather have my own clean slate to work on.”

“Ah, Doll, can’t we go back to my place and relax for five minutes?”

“I don’t need to relax.” She snipped each word with precision. “I need for someone to stop hunting me. Plan A is to remove what I think is their motivation. Someone didn’t want me to find out about Nikki’s affair. Once I knew, they didn’t want me to get the evidence to Don. Maybe it’s Nikki. Maybe that golf pro. He doesn’t look that smart, but you never know.”

“Sounds reasonable. If that’s not it, what’s Plan B?”

She leaned her head on the passenger window and stared at Skip.

“Peri?”

“I don’t know yet.”

“Peri.” His voice had that Father Knows Best tone she hated.

“I’m tired of being hit in the head, tired of being shot at. Granted it’s only once, but it’s enough. If they don’t leave me alone, well, I just don’t know what I’m going to do about it.”

“Well, I hope you’re not thinking about chasing after them.”

“Let’s not discuss it now. Let’s just get me a new toy to distract me for a little while so I can write my report tonight.”

"Okay." He turned right on Bastanchury and headed toward Imperial Highway and the Savi Ranch Center in Yorba Linda.

The worker bees at Best Buy were all fourteen years old, at least so they looked to Peri, and she quickly found one willing to sell her a laptop. She managed to sidestep the latest gadgets and add-ons and concentrate on what she needed. After rebuffing the salesgirl's attempts to sell her extended warranties, service plans and possibly an indentured servant to wipe the keys for her every morning, she walked out with a brand new Dell.

"Shouldn't you have waited for the insurance to see what they'd pay for?" Skip asked as he carried the box to the car.

"Maybe, but I need it now. I had a Dell. Someone shot it. I need a new one." She hopped in the seat. "Seems reasonable to me."

"Whatever you say, Doll. Can I take you home now?"

"I'm ready."

Skip herded his SUV back to Placentia and eased it into his garage. While he gathered his briefcase from the car, Peri entered the house and took her purchase into the family room. She placed the box and accessory bag on the floor in front of the fireplace, then turned to the open kitchen behind her and grabbed a pair of scissors out of a cabinet drawer.

At last, she sat down next to the box and began opening everything, while Skip foraged for lunch in his refrigerator. She lifted the new equipment from its spongy compartment and put it on the oak coffee table, then took out the instruction booklet and read.

Skip walked over with plates of sandwiches, turkey and cranberry sauce on honeyed wheat bread, with carrots and olives on the side.

"What do you want to drink?"

"Hmm? Oh, got any of that lemongrass iced tea?"

"I can make some, no problem."

She leaned back against the couch and popped a carrot in her mouth. Most of the instruction booklet was aimed at idiots, she decided.

"Why do they need to warn me about water—who uses a laptop in the tub?" She dug in the box and found the power cord.

"Because someone tried using their laptop in the swimming pool." Skip sat down on the couch and read over her shoulder. "Peri, we need to talk about this—this—predicament you're in."

"No we don't."

"You know I try not to say it, but I'm worried about you. You're not used to this kind of life. You're not equipped."

"I know, we've talked about the gun thing. I've been thinking—maybe I need to take some classes, get accustomed to handling one." She continued to plug the power cord together and refer to the manual as she spoke.

"That's not what I mean." He stood and paced to the sliding glass door, running his hand over his hair. "I think I'd worry more about you if you were carrying."

Peri powered up her new computer, and dug through a box of application CDs. "I thought you were worried because I'm unarmed. Make up your mind."

"When we started dating, you were a housecleaner. A smart, funny, sexy housecleaner. Sure, you went into strangers' homes, but I didn't worry so much. You never mentioned whether you had any problems with any of the homeowners, so I assumed you were safe."

"Of course I was safe."

"When you wanted to be a P.I., I was a little worried, but not so much. Surveillance, background checks, that kind of work is usually quiet." He sat down on the floor, across from her. "But this…"

"I didn't ask for this, Skip. It's not my fault."

"Of course not. But you're not safe, and you weren't safe on the last case, either."

Peri stopped working. “Only because Mrs. Cheavers couldn’t keep her mouth shut. I’ve now written a confidentiality clause into my contract.”

He took her hand in his. “When the dispatcher called me today, for a moment, I almost couldn’t keep it together.”

“Oh, Skip.” She reached forward and kissed him. “What about you? Not that you get a lot of violent crimes to investigate, but being a cop puts you in potential danger every day. I admit, I get worried when you’re late, but I know it’s your job and you love it.”

“I know, there’s no difference. I’m just having a hard time adjusting.”

“So what do you want me to do? Quit?”

He looked at her. “I don’t want you to quit and be unhappy.”

“But you wouldn’t mind if I happily went back to housecleaning.”

He shrugged.

“I’m pissed right now. All I was paid to do was get a few pictures, some receipts, proof of an affair. Instead I’m getting harassed by some faceless coward. Even if I happily quit and started scrubbing toilets again, I’d still want a piece of whoever is trying to scare me.”

The look on his face told Peri she’d frightened him, as much as she could frighten a man who outsized her by both inches and pounds. She smiled and massaged his hand with her fingers. “Eat your lunch and let’s talk about something else.”

“We need to get this talked about.”

“I know. But let’s do it when it’s over, when we can both have a clearer perspective.”

“Peri, how is my perspective going to be clearer? I love you. I worry about you. That’s about as clear as it gets.”

“And I love and worry about you. We are clear there. But let me get out of the middle of this madness before I decide what to do, okay?”

Skip moved to her side and kissed her neck. “Okay, Doll.”

Applications loaded, files retrieved from her external hard drive, internet connection established, Peri toiled to complete the Keller report. She retrieved her zip file from the email she sent earlier and printed the shots of Nikki and Tyler embracing on the green. She was still typing when Skip wandered in from the bedroom.

"It's two-thirty. You about done?"

She nodded. "I have one more page of notes to enter, then the report will take me about ten minutes to compile and print." She reached up and kissed his nose. "I'll give Keller a call in the morning to arrange a time for drop-off."

He ran his fingers through her long, blonde hair. "You have the softest hair. It's like silk or, I don't know, a really fluffy bunny."

Peri laughed, and leaned into his hand while his fingers massaged her scalp. "Mmm, that feels good. Let me finish this and I'll come to bed."

Skip kissed her and walked back to the bedroom. Forty minutes later, she joined him.

CHAPTER 16

The seven o'clock air felt painful against her sleep-deprived eyeballs, but she staggered to the bathroom and shook her head awake. A shower would refresh her, and she could smell the coffee Skip had made. *God bless that man,* she thought as she tested the hot water and stepped into the shower stall.

Clean and slightly more conscious, she shuffled into the kitchen, Skip's brown robe over her sweats and t-shirt, and poured a cup of coffee. Skip sat at the table, finishing a bowl of cereal and reading the Sports Section.

"Why are you up so early? You can't call Keller much before nine."

"I know," she said. "But I wanted to read the report one more time. I was so tired last night—this morning—whatever. I don't want any typos."

"Well, I'm supposed to go to a meeting at nine, but I'm getting one of the officers to come by and stay with you until I get back."

She sat down, wrapped her hands around her coffee mug and put it up to her nose, inhaling the strong bouquet. "I know, this is where I usually tell you not to worry about me, and I'm not a baby, and I don't need 24-hour surveillance, yadda, yadda."

Skip looked up, waiting.

"Not a peep," she said. "I'm peepless. Gimme shelter."

He chuckled. "Good girl. Tom Gomez will be over at eight thirty, and I should be back by noon. If you need to go anywhere, Tom will take you."

She read over the report as the minutes ticked past. At first, she thought she'd gotten up too early; the report looked clean. After the third read, however, she began to notice little things, an extra "the" here, a missing verb there. She cleaned it up and reprinted, just as the doorbell rang.

Skip walked into the kitchen with the leggy officer from yesterday's crime scene. "Peri, do you know Officer Gomez?"

"I remember you from yesterday. How are you?" Peri said.

"Fine, Ma'am. How are you feeling?"

"Much better. Thanks for the guard duty."

Skip gave her a quick hug and kissed her cheek. "I gotta run, Doll, but I'll be back around lunchtime. Want me to pick up anything?"

"I don't know. Call me before you come back."

Officer Gomez and Peri watched the door slam, then turned to each other in a moment of silence. Peri broke first.

"TV's over there, Officer. And help yourself to coffee, breakfast, anything. I'm going to get changed."

By nine o'clock, Peri emerged from the bedroom dressed in slacks and a button-down shirt, her blonde hair dry and curled and a swath of makeup on her pale face. She took the Keller folder into the living room, sat on the couch and dialed his cell phone number. It went to voicemail without ringing.

"Mr. Keller, this is Peri Minneopa. Please call me back."

Ending the call, there was nothing to do but wait. She played with her new computer, then used Skip's landline to call her insurance agent, and called Benny to see if he had fed the cat.

"He hates me, Miss Peri," Benny told her.

"I'm sure he doesn't hate you."

"He never smiles. He just sits and stares."

"Cats don't smile, Ben. They don't have the facial muscles. Did you feed him? Did he eat?"

"That food stinks."

Peri looked at her cell phone, wishing it would ring so she could end this conversation. "I'm not asking you to eat it. I'm asking you to give it to the cat."

"I found some meat in the refrigerator. He liked that better."

"My steak from Summit House?" She stood up, her voice tense. Summit House was a high-end restaurant, where she'd treated herself to dinner recently and had carefully saved half of her filet mignon to have for lunch later. "I was going to eat that."

She sat down and sighed. "I can guarantee, Benny, that even if he hated you before, he loves you now."

He was telling her about the intricate process he had developed for scooping kitty waste from the litter box without smelling or even touching it, when Peri's phone began to vibrate along the table.

"Gotta go, Ben, my other line's ringing," she said and hung up, then picked up the other phone. "Peri Minneopa here."

"Don Keller." His voice sounded flat.

"I have your report, Mr. Keller. If you'd like, I could drop it somewhere, or—"

"There won't be any need for that, Miss Minnowpia. I've decided not to pursue this investigation." He sounded like someone reading from a script.

"But I've finished it. I've spent a few days gathering data." She held back the information about being assaulted and shot at, for now.

"You'll still get paid for your services." His voice quivered so much Peri thought he might be crying. "But I've decided—I don't want to know. Mail me a copy of the invoice, to my post office box."

"Mr. Keller, pardon me if I'm out of line, but is everything all right?"

He snapped back into corporate executive mode. "You're right, you're out of line. Mail me the invoice and I'll send you a check. Thank you."

The line went dead. Peri sat for a few moments, staring at her cell, trying to process what had just happened. Don Keller, the arrogant, sonuvabitch who strode into her office last week, alternately ignoring her and making demands about her time, sounded frightened and suddenly didn't want what he had paid her to get for him. It didn't make sense, unless… what if Don Keller was being threatened in the same manner she had been?

Peri shook her head. When she was a little girl, Helen used to encourage her imagination. "What if the sky was green and the grass was blue?" she'd ask her daughter, and Peri would laugh.

She could blame her mother for her wild flights of fancy. But now she felt her imagination running off, like a spooked horse. Who had the balls to threaten Don Keller of Keller and Patterson? He was rich and powerful, at least by Placentia standards. And, truly, when had her sleepy little town had anything that smacked of intrigue?

Peri started to call Skip, then looked at her watch. He was still in the meeting. She went into his home office and found an envelope. Placing the bill for her services inside, she wrote Keller's post office box information on the outside and stuck on a stamp.

"Officer Gomez, could you take me to the police station, by way of the post office?"

CHAPTER 17

Skip knew the chief tried not to have many meetings, but he still found they ended up spending too much time rehashing material. Each time a topic was mentioned, five voices had to echo what one voice opined. He took another swig of coffee and tried to stay in the discussion, while the file on Dottie and Bob Peters lay in his lap, tempting him.

One of the younger officers began giving his status on a wave of car breakins at an apartment complex, so Skip pushed his chair out a little and opened the folder, intending to just skim the report from Bob's toxicology screen. The paper had columns and boxes with words and check marks, but he knew how to find what he was looking for. It confirmed what he suspected, that Bob had oleander in his system. It would have been easy to miss in an 80 year old man with a barrel chest and a preference for red meat.

Following the report, there were several pages of real estate jargon from John Patterson, outlining their offers to the Peters for the Palm Desert property. There wasn't much in the way of interesting data here. He leafed through the papers while his coworkers droned in the background. One of the forms had copied fainter than the others. Skip picked this up and looked at it more closely. There was a large white section in the left corner with handwriting. This sheet of paper had a note attached that the secretary had copied together. The note caught his attention.

"Use previous Quigley offer as basis."

What previous offer, he thought.

Chief Fletcher interrupted his study. "Detective Carlton, what's the status of the Peters investigation?"

Skip held up the paper. "As soon as this meeting is over, I've got another lead to chase down."

The chief smiled. "Well, then, what are you waiting for? Let's get to work."

Back at his desk, Skip considered his options. He could revisit Patterson's office to find out about this Quigley offer, or he could just call. He wondered if Patterson would be as forthcoming with more documents. A feeling in his gut told him this note meant more than a casual scribble.

A previous offer meant that Keller and Patterson had tried to purchase this land before. Patterson acted as though the parcel wasn't important to their development, but maybe he was lying. Skip looked over his notes. He was certain Patterson was lying about something in the interview.

When he requested the original file, he wasn't thinking of John Patterson as a possible suspect. Now he wasn't so sure. What if this "previous offer" turned out to be evidence against Patterson, or his firm? If even he suspected Patterson while he was asking for more files, should he get a court order? If he didn't and the files incriminated Patterson, would they be useable in an arrest? That is, if Patterson cooperated.

The world wasn't always black and white for a detective. At the end of his deliberation, he decided his gut feeling didn't count as probable cause for a warrant.

"Might as well see how far I get," he said to himself, picked up his car keys and headed out the door.

The clouds had moved west, revealing the sunshine, by the time Skip pulled into the Keller and Patterson parking lot. It was early, but he hoped someone would be in the office.

Tanya, Patterson's secretary, was at the front desk, talking on her cell phone and picking at what looked like a banana nut muffin. She was a pretty, zaftig woman, with dark brown hair and sparkling chocolate eyes.

"Good morning," she said. "You're the detective, aren't you?"

"Tanya, isn't it?" Skip replied. "Is your boss in?"

"Not yet. He's got physical therapy this morning, so he'll be late."

"I was going through the file you gave me and I came across this." He showed her the paper. "I thought maybe you could tell me what it meant."

She took the page and read it. "I'm not certain, but let me look up the file number." She turned to her computer and started typing.

He watched her work and thought about his conversation with Patterson. "Oh, I thought your boss said your system had crashed recently."

She looked surprised, then hesitated. "Um, well, sure."

"Tanya." He leaned across her desk. "There was no crash was there?"

"No."

"I probably misunderstood." He gestured toward the computer. "If I could just get the information..."

"Of course." She entered a series of numbers and read. "Would you like all the offers on that parcel?"

"Are there a lot?"

"It looks like we've tried to purchase that land four times in the last seven years." She pressed the mouse and turned to her printer. Two pages printed out. "Here's the information," she said, handing them to Skip.

"Thank you, Tanya. I appreciate this. Tell Mr. Patterson I'm sorry I missed him."

Skip walked out with a handful of paper and a head full of questions. Why did Keller and Patterson want this piece of property? Why pretend it was inconsequential? And why lie about a computer crash?

He drove back to the office, anxious to get some answers.

As he pulled into the police department parking lot, he wondered if Peri had come in for her interview yet. Having her knocked unconscious was worrisome to him. Having her window shot out by a bullet moved his worry up to a feeling of fear, something he was unused to dealing with. A certain level of apprehension when he was in the middle of a chase or a confrontation was part of the job. He knew how to incorporate it into his training, to control the adrenaline and use it.

But, he admitted as he walked to his desk, he didn't know what to do with that woman. He didn't know if he could get used to worrying about her. Besides, the Placentia Police Department could not spend all its time and resources protecting her, even if it was not her fault. If she didn't want to go back to housecleaning, maybe he could suggest another career she'd like just as much as sleuthing… maybe cat rescue…

Sitting down, he took a sip of the coffee he'd just poured, and turned on his computer. He'd start his search for previous owners in the public records. It was so nice to have things at his fingertips. In the old days, he would have had to travel to the Riverside County Courthouse and dig through books. Now he could access most public records online, as long as they weren't too old.

The information Tanya had given him looked like the firm's first offer to buy the land was about seven years ago. A man named Oscar Mendoza bought the parcel from the estate of Victoria Hagen. Then, two years later, Philip Hughes bought it from Oscar. Skip dug around a little more on the transaction and saw Hughes had actually purchased it from Oscar's estate. William Quigley purchased it three years later, from Hughes' estate. And just six months ago, the Peters bought the land from the late Mr. Quigley.

This was not looking like a good pattern. It did, however, look like a good reason for John Patterson to control the amount of material he handed over, even if it meant lying about a computer crash.

Skip sat back and reread the papers Tanya had given him. In each case, Keller and Patterson had made the estate an offer, only to be outbid by another buyer. On the one hand, if they had been intent on getting the land, he saw no reason why they would allow themselves to be bested by a private owner. On the other hand, there was just something wrong with all those owners dying.

It was now time to look into the deaths. He was almost hoping they weren't ruled heart attack, so he wouldn't have to order more exhumations. Sometimes it had to be done, but beyond all the paperwork, he hated the idea of disturbing the dead. He knew they didn't care, but their families did. Many times, it brought them right back to the beginning of their grief.

Before diving into more record searching, Skip stood, stretched, and walked down the hall to get another cup of coffee. He was returning to his office when he heard someone call his name.

"Do you have a minute?" Ella Mason walked up to him as he paused in his doorway. "I want to thank you for that brochure you gave me. Jorge thinks he'd like to take the photography class."

"That's great," Skip said.

"The only problem is that it's on Tuesday nights, and that's my one evening shift."

"Oh, that's too bad." He paused and looked at her. She wore the expression of someone who was looking for a favor. "I guess I could take him if you couldn't."

Her face lit up. He noticed she looked a little different today. Her hair was in the same bun, but her eyes seemed a little darker, and her mouth a little softer. "That would be so kind of you. I don't know how to repay you for being so nice."

"Really, it's no problem. Just let me know when class starts."

He was aware that Ella had somehow moved closer to him, almost sharing his space in the door frame. She smelled of pina colada, just like she did at the Peters house. His thoughts drifted toward the Caribbean cruise he had taken with Peri, and he smiled a little. He was thinking about the white sand of the beach when he heard someone calling his name. Craig Daniels was saying something, so he looked up.

Peri was with Craig, an odd, frozen smile on her face. Skip grinned and waved to her. “Hey, Doll,” he said as he walked toward her, without another thought of Ella and her son.

CHAPTER 18

Having dropped the invoice in the Placentia Post Office's outside mailbox, Officer Gomez drove Peri to the police station and escorted her toward Skip's office.

"Actually, Officer, I need to speak with Detective Daniels," she told him.

Through the window, she saw Craig Daniels sitting behind his desk, shuffling papers as if looking for something he'd lost. She noted the way his dark hair had been styled to a 'bed head' look. From his tanned biceps to his trendy ensemble of black jeans and plaid shirt over a Tommy Bahama tee, he had the look of a recently divorced, middle-aged man who was trying too hard.

He held up his hand when the officer opened his door, as if to stop him.

"Give me a minute, Gomez, I just got out of a meeting and I'm trying to find my phone."

Peri stuck her head in the door. "Why don't you try calling it?"

"Because it's on vibe—Oh, hi, Peri. You're looking good today. What can I do for you?" His demeanor changed completely, from annoyed to flirtatious in less than five seconds.

"I'm ready to discuss yesterday's shooting."

"Great. You know what? Let's go to one of the interrogation rooms. We've got recording equipment already set up, makes it easier. Plus, I think a lot better when I'm not in all this clutter."

Peri looked around at the chaos. "So, you don't spend a lot of time actually thinking in this room, huh?"

He laughed. "I guess I let it get out of hand. I'll clean it up when I get a free moment."

Skip told me all about you, she thought. *Your free moments are spent chasing skirts*.

After they sat down at the big grey table in the small beige room, she pulled the Keller folder from her tote bag and went through the evidence, beginning with the jogger and Officer Chou, and ending with her exploding window and dead laptop. Detective Daniels took notes as she spoke, but didn't ask many questions. At last, she sat back in her chair, looked at him, and waited.

"This is all very thorough, very methodical," he told her. "I wish all my witnesses had this kind of evidence."

"Except that I never saw Nikki, or anyone else, actually perpetrate any of these crimes." She pointed to the flash drive on the table. "The country club conversation might reveal something, but I wouldn't hold my breath."

"Maybe not, but we've got a starting point. And I think the key may be what happens next. I'm assuming you've delivered your report to Keller."

Peri crossed her arms. "That's another piece of the puzzle. I called Keller today. He doesn't want the report."

"What do you mean, he doesn't want it?"

"Suddenly he doesn't want to know. Oh, he'll pay me for my time. But no report." She leaned forward. "His voice sounded funny today, too. Insecure, scared, not like him at all. I don't know what's up with this case, but it feels like an awful hot potato in my hands, especially for just a standard, cheating-spouse assignment."

Craig was writing as fast as she spoke. "It does sound unusual. But what I was saying before, if you're finished with the case, you've written the report—even if you haven't delivered it, if it's Nikki who's after you, she should stop when you stop working on the case, right?"

"It's what I'm hoping. I'm really getting sick of the whole dead bird, head-whacking, shots fired, lifestyle. Maybe I should cross surveillance off my list of services offered. So far, these cases haven't been much fun."

"Oh, yeah, I remember—you were shot by that husband, weren't you?"

"Idiots." She rubbed her scarred shoulder in absent-minded response. "If it is Nikki and she just doesn't want her husband to know, I guess I'm in the clear. If it's her and she doesn't want anyone to know, she's going to have to take care of me, sooner or later."

"And if it's not her…"

"Yeah, we don't have a shred of evidence." She pointed to the bag of metal Allen had pulled out of her tire. "Unless you can get fingerprints off that."

Daniels stood. "We'll have Jason take a look at it, but I think I've got enough to start. Let's go back to my office and I'll make copies of your file."

They strolled back to his room. The detective moved stacks of paper out of Peri's way so she could sit, then stepped behind his own desk and began digging through a box on the floor.

She watched him hunt. "Can I help you find something?"

He pulled a beige folder out of the bottom of the box, spilling most of its contents. "Found one."

Peri shook her head, and thought about how glad she was to be out of the housecleaning business, although her fingers twitched at the sight of the disarray.

"Okay, let me stick a label on this baby," the detective said.

As the detective worked, Peri glanced up through the window to see Skip standing in the hallway, talking to Ella. Her gut feeling told her to put all her powers of detection into high alert; Skip was smiling in that paternal, helpful-cop, manner Peri had seen him use with witnesses.

Ella was smiling, too, but it wasn't a coworker's smile. Peri noted the tilt of her chin, which allowed her to look up with brown eyes, as large and luminous as Bambi on the big screen. Her lips were moist and she smiled with her mouth slightly open. If Skip were looking for a good time, Peri knew where he could get it.

"Your boyfriend's been trying to get us all to spend time with Ella's son," Daniels said.

Peri turned to see him looking out the window at the pair. "So he told me. He says he hates to see a cop's kid go astray."

"Well, take it from me, that boy's already strayed pretty far. I used to be the liaison officer at Kraemer Middle School."

"You knew her son then?"

"Oh, Sonny-boy and I go way back. The first day of sixth grade, he got caught tagging outside the boys' lockers. Then we had complaints about him playing grabass with girls as they came out of class. By seventh grade he was in one of the gangs." He shook his head. "I want to help, and I don't want to put the burden on Skip's shoulders, but it doesn't look good."

"Skip seems to think it's because he doesn't have any male influences to keep him on the straight and narrow."

Daniels laughed. "No male influences? Try too many. Don't get me wrong, Mason's a good cop, a nice gal, and all that. But she's always looking for a daddy for little Jorge. And that mom of hers—whew, what a, well, I don't want to gossip. But Grandma gets around."

"Hmm." The detective was not making Peri feel better about Skip's attempt to be a good influence.

He seemed to read her mind. Nodding toward the window, he said, "Good thing you don't have to worry. Skip's immune to her." He leaned back in his chair and stretched his arms up and out. "Too bad for me, though. If I thought Skip could be distracted, I'd ask you to the dance this Saturday."

"What dance? Oh, the party at Alta Vista?"

He acted surprised. "Aren't you going?"

The dinner-dance at the Alta Vista Country Club was held every year, on the second Saturday in October. It was the culmination of Placentia's Heritage Day, a daylong celebration for the residents of the city. The holiday started with a pancake breakfast, included a parade down Kraemer Boulevard to Tri-City Park for an afternoon of games, food, and festivities, and then ended with the Heritage Dinner-Dance at the club.

The party was a formal affair and came with a sizeable price tag, but members of the PPD were invited, no charge, as a way of saying thank you. Skip had been invited every year for awhile, and had declined each time.

"Spending the evening in a monkey suit isn't my idea of a good time," was his excuse.

"You know Skip never goes to that party," Peri told the detective.

Craig held up a piece of paper. "Well, this year, he's supposed to. We got a memo from the chief. He wants us all there. Good PR and all that." He smiled. "Skip didn't tell you? Maybe there's hope for me yet."

She smiled and stood. "Are we done? Skip's taking me to lunch."

"Let me make some quick copies and we're all set." He walked around and opened the door for her. "Hey, Skip," he called down the hallway. "Friend of yours stopped by to see me."

Peri saw Skip glance up, and then wave. He smiled and moved toward her, leaving Ella to stand alone.

"Is it lunch already?"

Peri glanced at her watch. "Eleven thirty. Close enough."

CHAPTER 19

"So were you planning to tell me about the dance on Saturday, or do you like having the chief kick your butt?" Peri waited until they were diving into chips and salsa at El Farolito before launching her inquiry.

"Oh, yeah, kind of forgot that. Want to go to the dance on Saturday?'

She frowned. "It's black tie, Skip."

"I've got a tux."

"But I don't have a dress. I need a haircut, my nails done, I'm not ready."

"Maybe you can get Blanche to go shopping with you tomorrow."

A young Hispanic man brought their food to the table. Peri sat back in her chair and allowed him to put the hot plate in front of her. The steam from the enchilada verde rose toward her, filling her senses with spices, garlic, onions, and more. She managed to exchange smiles with the waiter before she picked up her fork and filled it with a beginning mouthful of rice, beans and green sauce.

"Mmm." Her eyes closed to better concentrate on the flavors. Looking up, she saw Skip smiling at her.

"That hungry?"

"No. That good."

He laughed, then took a few bites of his own lunch before speaking again. "So, I'm guessing you got that report turned in."

"Yes and no. After all that work, suddenly he can't stand to look at what I've found. Doesn't want it anymore."

"But he's going to pay you, right?"

"So he says. And if these attacks are because of my work on that case, I have no idea whether they're going to stop now that I'm done. What do you think?"

Skip reached out and brushed her hand with his fingers. "I don't know, but you'll stay with me until…"

"Until when, Skip? Until people stop trying to hurt me? If I'm protected all day and night, how will we even know if they've given up?"

"Well, Daniels will do his investigation first. If we get lucky, we'll find the person."

"Like I've ever been lucky."

"You know what I mean."

"Yes, there will be interviews and investigating and solid police work, and if you get enough pieces of information, you'll be able to figure it all out. But luck would be nice. And there's a reason I don't buy lottery tickets."

"Peri—"

She held her hand up to stop him. "In the meantime, I'll be a good girl and let Daniels do his work."

They finished their lunch and walked out of the restaurant. The afternoon sun bounced from the white stucco of the building to the sidewalk, aiming its heat at Peri. She stepped into Skip's black SUV and fanned the door to chase the hot air out of the car. The weatherman had predicted highs in the 80s, and it felt like the temperature had achieved that goal, and more. She fluffed her hair from the nape of her neck, happy to be in short sleeves and light cotton slacks. Who the hell decided that autumn in southern California was the right time to drag out the suede boots and tweed jackets?

"Back to my place, right?" Skip stepped into the driver's seat.

"Actually, I was hoping you could run me past the office so I could talk to the landlord."

"Sure."

"And maybe look at the damage?" Her voice rose a little, like a child asking permission.

He kept his eyes on the road, his expression stern. "I really don't want—oh, what the hell. Okay."

As they pulled into the parking lot, Peri felt her lungs grow tight and stiff. She was surprised at such a visceral reaction, and kept close to Skip for support as they walked through the wrought iron gate, down the corridor toward the door with yellow police tape. Just before they reached the office, she stopped and sank backward into him.

"You ready to do this?" he asked.

She thought for a moment, reliving the exploding windows, the incredible swiftness of the event, and her feeling of wonder that she and Benny survived it. The tightness in her chest did not relax, but finally she nodded and walked forward.

"I'm ready."

Skip opened the door and cleared the tape. The small room was completely dark, windows boarded up with plywood. Peri stepped in and flipped the light switch.

The first thing she noticed was the glass pebbles. Small fractions of the window, random, jagged edges like cornflakes, lay everywhere on her desk and the floor. The desk was bare, except for the lamp and her pencil holder.

"Where's my dead laptop?"

"Jason probably took it to process the bullet."

"Of course. They'd have to take it to the lab."

She stood and stared for several minutes, looking right and left, memorizing each detail.

Skip interrupted her thoughts with a gentle caress of her shoulder. "You ready?"

Peri nodded and backed out of the door, then stopped and turned. "Where's my picture?"

"What picture?"

"The one of you and me, that day we went whale watching."

"Maybe Jason took that, too."

"Why? Was it shot?"

"I don't know." Skip stepped into the office and looked around the desk, before opening his cell phone. "Hey, Jason, did the evidence from Peri's office include a framed picture of her and me? Okay, thanks."

He turned back to her. "He didn't take it."

She looked again at the spot on the desk where she last saw it. "Someone took it."

"Who?"

"I don't know, Skip, but I know that picture was on my desk."

"Maybe it was, but what's so special about a picture of us?"

"I hid my camera's memory card behind your face. I was feeling paranoid." Gesturing to the plywood-covered window, she added, "I'd say I was justified."

She took another step toward her desk, but he stopped her. "Stay out, Peri."

"Why?"

He called Jason again. "We may have had a breakin here after you processed the scene. Can you come back and go over the office again? The sooner the better. Thanks."

She looked at Skip's hand on her arm and exerted a little pressure, but he didn't budge. "We can look around, right?"

"No, we can't. We need to wait for CSU."

"You're kidding."

Skip pulled her out the door. "We need to be as far from this office as possible."

"Stop dragging me. This is my office—I think I should be able to look around my own office to see who's been in here."

"I know you feel that way, but try to understand. It's a procedural thing. I'm worried about our presence in the office as it is. Say we look around and find evidence. We catch the person, and the DA reads the case file and finds out who discovered it.

They are not going to want to explain to the jury how you and I got involved without compromising the case."

"Why would we compromise it? I just want to find the person who did it."

"And if it's Nikki Keller? And she says you were prejudiced against her and planted the evidence?"

"Oh, Skip, that's stupid."

He moved his hand down to her back and pointed her toward the corridor. "It may be stupid, Doll, but in the world of juries, it's called reasonable doubt." Locking the office door, he said. "Let's go visit the landlord."

Michael Steuben was at his desk, opening the mail when they entered. A slight man with dark features, he looked relieved to see them.

"Peri, I'm so glad you're okay. What happened?"

"The police are still checking that out," she told him. "Have they talked to you?"

"No, a detective called, um—" He searched around on his desk until he retrieved a scrap of paper. "Detective Daniels. I'm supposed to talk to him on Monday."

Skip introduced himself. "Has the insurance company contacted you?"

"Actually," Peri said, ignoring Skip's grip on her arm. "I wanted to know if anyone wanted to see any of the available offices yesterday."

"Not yesterday, but the day before, I had a gal looking for space."

"What did she look like?" Peri felt Skip's grip tighten.

"Tall, brunette. Attractive gal, maybe in her thirties."

Peri looked at Skip, then back to Michael. "What offices did you show her?"

"All she wanted to see were the second-story locations, so I showed her the three offices I have upstairs."

"Are any of those across from my office?"

"Closest one is that corner space." He pointed toward the southwest corner of the complex.

Skip interrupted their conversation. "Thank you, Michael, we'll pass this on to Daniels, although I'm sure he'll have more questions."

"Michael—" Peri started, but Skip's grip began to pinch. "Thanks for being so understanding. I'll be in touch."

They left the office, Peri being escorted with gentle force by her boyfriend. She waited until they were at the gate before speaking.

"Oh, come on, can't we at least check the office upstairs? It didn't sound like Nikki, but it could have been one of her friends. What if she's got all her besties involved? There could be evidence."

"If there is, Jason will find it." As he opened the SUV door for her to get in, he leaned over and kissed her. "Craig Daniels is a good detective. I want this done by the book."

"And in the meantime?"

"In the meantime, let's go home. You need to schedule some shopping time with Blanche."

"Not to mention the hairdresser, the manicurist and perhaps the personal trainer." She buckled her seatbelt as Skip stepped into the car. "Do you think I can lose ten pounds in two days?"

He laughed. "Don't you dare lose any weight. I like those curves."

CHAPTER 20

Blanche stepped into Skip's foyer. "You ready for some shopping, Girlfriend?"

"Let's see," Peri said. "I'm wearing a skirt and blouse that can be removed easily, and I'm bringing my best stilettos. I'm either ready for shopping or a night of streetwalking."

"Hey, I heard that." Skip came out of the kitchen, a sandwich in his hand.

"How else am I supposed to afford a dress at Nordie's?" Peri smiled and gave him a kiss before taking a bite out of his lunch. "Mm, needs avocado."

"Have fun, ladies," he said, then nodded at Blanche. "Take care of her."

"You bet, Boss." Blanche's throaty alto accentuated her sarcasm.

As they walked out of the house, Peri gave the front door an extra tug to close it. The two friends got into Blanche's white hybrid SUV, and rolled out of the driveway.

"I wish you were going to this soiree," Peri said as they headed toward the Brea Mall.

"I know, but Paul's still out of town on business. I've gone to dinners solo before, but I decided I'd rather curl up with a book."

"But we'd have fun. You could always dance with Skip."

""Well, I didn't know you were going until, like, yesterday. I had already told my boss I'd be on call Saturday night." Blanche pushed her sunglasses back up on her face. "So, what kind of dress are you looking for?"

"One that will make me look younger. Svelte and hot would be nice, too."

"Well, I think you're damn hot for—"

Peri cut her off. "God, don't say it, Beebs. 'Damn hot for your age.' I don't want to be my age. I want to be thirty. Well, maybe thirty-five."

"Don't be silly. I remember you at thirty-five. You were still trying to chew your way out of that third marriage."

"Okay, I don't want to be thirty-five again. But I sure would like that body back."

Blanche laughed. "Who wouldn't? You're preaching to the choir."

"You're always so stylin', though." Peri dug her fingernails across her scalp, fluffing her hair. "I feel like I crawled into a Land's End rut, and by the time I climbed out, I didn't know how to dress my age anymore."

They pulled into the spartan, tiered parking structure and Blanche eased the car to a stop in a space on the second floor.

"Well, honey, put yourself in our hands. Me and Nordie's are here for you."

Blanche stepped out and retrieved her chestnut leather hobo from the backseat. Peri met her at the back of the car and they strolled across the skyway toward the world of fashion enchantment.

Although most people called Nordstrom's a department store, it did not quite fit the description. The Seattle-based chain sold clothing and accessories for men, women and children, and boasted high quality apparel at prices to match. They offered everything from classic styles to designer collections and the latest fashions, but they did not sell electronics, furniture, or power tools.

Peri felt the atmosphere change as soon as she entered. A layer of quiet blanketed the large room, as if a machine sucked the extraneous sound away, leaving only the gentle tones of the baby grand piano on the floor below. The pianist was playing a medley of Andrew Lloyd Webber songs. Even ambient odors seemed to have been eradicated, leaving only a vague smell of powder-fresh cleanliness. Peri paused at a rack of blouses, hung at precise intervals, separated by size and color.

"Not those," Blanche told her. "Those are petites."

She looked up, stretching her short frame taller. "Occasion dresses, that's where we want to go."

Peri followed her friend, feeling like a child to be dressed, by adults who knew better. Her flip-flops made a shooshing noise as she walked toward the racks of sparkling dresses.

Blanche stopped at a display of a chocolate chiffon skirt with a sleeveless, beaded top. She ran her fingers down the blouse, then picked up the layers of the skirt and examined them. "Do you have any idea of what color you want?"

"Um, I don't know. Black?"

Blanche pursed her lips. "It's a little boring."

"Beebs, you're here with me because I don't know what I'm doing. Why would you ask me what color I want to wear?"

A salesgirl appeared, her classic pumps snapping along the floor. "Can I help you ladies today?" She looked to be in her very early twenties, her henna-red hair in a sharp bob, and plenty of dark eye makeup to match her black-on-black outfit.

If I wore that, I'd look like a mime, Peri thought. *She looks like she's posing for Vogue*.

"My friend is going to a country club dinner and dance and needs a dress."

The girl turned to Peri. "Did you want a formal gown or a cocktail dress?"

Peri turned to Blanche. "I don't know, what do I want?"

The small brunette pulled at her bangs for a moment. "I've been to this thing before, and I've seen both long and short dresses." She looked at Peri, her eyes narrowing as she stared. "Let's try a cocktail dress."

"Okay, the cocktail dresses are over here." The salesgirl led them to a group of dresses that hung against the wall. "What size are you?"

"It depends on the cut. I'm usually a ten or twelve."

The girl picked up a pale mint sheath with a jeweled shrug and held it up to Peri. "Hmm, maybe a twelve in this."

"No," Blanche said. "That's not a good color on her. See how pale she is? That pastel will wash her out."

"Oh, okay." The salesgirl shuffled through the clothing before picking a frothy coral chiffon with a full skirt. "This would work."

"Not that one," Blanche told her. "Coral will make her complexion too ruddy."

Peri took a seat and watched the battle of the fashion titans, while Blanche and the young woman picked out choice after choice, just to shoot each other down. Ten minutes later, the two had picked out several dresses in various jewel shades, and a few in black.

"Peri, what do you think?" Blanche turned toward her friend. "What are you doing?"

"You didn't seem to need my input, and I was tired of standing."

"Oh, for Pete's sake, get in the dressing room and start trying things on."

The salesgirl led Peri into a long hall and opened the bleached wood door to one of the rooms. "Let me know if you need anything," she said as she hung the dresses and left.

The first dress was a cobalt wrap with large ruffles and a bow. Peri slipped into the dress and her black peeptoe heels.

"I look like one of those Christmas poppers they sell at Cost Plus," she told the mirror.

Blanche had the same opinion when she walked out to the dressing room foyer.

"Dear God, get out of that thing."

The burgundy dress with the jeweled bodice was too short. The black empire with sequins made her shoulders look like a football player's. The next two numbers thickened her waist. The teal chiffon made her look pregnant.

"How many are left?"

"A black one and a blue one, which is pretty much how my ego feels." Peri turned to go back into the dressing room and stopped, leaning her head against the door. She rested there a moment, her body sagging.

"You okay?" Blanche's hand squeezed her arm.

Not wanting to cry, Peri stood for a few seconds before answering. "Ah, Beebs." She stopped and fanned the tears pooling in her eyes. "I can't remember ever feeling so old and dowdy before. I used to throw on any old thing, and it would fit and I'd look good."

Blanche put her arm around her. "Believe it or not, I go through the same thing. I used to shop at Target. Now I have to shop high-end stores and buy the same label if I want to look good. It's boring but it's the only way I can keep the image thing up."

"So that's your secret. You been holding back on me."

"All ya had to do was ask." Blanche opened the dressing room door. "Now, get back in there. You've got two more dresses. And if they don't work, we've got a whole mall full of stores."

Peri did as she was told. She decided on the blue dress, a silk chiffon, Grecian style with a keyhole from the neckline to the beaded empire waist. It took a minute to shimmy into the dress and slip into the heels, but when she looked in the mirror, it was worth it. She strutted out the door.

"Why, Miss Marple, you're beautiful," Blanche told her.

They were still laughing when the salesgirl returned. "How are we doing in here?"

Blanche leaned forward and grabbed the price tag on the dress. "Even with tax and tip, it's less than two hundred."

"We have a winner," Peri told the girl, and spun to make the skirt twirl before going went back in to change.

Blanche held the dress while Peri completed her purchase. "Where's lunch?"

"How about Islands?"

"China Coast Salad?"

Peri took her bag. "Dressing on the side, if I want to wear this on Saturday."

"I don't think you'll have a problem." Blanche gestured toward the restroom. "I need to stop by the ladies' room before we leave."

Only at Nordstrom's would the restroom be called the Women's Lounge. It consisted of several rooms, with everything from bathroom stalls to couches, makeup vanities with appropriate lighting, and a baby-centric room for mothers to change diapers and breastfeed in quiet comfort. Peri was always waiting for them to install the hot tub.

Women's voices could be heard as she opened the door. She had taken two steps, when she recognized who was speaking. Backing up, she grabbed Blanche's arm and yanked her outside.

"Oh my God it's Nikki and Kim." She had a hard time keeping her voice to a whisper.

"Are you sure?" Blanche peeked into the open door.

"Of course, I'm sure." She closed the door and pulled her friend to the side. "You need to go in there alone and tell me what they're talking about. If they see me, they'll get suspicious."

"Won't they have seen me, too?"

"Yes, but I'm pretty sure I'm the blonde they were talking about at lunch. You're a member of their country club."

Blanche raised an eyebrow. "So, I'm one of them?"

"Yes, in that they wouldn't think twice about you being in Nordie's. They wouldn't suspect I'm with you today."

"Okay, Thelma." Blanche tossed her the car keys. "Meet you in the parking lot."

"I'll be waiting, Louise."

Peri sat in the SUV for what seemed like hours, playing with everything from the satellite radio stations to her seat adjustments. She went through the glove compartment, checked her email from her phone, and was almost ready to go back in and see if the girls had hit Blanche over the head, when she saw her friend on the walkway.

"Well, that was weird," Blanche said as she got into the driver's seat and started the engine. The radio blasted polka music. "What the hell have you been doing in here?"

"Sorry, I was bored. What happened? What did they say?"

"First of all, they weren't in the stall area, they were in the mommy room." She rolled out of the space and started down the exit ramp. "But they were talking pretty loud. Nikki said, 'What's the harm? I'm just having some fun.'"

"Must be a reference to the boy-toy."

"Maybe. And then Kim said, 'The harm is when your husband finds out and kicks you out of the house. And if that bitch shows him the pictures – well, are you prepared for life at the homeless shelter?'"

Peri frowned. "So I'm a bitch, huh? At least I'm not shooting people's windows out."

"Then Nikki says, 'No. Why didn't she stop when Susan scared her?' And Kim says, 'She must be too stupid to scare.'"

"Geez." Peri leaned back in the seat. "Which scare was Susan's? And I am not too stupid to scare."

"No, too stubborn." Blanche scowled at her. "Meanwhile, the rest of us are scared for you.

"Anyway, I heard them walk out to the foyer, so I moved a little further back toward the stalls and hoped they couldn't see me in the mirror. God, Peri, I don't know how you do it. My heart was trying to climb out through my trachea."

"Mine does, too, Beebs. I just stuff it back down again. So did they say anything else?"

Blanche steered the car into the Islands parking lot. "Oh, yeah. Nikki says, 'Don't you worry about Don. I can handle him.' And then Kim says, 'You'd better, or I'll have to do it.' And then Nikki sounds kinda funny and says, 'Really, I'll handle it,' and Kim says, 'Nikki, you're my best friend. You know I'll never let anyone hurt you.' And then they both left the lounge."

"So Nikki and Kim know Don hired me. They got Susan to try to scare me off – I wonder if it was just one of the incidents or all of them – and they know I got pictures of Nikki and her boy-toy. I wonder how Nikki plans to handle her husband."

"I know the way most women handle their hubbies. But with this crew, she could be planning a little hemlock in his tea." Blanche turned the engine off. "Let's go. I'm starving, and I forgot to actually use the restroom in Nordie's."

CHAPTER 21

They walked in to the restaurant and were led to a table. Peri sat down, while Blanche proceeded to the back.

As she waited for her friend to return from the restroom, Peri looked around at the tropical décor. She wondered if the booths were real bamboo, or the thatched roof over her head was really palm fronds, and why they didn't complete the look with Polynesian servers. Granted, it would be discrimination, she thought, but if you're trying to establish an island mood, tall white boys with Germanic features didn't quite scream "Aloha."

Blanche returned to their booth, flitting into the seat with her usual quickness. Peri watched her rub her hands together and noticed they were still damp.

"Dryer not working?"

"They don't have a dryer. They only have paper towels." Blanche took the paper from her straw and sipped her passion fruit iced tea. "Completely unacceptable."

"You worry too much about germs."

"I don't get sick, either."

The server, a young, blue-eyed man in a Hawaiian shirt, took their order and soon returned with their drinks and two large salads. Peri poured half of the dressing container into her bowl and stirred it into the lettuce, trying to coat as many leaves with as little oil as possible. She looked up to see Blanche staring at her.

"By the way, what was all that drama about in the dressing room?"

Peri shook her head. "I don't know, Beebs. I mean, I know I'm in good shape, but I've put on a couple of pounds that won't go away. My clothes have gotten comfortable, instead of stylish, or sexy."

"Is Skip complaining?"

"Just that fight we had about my running clothes the other day. He's been on a whole image binge since that stupid article in the paper."

"Ugh." Blanche curled her nose. "Placentia's most eligible bachelor. How special."

"That's what I thought. And then there's Ella Mason."

"Ella? The officer who spent her time at Dottie's house trying not to puke? That rookie can't even handle a dead body."

Peri watched the woman behind Blanche put her fork down and lift her napkin to her mouth. She smiled. "You might want to lower your voice, McGruesome. Yeah, her. I think she's gunning for Skip."

"Why do you think that?"

"I've seen them at the station. She's always making doe eyes at him, standing so she has to look up, lips open, you know the drill. It all started when she cried on his shoulder about her poor, misbehaving son. Now he's trying to find a way to mentor the boy."

"Maybe it's just your imagination. I mean, I hate to say it, but it's hard to complain about him wanting to do a good deed."

"I know, don't you think I feel like the Wicked Witch of the West?" She speared a combination of lettuce, chicken and spring onion, and carefully placed it in her mouth. The sesame and ginger dressing filled her senses, from her taste buds to her sinuses. "But I know goo-goo eyes when I seem them. Doesn't seem like she's making a dent in Skip, but she sure is making me cranky."

"Well, cut yourself some slack, Honey. You've got a lot more than an office vulture to worry about. Have they discovered any evidence pointing to whoever's been after you?"

"Not yet." She put her fork down and sank into the back of the booth. "Although I may ask you to stop by Craig Daniels' desk and tell him about the conversation you just heard."

"Peri, you know how proud I am of you for starting a new business—"

"But?"

"Can you blame me for being worried?"

"Are you kidding? I'm worried. Skip's worried, we're all worried." Peri leaned forward and grabbed another forkful. "Actually, I'm only part worried. I'm mostly pissed."

"Good thing you've got the Placentia Police Department to keep you safe."

She nodded. "Craig Daniels is investigating, and I'm staying at Skip's until…" Her hand gripped the fork and tapped it against the plate. "Until when? Until Daniels has a suspect in custody? Until no one's threatened me in a week? A month?"

She looked at Blanche, who shrugged.

"I'm sick of this, Beebs. I want to sleep in my own bed. I want my life back."

"I know patience isn't your virtue, but you should be able to go back to normal soon."

"Yea, but I want normal now." She leaned forward. "And I'm going to get it."

"Now, Peri—"

"Why shouldn't I lead my own investigation? I'm tired of feeling like the prey. It's time for me to go hunting." She stared at Blanche as she thumped the table with her index finger.

"Girlfriend, you know I love you, but I am not going to help you do this. You could get yourself killed."

"I'm not asking you to help me kick in any doors. I promise to be careful. I might ask for a little information, now and then. And, of course, no blabbing to Skip."

Peri watched her friend sip her drink, and noted the creased forehead. "You're going to get all wrinkly if you keep thinking so hard."

"You know I don't like this."

"I know."

"But I'll do it."

"I know."

"Let's get the check and I'll drop you back off at Skip's." Blanche flagged the server with a wave. "Honest to God, Peri, I don't know how I'm going to lie for you."

"The same way you did in high school when my mom asked if I was at your house."

"I'm pretty sure your mom knew I was lying." Blanche laughed. "I mean, every time she called, you were either in the shower or going to the bathroom."

Peri giggled. "I was the cleanest girl with the most regular digestive system ever."

They paid the bill and strolled out of the restaurant. The afternoon sun stabbed Peri's shoulders and neck. She reached up and rubbed her arms, as if trying to brush the rays away.

"Beebs, what are you doing Saturday?"

"I'm not helping you do anything dangerous."

"Puh-lease. I want to go to the Heritage Day festival in Tri-City and need a body guard. Want to go with me?"

"Oh, okay. Yea, sounds like fun."

The two friends laughed and talked as they returned to Skip's house. A black, older model Toyota sat in the driveway.

Blanche pulled up to the curb. "Whose car?"

"Damned if I know."

Peri opened the door and reached into the back seat for her purchase. "Well, thanks for the ride."

"Wait, let me go with you."

"You don't have to hand-deliver me. I can make it to the door by myself."

Blanche reached over and grabbed Peri's arm. "What if the car belongs to someone looking for you? What if they've disposed of Skip and are lying in wait?"

"What if it's a surprise party for me?" She rolled her eyes. "Beebs, why would criminals, intent on murder and mayhem pull up in the driveway? Trust me, if they're that stupid, Skip has disposed of them." Stepping out of the SUV, she turned to her friend. "Thanks for watching out for me."

Blanche got out of her car and followed Peri to the front door. "Sorry, but I can't drive away without knowing you're safe."

Peri turned the key in the lock and announced herself. "Hey, Skip."

Skip's deep voice answered. "In the kitchen, Doll."

She turned to Blanche. "Okay?"

"He could be tied up and enticing you in, under duress."

"Argh." Peri raised her hands to match the disbelief in her voice. "Come on, then. We'll get captured together."

They walked around the corner to see Skip at the kitchen table. He was having iced tea with a couple of visitors. Peri recognized Ella Mason at once. She guessed that the large doughy youth next to her was her son, Jorge. They were all looking at a piece of paper on the table.

Peri took careful stock of the situation. She could see the top of Ella's outfit. It was tight, low-cut and bright red. She also saw the blink of a moment when Ella went from flirtatiousness to annoyance at her arrival. Skip looked relaxed, innocent as a newborn lamb. Jorge also looked unruffled by her appearance. He sat like a lump of flesh, his mouth slightly ajar and eyes staring.

Skip got up and met her at the door, giving her a kiss. He looked behind her. "Hey, Beebs," he said.

"Hi, Skip. Just thought I'd come in and turn her over to you officially."

"Thanks, I appreciate it." He turned to Peri and ran his hand down her arm. "Find a dress?"

She held up the bagged hanger. "A real killer."

"Great. I was just helping Ella and Jorge sign up for some community classes. She had some questions I couldn't answer over the phone."

"Of course." Peri hoped she didn't spit this out in as sarcastic a tone as she felt. "I'm going to see Blanche out, then go hang up my dress. Nice seeing you, Ella. Nice meeting you, Jorge."

Ella matched Peri's pasted-on smile. Peri thought she saw a slight movement of Jorge's head in her direction, but it was difficult to tell. She walked to the door with her friend.

"Okay, am I imagining?"

"No, you're right. She's fishing." Blanche hugged Peri. "But she ain't got the right bait for him."

By the time Peri had taken her party dress from the bag, hung it up, and freshened her hair and makeup, the two visitors were gone. She prepared a glass of iced tea and joined Skip in the family room, where he was watching a baseball game.

"Hope they didn't leave on my account." She melted into the tan leather couch beside him.

"No, we had finished the paperwork before you came. I was trying to get to know that boy of hers." He whistled. "That's a tough nut. I've seen mushrooms with more personality."

"Craig Daniels expressed some doubts about your mission. Said he'd been dealing with young Jorge since sixth grade."

"I hate to just give up on any kid, but one of our own—it doesn't seem right."

She laid her head on his shoulder. "I know, Skipper. I only saw him for a moment and he looks like an uphill battle."

"Well, I signed us both up for a class on digital photography. Ella says he's interested in it, but you can't prove it by me."

"Does he have a digital camera?"

Skip chuckled. "What doesn't he have? Between Ella and Nana and all the aunts, they've lavished gifts on that kid. He has a camera, an iPhone, an iPod, three different gaming systems. If he's grateful, no one knows it."

"Craig said he was in a gang."

"Craig, hmm? When did you two get so chummy?"

"Who said I was chummy?" She reached up to kiss his cheek. "Although, he said if he thought Ella could turn your head, he'd be asking me to the dance on Saturday."

"He did, did he?" Skip turned to Peri and wrapped his arms around her. She eased back on the couch and took his face in her hands.

"Jealous?"

He kissed her, his lips pressing deep yet tender. She kissed him back. They spent some time on the couch, kissing, until fingers began searching for buttons and zippers, and they moved to the floor. Their lovemaking consumed them for some time, until at last sated, Skip sank back into the pillows propped on the fireplace. Peri joined him, her head on his chest.

"You know you're the only one for me," she said.

"Ditto, Doll."

CHAPTER 22

Peri began calling Benny at nine the next morning. He finally answered at nine-thirty.

"Why are you calling me?" His whine pierced her eardrum.

"Good morning, Benny. Get dressed and come over to Skip's house. We have work to do."

"Ah, Miss Peri, do I hafta? I was up late last night."

"Sorry, but I need you today. Just get to Skip's. I'll be driving us around, so you can sleep in the car."

"You mean we'll be in your car? It looks so cramped in there."

Peri stopped to breathe in, take a sip of coffee and stop her fingers from wanting to reach through the phone and grab him by the neck. "I'm sorry you'll be cramped, but you're just going to have to suck it up. I need to get to a few places and I can't be so conspicuous."

"Miss Peri—"

Mornings did not improve her patience. "Benny get your ass over here in the next ten minutes or I'm calling your probation officer." She ended the call without waiting for his answer.

Eleven minutes later, the black Caddy pulled up in Skip's driveway. Peri came out of the house to see Benny running to the porch, the perspiration beading around his face.

"Don't call her, don't call her." His voice huffed each word, in terror or exhaustion, she couldn't tell.

"You're safe. As a matter of fact, I've even changed my mind. We'll take your car if you want."

She watched him bobble up and down like a buoy in the ocean before his feet began to shuffle back and forth in no discernible rhythm. His mouth twitched a smile, bigger and smaller and bigger again. The effect was both laughable and disturbing.

"What are you doing?"

His movements jerked to a halt. "I'm just so happy. I had to do a little happy dance."

"Well, don't. It's— " Peri stopped her critique when she saw his shoulders droop. "It's just that we need to get moving. You can do the happy dance later. Let me get my tote and we'll go."

She grabbed her pink snakeskin bag from the table by the door and scurried out to the Cadillac. Benny was standing by the driver's-side door, fanning his cream and navy bowling shirt away from his body to dry it out.

"Nice shirt," she told him. "From the Dino collection?"

"Don't be silly, there's no such thing." He slid into the front seat, behind the wheel. "Or is there?"

Peri took her place on the passenger side, again marveling at how pristine everything was, in both look and scent. "Not that I know of," she said as she sank into the velvety leather.

He started the engine. "Where to?"

"I need to go to my office first."

Benny's joy evaporated. "Oh no, we are *not* going back there. They shot at us."

"We're not actually going into my office. We're going to the landlord's office. No one will shoot at us. They were just trying to scare us that day."

"Yeah, well, they succeeded. I'm not going back there."

"I need to talk to Michael. You can come with me if you want."

He started the car and backed out of the drive. "You can talk to the landlord, but I think I'll wait in the car."

"Fine by me."

The ride to Founders Plaza was without conversation although it was hardly silent. Dean Martin crooned at an ear-splitting volume for the entire trip. Peri liked Dino, but no one was enjoyable when they were that loud. Just when she thought she might need either an aspirin for her headache or a sledgehammer for Benny's stereo, he pulled into a parking space and shut off the motor.

"You can wait here," she said. "I just want to check a couple of things."

She hopped from the car and entered the complex through the wrought iron gate, intending to visit Michael Steuben. Halfway there, she had another idea and took a right turn toward the second story.

At the top of the stairs, she stopped and looked toward her office. Although she could see the plywood still covering her window, she could not find a position in which she thought someone could fire a rifle with any degree of accuracy. They'd have to lean over the staircase railing; she attempted this while pretending to line up a weapon and had a difficult time maintaining her balance.

Peri looked at the first office on the second floor. Michael said this was available, and she wondered if there was a window that could be opened. She tried the door, and wasn't surprised that it was locked.

Perhaps Michael could open it for me, she thought, and turned to go find him. A small, round shape barred her movement.

"Jeepers, Benny, would you stop sneaking up on me?"

"Sorry."

"I thought you were going to wait in the car."

His hands wrung together, a sign Peri recognized as stress. "I didn't like being alone out there."

"Okay, well, let's go to the landlord's. I want to see if he'll open this office. I think this is where the shooter was." She scooted around Benny and headed down the stairs. At each step, she could feel his breath on her neck. Finally, she turned to face him.

"Benny, if you walk any closer to me, I'm going to have a heart attack. Back up a step, okay?"

Pouting, he stopped; she felt the air flow between them, as he let her move ahead a few steps before following.

She walked to the heavy tan door that said, "Manager" and rapped twice with her knuckles before turning the doorknob and entering.

The first thing she noticed was the smell—a coppery odor mixed with something horribly bad and vaguely human. She stopped in the doorway, causing Benny to bump against her. Whipping around, she caught her temper just as it was about to rain down on her hapless chaperone.

"Benny," she said with a deep breath. "I need you to stay outside a minute, okay?"

He did as he was told and stepped back to the walkway. Peri went into the office and shut the door. The curtains had been drawn across the large atrium window, so she turned on the light. She saw a pair of shoes sprawling from behind the desk, shoes with feet in them. In a slow motion attempt at denial, she walked around the desk before looking down.

It was Michael Steuben. There was a dark stain on his torso, a stain that spread down his shirt, where it had trickled to a stop on the carpet. Michael's eyes were open and lifeless.

In the silence, Peri allowed herself some tears. She liked her landlord. He had been easy to get along with, firm about rules, but friendly to everyone. She couldn't imagine who would do this to him, but of course she didn't know anything about his personal life. Did he have a wife and children? A significant other, of either gender? Debts? Addictions?

There was once a boy she knew in high school—the quiet, easy going type—who hanged himself in the locker room. The tragedy had taught her not to assume everyone's life was roses.

After composing herself, she moved toward the door and then paused. What if this was related to her office shooting? She surveyed the top of his desk, making certain to stay away from the body. The first thing she spied was his cell phone. She took a pencil from the blue ceramic cup on the corner, and used it to turn the phone toward her. The display was dark, so she pressed a button.

It looked like the last function he used was his calendar. Today's date, with several appointments, was displayed. The first meeting was about an hour ago.

"Mrs. Keaton, call P," she read.

Peri didn't remember a Mrs. Keaton on Nikki Keller's list of friends, but she suspected anyone who might do this to poor Michael would probably not have used their real name. She returned to the calendar and looked up the day her window was shot. No Mrs. Keaton was listed. On a hunch, she flipped through previous days and found Mrs. Keaton two days earlier.

It had to be more than coincidence, she thought. *It had to be related to the shooting. And what did "Call P" mean? Call Peri? Call Police?*

She tried to find Mrs. Keaton in his contact list, but had no luck, so she poked through the trash for errant notes or phone numbers. There wasn't anything unusual. At last she stepped outside and closed the door behind her.

Benny grabbed her arm. "He's dead, isn't he? He's been shot. You said they wouldn't shoot anyone. You said they were just trying to scare us." His voice rose with each word.

"Yes, he's dead." She pried his fingers from her skin and then reached into her tote for her phone. "I don't know that he's been shot, or even if it's the same people. We need to call the cops."

She stood for a moment with the phone open, wondering whether to call Skip, Craig Daniels, or 9-1-1. In the end, she voted with her heart.

"Hey, Doll, what's up?" The dulcet tone of his voice gave her strength.

"Skip, can you come over to Michael Steuben's office? He's been killed." Her voice quivered at the last word.

While they waited for the police, Peri noticed how Benny was trying to flatten himself into the stucco.

"I know it's nerve-wracking." She patted his shoulder and felt his muscles like tight springs flinch at her touch. "I really hate this. But the police will be here soon."

"I'm scared. What if that person starts shooting again?"

Peri stood tall and smiled. "Not a chance." Not getting any response from him, she added, "What would Dino do in this situation?"

Benny unfolded from his slumped position, a sly grin at the edge of his mouth. "He'd play it cool."

"That's right. He'd play it cool." She heard car doors in the parking lot, lots of them. "Sounds like the Cavalry's here."

Skip strode ahead, followed by two uniforms. "Where is he?"

Peri pointed to the office, and watched Skip enter, with the officers. While she waited, Craig Daniels appeared.

"What happened?"

"I came over to talk to Michael about the insurance company, and found him like this." Her hand swept toward the door.

Daniels looked over at Benny, who looked at Peri, sweat beading on his hairline. It took the little man several seconds to blink at Daniels, then the ground, and finally nod. "That's right."

The detective stared at Benny. "Do you have anything to add to that?"

"No." It came out as less of a human voice and more of an animal's squeal. "I-I-I don't have a thing to add. It's just like she said."

"You'll have to forgive him," Peri said. "Police officers make him a little nervous."

"Yeah, nervous." Benny added a little high-pitched giggle to convince the detective.

Skip came out of the office and nodded to Daniels. "Looks like he was shot, through and through, stippling on the shirt. Coroner's on the way, so she'll be able to give us a better picture."

Peri stepped forward and touched Skip's arm. "Do you need us to stay?"

"Did Daniels get your statements?"

"Yes."

"I guess you can go." Skip looked at her. "Wait a minute—why do you want to leave? You never want to leave the scene of a crime."

"I know, but Benny's kind of traumatized, and I'd like to get him home."

He continued to stare in silence.

"What?" she said. "It's not my crime. That's what you always tell me, right?"

"Yes, but you don't usually listen."

Peri took a playful swing at his arm, punching him in the shoulder. "See how far I've come, Skipper? I'm learning to listen."

His face relaxed a little, but he didn't smile. "If we've got more questions, I guess we can ask them later."

She leaned up and kissed his cheek. "Thanks."

Her hand on Benny's arm, she steered him toward the parking lot. Once out of sight, she swung him to the left.

"The car's over there." He gestured in the opposite direction.

"I know, but we're going back to that upstairs office."

"Why?"

"So you can pick the lock and I can look inside."

Benny stopped walking. "Miss Peri, do you think that's okay?"

"Do I care?" She saw his expression and adjusted her answer. "It's probably not okay now, but it will be okay later. I'm trying to find out who's trying to get to me, and right now, the only step I know how to take is to look around that office."

She turned to face him, putting both hands on his shoulders. "I need your help, Benny. We need to find out who shot at us. Will you help me?"

He nodded as if in a trance. She turned and started up the stairs, Benny following like an obedient puppy. When they got to the office in the corner, Peri stepped out of the way and let her partner in crime take over.

"Chili says it's all in the feel," he said as he placed two pins in the lock and made small, methodical adjustments.

Peri heard a clicking noise, and he opened the door. "You kind of amaze me, Ben."

As usual, her praise looked like manna from heaven reflected in his face.

The noon sun was hitting the window toward the atrium, which Peri hoped would cause a glare. She didn't want any of the police force to glance up and see her snooping around. Stepping inside, she motioned Benny to follow, and then shut the door.

"Stand by the door, okay?" she told him, snapping on a pair of disposable gloves. "I need to look at the carpet and windows for any evidence."

She took a quick look around the room. It was about twice the size of her office, newly painted and carpeted in neutral tones, with no furniture. There were curtains, but they were pulled away from the window. Peri was somewhat happy about this, since she didn't want to call attention to the room by moving the curtain out of the way to see what the shooter saw.

For the next ten minutes, she worked her way toward the windows, kneeling and examining the carpet surface for unusual footprints, combing the carpet for something left behind, and looking at all angles for anything out of place. At various points, she took pictures of the carpet, sometimes with a ruler lying on the floor.

"Why are you photographing the carpet," Benny asked. "It's not doing anything."

"I know. It may be nothing, but it looks like someone walked around in high heels. The carpet is new enough that it retained the impressions, especially those little stilettos."

At last, she made it to the windows, floor-to-ceiling on half of the far wall, with another pair of smaller windows facing the stairway. The small panes were segmented by black frames. Peri kept to the wall, twisting around to examine them.

They all had screens on the inside, and a hand crank to open the glass outward. Peri felt the closest screen edge from top to bottom. It was smooth. She moved to the next edge and ran her gloved fingers down. This edge had some roughness to it, as though the screen material had not been properly trimmed in the frame.

One piece seemed longer than the rest. Peri gave it a little tug and found a large tear at the side that had been tucked into the frame. She looked through the hole at her office. It lined up perfectly. Excited by her discovery, she got out her camera and took shots of the hole, her ruler beside it to show the size. She was so busy taking pictures, she didn't hear the footsteps.

"Miss Peri, I think someone's coming." Benny's whisper had a note of hysteria.

"Shh, it's okay." She scampered to the wall next to the door and pulled Benny over with her. "Hopefully, if they open the door, they won't look behind it."

The footsteps stopped outside the office, and the doorknob jiggled. Peri held her breath and backed further against the wall. It was quiet for a few moments, then she heard jingling. One after the other, the lock was tried with a succession of keys, until a click resounded and Benny gasped.

Peri threw her left arm across Benny's chest to keep him from running and looked at him, her finger over her lips in the universal sign for *shut up*. The door crept open, until she could see daylight in the crack. She could also see a gun. It advanced, along with the hand holding it, attached to an arm covered by a beige knitted shirt.

The door yanked away from her and a man leapt toward them, gun held firm and steady.

"What are you doing here?" he demanded.

"Hey, Skip." Peri attempted a smile. "Fancy meeting you here."

CHAPTER 23

"What the hell is wrong with you?" Skip's cheeks flushed crimson as he spat his question at her.

"God, you scared me," Peri told him, supporting Benny, whose knees had buckled.

"What was all that crap about 'not my crime' and 'need to get Benny home'? You lied to me."

"Not exactly. Benny is upset. I was going to take him somewhere to calm down. But I got this sudden urge to see the inside of this office. This is where the sniper stood. Let me show you the hole in the screen."

She started to walk toward the window, but Skip grabbed her arm. "We had the talk about compromising a scene, didn't we?"

"I wore gloves." She held up her hands. "I took pictures. It's all I did."

"You're missing the point."

"I'm not. I know. I get it. If I discover evidence that puts Nikki Keller in here, she can argue that I'm prejudiced, even that I'm framing her." Peri removed her ball cap and rubbed her scalp with her fingertips. "I can't do nothing, Skip. Michael's dead. He may be dead because of me."

"No." Skip took her face in his hands. "Listen to me. Do not go there. We don't know why any of this happened yet, and even if it turns out, the person who shot at you didn't want to leave witnesses, it's still not your fault. You didn't make them killers."

"You're right. I didn't make them killers, but maybe my job started them on this particular binge."

She rubbed her eyes. "I just want to go home. I want my life back. You and Craig are doing your best. I know you're good at your job. But I'm not the princess who sits around the castle watching the knights duke it out with the dragon. I'm gonna take a swing at the beast, too."

Skip glared at her, so she added, "And you know that about me."

She stood motionless, waiting for him to either accept her or yell some more. Instead, he matched her in silence. After a few moments, she heard sniffling. Looking over to the corner, she saw Benny, a handkerchief in his hand, dabbing at his eyes and nose.

"Benny, what's wrong?"

"I don't like it when you fight."

"It's okay," Skip told him. "I want you to take Peri back to my place and wait with her. I'll be home later."

"Not yet," Peri said. "I need—"

"Now, Doll, let's not argue in front of the kids."

"I was going to say, I need fuel. Can Benny and I go to lunch first?"

"Of course. Then go home and do some work on the computer or something. I want you safe until we've done a little preliminary investigation."

Peri looked at Benny. "Pizza or Chinese?"

"How about Capones?"

Skip and Peri exchanged glances. During Benny's brief incarceration, his favorite Italian eatery had closed. It sounded like he hadn't noticed yet.

Peri patted Benny's shoulder, turning him out of the office and toward the stairs. "I've got some bad news, Ben."

"No, this is horrible." Benny stopped on the top stair, his face crimson. "Why didn't you call me? We gotta do something. File a complaint, organize a protest."

"I feel your pain," Peri told him as she directed him forward down the steps. "But the economy's been rough on a lot of businesses. Let's go to Antonia's. You like their lasagna, right?"

"Yeah, I like their lasagna fine. It's just, they just don't have the upscale dishes. No spinach ravioli, no veal parmesano."

"Did you order the upscale dishes?" She opened the passenger-side car door and got in, as Benny slipped behind the wheel.

"No, I always ordered the lasagna." He turned the key in the ignition. "But the servers at Capone's all knew me."

"Drive to Antonia's. I'll introduce you to the staff."

Once at the small restaurant, Peri pulled the manager aside while Benny was in the restroom.

"My friend is mourning the loss of Capone's, mostly because everyone knew him there. He loves lasagna and lives just around the corner, so I think you'd have a regular customer if you and the staff greeted him by name."

The short, round woman smiled, her dark eyes sparkling atop her high, pink cheeks. "We'd love to take care of him. It's what we do best."

They watched Benny come around the corner.

"Benny," Peri said, "I'd like you to meet Angela. She's the manager here and has a table and a slab of lasagna with your name on it."

Angela shook Benny's hand and escorted them to a table. She sent two iced teas over with the server, with half ice and four lemon wedges for Benny, just the way Peri had asked. He looked at his iced tea and sniffed it, before taking a cautious drink. Peri watched the smile unfold on his face.

"Did they get it right?"

"I may like this place," he told her.

While they waited for their food to arrive, Peri dug a notebook out of her tote and began to write.

"Watcha doin?"

"Trying to make sense of this mess. I've got a flat tire, possibly not an accident. There were four women at Nikki's table at the club, but I only saw three women leave. If the flat was deliberate, it could have been by Kim Patterson." She looked up from her writing.

"Then there's the golf course. I'm pretty sure the whack I got in the head wasn't accidental. Skip said it might have been a stray golf ball, but I don't see how it would have been coming from that direction—I mean, I was still fairly close to the clubhouse. Nikki was on the premises. She could've done it. Or her friend, Tyler."

The server interrupted her to bring their lunches. Benny's eyes widened at the sight of the extra large slice of lasagna in front of him. Peri had ordered a small pepperoni and pineapple pizza. It was a favorite of hers, but not Skip's, so she indulged herself. She picked up a slice, blew on it, and took a bite of the tomato and cheese gooiness, punctuated by the savory meat and sweet fruit. It was a little too hot, so she sipped her iced tea and returned to her notes while her meal cooled.

"Next is the headless crow. What is up with that?" She kept writing the incidents in the book, until she had caught up with today's tragedy. Sitting back against the booth, she watched Benny enjoying his pasta and sauce. The image of Michael's body flitted through her mind, and she pinched her nose to keep the tears from flowing.

"You know what I need?"

Benny stopped long enough to mumble "What?" through a mouthful of food.

"I need Jason's test results. He's been working on this mess full time for a week now. I think I deserve to know what he's found out."

"So ask him."

Peri took another bite of her pizza and thought about it. "I'm pretty certain Skip won't approve. I know Chief Fletcher won't. He thinks I'm wearing out my welcome in the department."

"What does Jason think?"

"Good point, Ben. I don't know if he'll want to share the information, but I might be able to get him to talk about it anyway."

They finished their lunch, paid and left.

Peri opened her car door. "Did you feed Mr. Mustard today?"

"Not yet, Miss Peri." He got behind the wheel, as Peri sat down and fastened her seatbelt.

"Maybe we should run by my house and take care of that."

"Okay." Benny backed out of the parking space, then stopped. "Oh, no. I'm not supposed to take you there. Mr. Skip told me to take you to his house."

"C'mon, Benny, it's just for a couple of minutes while you take care of the cat. What's the harm?"

"The harm is that Mr. Skip is a policeman and I need to stay out of trouble." He shook his stubby index finger at her. "I can't go back to jail. I won't."

She surrendered, if only out of shock that she couldn't manipulate him as much as she thought. "Okay. Take me to Skip's."

The drive down Kraemer Boulevard toward the detective's cul-de-sac was quiet. Peri watched out the window, noting the overgrown bougainvilleas flowing across the block walls. She looked at the houses and saw a continuous row of satellite dishes and swing sets, windows and roofs. Everything looked well-kept; still, she wondered what kind of people liked to live with such a busy street outside their backyard.

Maybe deaf people.

They turned into Skip's drive and Benny parked the car, but kept the engine idling. After making him promise to go straight to her house and feed the cat, Peri walked to the front door and turned to watch the long, black Caddy pull away. She fiddled through her key ring until she found the right key and let herself in.

Without a case to work, Peri wandered through the ranch-style house, her frustration and energy level pushing her toward some kind of action. Skip would be angry if she went for a run. He had a treadmill in his office, so she decided to try to work off a few calories. She found Turner Classic Movies on the TV in the room, hopped onto the machine and started it up.

After three minutes, she was already checking the time and looking around the room for a distraction.

"There's a reason I don't have one of these contraptions," she told William Powell as he solved The Kennel Murder Case. "This is boring."

She played with the treadmill's speed, tilt, and degree of difficulty, watched more of the movie and kept running. After ten minutes, she started hopping and skipping as the track rolled under her feet. She then turned around and ran backward; that's when she spied Skip's computer.

Peri watched the Windows logo bouncing around the screen and thought about how much information Skip might be able to access from home. She also thought about where he kept his password written.

It would be wrong to break into his account, she told herself. *If he found out, he'd be more than angry. I know I'd be hurt if he did it to me. It's a trust thing. We need to trust each other.*

She turned back toward the TV and watched the end of the movie, while the computer sat behind her, like someone staring at the back of her head. Sweaty and tired at last, she ended her treadmill session and went to the master bedroom to clean up.

Standing in the shower, she thought about the kind of reports Craig Daniels might be sharing with her boyfriend. Jason might have copied Skip on his analyses. Maybe Skip would let her read them when he got home tonight.

It's not like it's personal information, she reasoned. *It's business. Not only that, I'm a P.I. I've got a license to snoop.*

She argued back and forth while she shampooed, rinsed, dried and dressed. In an attempt to take her mind off the debate, she sat down in the family room with a bottle of nail polish and turned the classic movies on again. Unfortunately, it was another Philo Vance episode, this time with Warren William in the title role.

Each methodical stroke of ruby polish ticked another reason in Peri's mind why she should use Skip's computer to investigate. When all ten fingers and ten toes had been painted, she sat and waved them dry, thinking of the same number of reasons to leave his computer alone. At last, she decided to call Skip and talk to him.

His cell phone went immediately to voicemail, so she tried his office number. When she heard another version of why he couldn't answer the phone, she hung up and walked back into his home office. Being away from his desk and not answering his cell phone meant he was either in a meeting, or doing some field work that required silence.

Peri went to his computer, but didn't sit down. Instead, she rolled the mouse over the pad and woke the monitor. The desktop had a picture of the two of them, the same photo that was stolen from her office. The email icon was in the left corner, along with Spider Solitaire. She eased into the chair and opened the game, to distract herself. Three games won, two games lost, and she couldn't stop thinking about what she wanted.

Wait, there's the audio software. I could try to listen to that recording again.

Saved by a useful diversion, Peri went back into the family room and opened her laptop. She had downloaded the audio processing software, but hadn't tried it out, although she did give a copy of the recording to Craig for Jason to process. Jason had more sophisticated equipment for isolating and removing background noise. She assumed he'd have better luck, but if it would keep her away from temptation…

After cruising through a brief tutorial, Peri imported her file and went to work. She hadn't imagined it would be easy, especially since her knowledge of frequencies and bandwidths was limited. It took her three tries to isolate the part of the conversation she wanted to manipulate, and then she didn't know which menu option she wanted to use. *Edit? Analyze? Help?*

Half an hour later, she had separated tracks by frequencies and could hear the conversation, although she could not bring the volume up past a whisper. She listened to the entire section, easily identifying each woman's voice.

Kim spoke first. "See the blonde by the window? She was parked on Dunnevant this morning."

Susan was next. "So?"

"So I think she's following one of us."

Nikki's voice was next. "It may just be a coincidence, Kim."

"I don't believe in coincidences." Even with the bad quality of the recording, Kim's voice sounded almost pathological in its coldness.

Lisa's slight drawl sounded grainy. "What should we do?"

"Discourage her," Kim said.

"How much?" Nikki's voice sounded whiny.

Kim's words made Peri's body go numb with fear: *"With as much force as necessary."*

These women definitely knew about her, and it sounded like they would go to any lengths to make her stop her investigation. She had a sudden urge to know as much as possible about the crimes against her. How much force was Kim capable of using?

She strode down the hall to the office, sat down at Skip's computer, and clicked on the email icon.

Every appliance in the house amplified its creaks and groans as Peri entered his password. She barely breathed, she was so frightened he'd come home early. A formatted screen popped up on the monitor, contacts and folders in the left column, advertisements to the right, and 1500 messages down the center.

Peri quickly scanned the subjects, looking for anything that would pertain to her.

There were four, all from Jason Bonham, all with attachments, and all previously opened. She clicked on one and read the note. "Thought you might want to be kept in the loop," it said. She opened the attachment, saw it was from the dead bird at her house, and printed it. The next were from the golf course, the office shooting, and the subsequent breakin. She printed those, too.

Another subject caught her interest. Jason and Blanche had both sent reports to Skip about Dottie's death. *As long as I'm snooping, I might as well go all the way*, she thought, and printed those.

A slamming car door outside made her jump. She moved the cursor up to close the mailbox when she read the subject line on the bottom of the screen. It was from Ella Mason, and it said, "Thanks for a lovely time."

It hadn't been opened. Peri knew how to open it, and then mark it as unread, but she felt guilty enough reading his business mail. Exiting the application, she grabbed her printouts and went back into the family room. She pulled a folder from her tote and stuck the papers behind a spreadsheet containing her current tax information.

As she walked to the kitchen to get something to drink, her cell phone began vibrating. She recognized the caller and answered.

"Hey, Skip."

"You called me? Sorry, I was in a meeting."

"It was nothing, really." Peri's face felt warm. "I just wanted you to know I was at your house. What do you want to do for dinner?"

There was a long silence. "Dinner, yeah. I've got a thing this evening. There should be plenty of leftovers in the fridge."

The image of a certain police officer in a red dress crossed her mind. "A thing? Since when do you have 'a thing'?"

"It's just something I have to do before we go to that shindig tomorrow."

"Why are you being so secretive?"

"Oh, for Pete's sake." His deep voice growled even lower. "My tux doesn't fit, okay? I gotta go rent one tonight."

"Oh. Okay, then I'll see you later." Peri was going to end the call, but had another thought. "Skipper, are you coming home before you go shopping?"

"No. I'm hoping that store by the mall has something to rent at the last minute. If everything goes well, I'll call you and see what I can bring home for dinner."

"Okay, well I hope you can get something. Love you."

"Ditto, Doll."

Peri ended the call and poured another glass of iced tea, then assumed a comfortable position on the leather sofa where she could read all the reports she had printed.

There was nothing from her golf course attack. The manicured grass had been too trampled by emergency personnel to discern any pattern, and the assailant hadn't been kind enough to toss the weapon where it could be found. Everything about the incident had been inconclusive, except for Peri's suspicions that it sounded like a golf club. At least they didn't find a golf ball at the scene, discounting the theory of a stray shot.

The headless crow and office shooting were slightly more interesting, as Jason had discovered hairs at each scene. There were no skin tags attached, so no DNA could be typed, but a long, brunette strand was found under the dead bird, and a short, brunette hair was on the lamp in Peri's office. A partial print was also found on her desk, but so far hadn't been matched in any database. The bullet was too banged up from hitting the window and the computer to identify, but Jason's notes indicated it was likely fired from a rifle.

He was probably at her office building now, processing Michael's death, and the second-floor office. She wondered how long those reports would take to process and send to Skip. Maybe there were more hairs to be found, or even a fingerprint. Hopefully, something more than those stiletto impressions, if that's what they were.

Darn stilettos, she thought, remembering the shoe prints in the carpet, *it's hard for a gal to aim when her heels are that tall.*

Stilettos reminded her of Ella Mason, sashaying through Antonia's in those little strappy numbers. She was trying not to dislike that woman, but it wasn't easy. The problem was not about Skip being friends with a woman—he had other female friends, some of whom liked to flirt. Peri knew and liked them. Maybe Mason's flirtatiousness wasn't as predatory as it seemed. Maybe Peri just didn't know her well enough to gauge her motives.

"But if it walks like a duck and talks like a duck," she said, and read another page.

She thought about the unopened email message on Skip's computer. It was only five o'clock. Skip would be at work for another hour, after which he'd be at Friar Tux's, trying to find something to rent for tomorrow evening's dinner. She had plenty of time to see what he'd done to make Ella thank him so sweetly.

Peri was halfway down the hall when she stopped. *This would be wrong. I shouldn't have read the police files, but sometimes that's my job. Reading Skip's personal messages means I don't trust him. And I do trust him. If there's anything for me to know, he'll tell me.*

Returning to the family room, she put away the folders, settled into the couch, and turned on the TV. Abbott and Costello were in a haunted mansion. The creaking of an old door was overridden by the sound of Skip's garage door. Peri sat upright as she heard the kitchen door slam.

"Hey, Doll, I decided to stop by on my way to the tux shop. Want to help me get a monkey suit?"

CHAPTER 24

As they drove down Imperial Highway, Peri squinted against the brilliant California sunset, the car's visor useless due to the angle of the light. She finally lifted her hand across her brow and turned her head to watch the generic, All-American strip mall roll past. Wal-mart, Home Depot, McDonald's, common EveryStores filled the city block to her right.

She closed her eyes and rolled her head left. Opening one eye, she watched Skip drive, his expression set in concentration. They had reached the five o'clock crunch of Imperial, a slow-and-go inching of cars toward the 57 freeway. Skip chose the middle lane. Peri leaned back into the headrest as he maneuvered away from the stalled bumpers trying to merge right onto the freeway.

"Always a lot of traffic this time of day," she said.

"Hmm, Mmm."

"How was your day?"

"Good."

"Any news on my case?"

She saw him smile. "I was wondering when we'd get to that question. Jason sends me copies of everything, but Daniels isn't exactly keeping me in the loop."

"I love you, Skip, but I want to move back into my own home."

"I know, Doll. I love you, too, but I'd like you to go home."

She laughed. "At least we're okay with that."

They managed to cross the freeway, at which point Skip danced the black SUV over two lanes, to turn right on State College Boulevard.

"What about Dottie? Did you find anything out?"

"A little. Turns out Bob had oleander in his system, too. Jason's tests showed it in Dottie's coffee, so we ran the only can of coffee in their house. It was laced with the poison. At this point, we're assuming that's how Bob got it, too."

"Oh my God, is it some kind of mass market poisoning?"

"We don't think so. We alerted the company and gave them the lot number. Here's what's weird—that lot was sold at Henry's Market in Yorba Linda. Did Bob and Dottie drive that far for their groceries?"

"Well, granted I hadn't cleaned their house for awhile, but they always went to the Ralph's down the street. What brand was it?"

"Starbucks."

"Seriously?" Peri sat up. "The Peters weren't fancy schmancy coffee drinkers. As a matter of fact, it gave Dottie heartburn. Bob thought Folgers was high end."

"Maybe they got it as a gift," Skip told her. "It was a fancy tin with a ribbon on it. Or maybe they won it in a raffle."

"Maybe. Did you get prints?"

He nodded. "Quite a few, but apart from Dottie and Bob, nothing recognizable."

Skip pulled the car into the parking lot, and found a space at the front of the tuxedo and formal wear shop.

"Who are all these people with no hits in any database? Prints on a coffee can, prints in my office…"

As soon as the words came out of her mouth, she knew she was in trouble.

"How did you know about the prints in your office?"

She could feel her face freeze, in that look of a deer before impact. She sucked in, a sharp breath, before she spoke. "Here's the thing—"

The sun bounced off the hood of the car, into her eyes, causing her to wince. "No one was keeping me in the loop, so I went looking for information."

"Where?"

The words stuck in her throat. At last, she pushed them out. "In your emails. But I only looked at—"

Skip held up his hand. "Don't say it."

Peri watched his jaw clench and unclench. He got out of the car, walked around, and opened her door. The silence was worse than any screaming match. She got out and followed him toward the entrance to the store, a one-story, beige stucco building in a cul-de-sac of restaurants and banks. Even her long stride could not quite catch up with his quick pace. When he got to the glass door, he turned and waited. She could feel his disapproval, radiating him like a force field.

A slim young man met them at the foyer, dressed to the nines in a pair of charcoal slacks, jewel-blue shirt and wine-patterned tie. "May I help you this evening?"

"I need a tuxedo." Skip's voice made it sound like he was asking for a colonoscopy.

"Certainly, sir. We have several styles. Did you want to rent one or purchase?"

"I need it tomorrow night."

The salesman's eyes widened for a second. "Well, I would recommend rental, then. We can have one ready for you tomorrow, and you don't have to be rushed into making a commitment to a suit."

Skip walked forward, leaving Peri behind, while he and the salesman discussed color, style, and measurements. She took a seat by the three-way mirror and waited.

It took about half an hour to fit into a slim, black suit with a satin stripe down the pants legs. Skip eschewed a cummerbund, opted for a regular satin tie instead of the traditional bow, and bought a new white shirt with French cuffs. Peri sat and watched the transaction, joining Skip at the counter when he was paying the bill.

The silent pair returned to the SUV. Skip walked slower this time, which enabled Peri to keep up. He held the door open for her, shutting it just as she pulled her leg into the car. She watched him walk around the front of the car. His face looked expressionless. He slipped behind the wheel and eased the car out of the parking space.

"I know it was wrong," she said at last.

"I know you know that."

"I only snooped into those files, not any of your personal emails."

"I know that."

Peri touched his shoulder and let her fingers run down his arm. "I don't want you to ever think I don't trust you. I'd never snoop into anything personal of yours."

"I know you trust me, Peri. That's not the problem. I'm unhappy that you snooped into police files, and I'm really unhappy it was from my email account. You could get me in trouble for disclosing sensitive information."

"You didn't disclose it. I found it."

"Because you were sticking your nose where it didn't belong. I can't believe you went into my email account." He tossed his cell phone at her. "Here, want to check my voicemails and texts, too?"

"No, I'd never—"

He cut her off. "Don't tell me you'd never do something. You'll do whatever you want, then justify it later."

"I didn't open your files because I wanted to. I did it because—" She was going to tell him about the recorded threats, but it suddenly felt like an excuse. "I just did it."

He kept his eyes on the road. "I need time to process this. I know it's not about trusting me. It's about me trusting you. If I can't trust you not to turn into one of those sleazy private dicks—"

"Sleazy? Looking at police reports is sleazy?"

"How would you define looking at my reports without my knowledge or consent?"

"I'd call it doing my job."

Peri watched his face turn crimson. "What job?" His voice boomed through the SUV. "It's not your case."

She matched him, loudness for loudness. "No, it's not my case. It's my life. And I want it back."

Her intensity startled her into silence. She leaned back and turned her face to the passenger side window. "From now on, I'll admit I'm capable of anything. Can we get some dinner?"

"Lucille's is at the next light." Skip's voice was quiet and flat. "Want something from there?"

"Okay." She rubbed her eyes, fighting tears. "Let's get it to go. I'm not in the mood for a crowd right now."

Dinner at home was served with a large side-order of awkwardness. Peri ate at the table, while Skip took his plate into the office. She thought about apologizing. A simple "I'm sorry" would make this all go away. Unfortunately, she didn't know how to say it and mean it. She only wanted to say it to make him stop being mad. And she knew he wouldn't accept it unless she meant it.

When she finally went to bed around eleven, Skip was still on his computer. By the time she fell asleep at midnight, he hadn't come to bed, and he was gone when she awoke.

Gone to the office, she thought as she wandered into the kitchen, *to work with Ella Mason*.

CHAPTER 25

After pouring a cup of coffee, Peri did some long, slow stretches to wake up her muscles. She actually wanted to run on the treadmill this morning, to work off the excess energy, but she didn't want to enter that room. It felt off-limits now. Instead she made some toast and eggs that she picked at, and drank a little orange juice. She turned on the TV and let the morning news show wash over her until it was time to get ready to meet Blanche.

The doorbell rang at nine, bringing her running, zipping her white capri pants as she scampered. Blanche stepped into the foyer.

"You ready?"

"Almost."

"Wow, new outfit? It's cute." Blanche looked at the white pants topped with a royal purple knit blouse.

Peri shrugged, her expression blank. "I ordered it online."

She felt her petite friend's eyes boring into her. The good thing about best friends is they know how you feel before you even tell them. It's also the bad thing about best friends.

"Okay, what's up?"

She couldn't look Blanche in the eye. Instead, she looked at the floor. "Oh, Beebs, Skip and I had a huge fight last night."

"About what?"

"About my snooping." She reached up with the back of her index finger and caught a little excess moisture from her eye. "It's all my fault. I snooped in his emails to find out about my case."

"Oooh, email snooping. Was it just police business or private emails as well?"

"Just the files from Jason about my case. Oh, and your tox screens from the Peters."

"My files? I feel so violated." Blanche hugged her. "I'm kidding. You guys have fought before. He'll get over it."

Peri shook her head. "I hope so, but I don't know. I know he'd get over it faster if I'd just tell him I'm sorry, but I'm only sorry I got caught. That's not gonna do."

"Well, did you tell him about the conversation I heard in the ladies room?"

"I keep holding things back because he's so fussy about my safety. I don't want to fight about it."

"And yet you're fighting anyway. Maybe he'd understand if you told him. I mean, I think your snooping was totally justified, after listening to those women."

"Maybe." She picked up her pink snakeskin tote. "It wasn't a big argument, but it was a really deep one. I broke a fundamental rule. I read his emails. They were work emails, but still. I tried not to, but Chief Fletcher has frozen me out of the office, Craig's not telling me much, and I can't just sit still and do nothing. After I heard what those women said on the tape…" She told Blanche about the conversation she had extracted.

"Good God, Peri, this is a dangerous crew." Blanche's husky voice sounded worried. "I think it certainly justifies your snooping, for your own survival. Skip has to understand that."

"Doesn't matter. The problem now is, I don't regret it. I got information out of it. I'd do it again if I had to." She sat down and rubbed her forehead. "Skip can't trust me now."

Blanche hugged her again. "Do you still love him?"

"Fiercely."

"And he loves you. You'll get through this." She picked up Peri's straw hat from the table and moved to the entrance. "Here, put this on and let's go have some fun."

"Yes, Ma'am." Peri rose and put on her hat. Smiling at her friend, she reached down and gave her a quick hug. "Thanks for listening. I really appreciate you."

Being at Skip's made it easier to walk to the parade, rather than try to find a place to park near it. The Placentia Heritage Parade was mostly high school bands, city groups and charities, all waving at the crowds who waved back from their seats along Kraemer Boulevard. Grand marshals ranged from local heroes and celebrities to costumed characters, like Mickey Mouse and Snoopy. It was all very enthusiastic and a great kickoff to the celebration in Tri-City Park later in the afternoon.

Peri looked for a change of subject as they walked toward the boulevard, the morning sun already warming the October air. "So how's the fam?"

"Paul's still on travel this week, back in D.C., trying to convince the Department of Defense to invest in the next generation of tracking systems they're building. Nick's driving me nuts because he won't get his driver's license."

"Why does that bother you? Doesn't it save you money?"

"Yea, but in the meantime, I'm the one schlepping him to his soccer games and his saxophone lessons."

"Can't Danielle do that?"

"Didn't I tell you? Dani decided at the last minute she didn't want to live at home and go to Cal State Fullerton. She got an apartment with a girlfriend over on Nutwood."

"Is she still seeing the Goth boy?"

"Chad? No, she told him she thought it would be too hard to maintain a relationship and keep up with the demands of college."

"Wow, she sounds so mature."

"I know. We were just getting to like him, though." Blanche dug her sunglasses out of her purse. "We may see her today. She said she and her girlfriends were going to come over and peruse the booths, have some unhealthy fair food, etc."

“Everything tastes better when it’s on a stick,” Peri said. “I hear they’ve got a beer garden this year, too.”

The neighborhood block walls still shaded the west side of Kraemer, so the two women parked themselves along the sidewalk a block down from the entrance to Skip’s street, nearly across from the park.

“Maybe we should’ve brought chairs,” Peri said

“We could sit on the curb.”

“Nah, it’d get my white pants dirty.”

Blanche laughed. “From Land’s End reject to fashion diva, in one step.”

“Call me crazy, but I don’t want to walk around with a dirty butt all day.”

“Fine. Just don’t lock your knees. You’ll pass out.”

“Remember that bridesmaid at your wedding?” Peri laughed. “What was her name, Cambria?”

“Camilla.” Blanche giggled. “It’s one thing to faint, but she took out a row of flowers and the ring bearer.”

“Your poor little nephew. And your mom’s face—I thought her head was going to spin like that scene in The Exorcist.”

They stood there, laughing at the memory, until they heard a small child calling out, “I hear something.”

A distant drumbeat could be heard, along with staccato bursts of brass notes. The first band was on its way. Soon, the banner came into view, *46th Annual Placentia Heritage Day Parade*, carried by two Eagle Scouts. The Valencia High School band followed, then a group of dancers, a restored old car carrying city officials, and so forth. This year’s Grand Marshall was a local author who’d made the front page of the newspaper; she smiled and waved, turning to include both sides of the street.

It took a good hour to see the bands from all the district’s high schools, plus the specialty groups, who strode gaily down the street. Fortunately, the parade route was only a couple of miles long, so everyone ended their trek with almost as much energy as when they began.

After the last group marched down the street, Peri and Blanche made their way over to the park. Tri-City Park was a 40-acre site managed by a board representing Brea, Fullerton, and Placentia. It had a walking path, a small lake, picnic areas, and lots of rolling green hills and trees.

Plenty of places to hide a body, Peri always thought.

For the Heritage Day festivities, booths were set up along the paved path, which curved around the south side. Everything was arranged according to what was being sold. The food stalls were the first thing visitors saw to the right, and led to the Classic Car Display. The craft booths backed up to the food with a fence separating them, and were accessible by leaving the path at the classic cars and heading back to the left. Nonprofit organizations got the short end of the stick, appearing to the left end of the food and out of the general path of traffic.

"Oh, look, churros," Peri said, pointing to a cart. She and Blanche bee-lined toward the smell of cinnamon and forked over a couple of dollars, in exchange for the spongy Mexican treats.

Blanche looked around the park. "Where's the coffee?"

"Over here, ladies. My treat." Peri looked across the path and saw Craig Daniels at the coffee cart.

"Craig, good to see you." She walked over, Blanche following. "Skip told me you pulled park detail."

"Yea, he got the short straw—he's playing golf with the chief and a couple of country club Got-Rocks." The detective bought two more coffees and handed them to the women. "You're both looking lovely today."

"Thanks," Peri said, taking a deep sniff of dark roast. "So, find out anything about my case?"

Daniels laughed. "You don't waste time, do you?"

They strolled together toward the classic cars, Blanche in their wake.

"Gotta tell you, Peri, I don't have a lot to chase. We've got some evidence, a few hairs, a couple of fingerprints, but nothing to match anything to. The bullet in your laptop was fairly smashed, so no info there. Jason did match the elements of that shrapnel in your tire to mini-tire spikes—it's the same metals, but we still can't call it a dead match. There are other things made of the same material."

"A couple of fingerprints?"

"Yeah, there was a partial on the desk in your office, then a full on the window ledge in the upstairs office, along with a short, blonde hair on the carpet."

"Good thing it was a short hair." Peri gestured to her medium-length locks. "You do know I was in that office."

He nodded. "Skip told me."

"I was very careful. I used gloves."

"Don't worry. You didn't leave anything behind to contaminate the scene." Craig smiled. "Skip worries too much. I completely understand your curiosity. Who wouldn't want to know who's behind it all?"

She smiled back at him, validated by his words. "Has Jason been able to listen to my recording yet?"

"Not yet. He's been a little busy."

Peri frowned a little, disappointed. "What about Michael's murder? Any leads?"

"That one's the most interesting. We just got this software that takes bullet striations and tries to match them to others in a huge database. The bullet that killed Michael Steuben came from the same gun that's been used in another killing in San Diego."

"Who?"

"Guy named William Quigley, about six months ago, still unsolved. There's no immediate connection between the two men, but I'm going to meet with the detective that handled the case. He sent me the report, but sometimes there are details that don't get written up."

She nodded. "Don't suppose you could email me that report?"

"Well, it's really frowned on, Peri."

"I know, Craig." She used his first name, hoping to cash in on his naturally flirtatious nature. "I wouldn't be acting on the information. I'd just be one more pair of eyes looking at the data."

"And a pretty pair of eyes at that."

Bingo, she thought.

"Well..." He smiled. "As long as you promise not to act on it, I don't see any reason not to share it with you."

As he spoke, Peri became aware of a petite woman to her left. Her back was to them and all Peri could see was a straw hat atop a pair of khaki shorts and white t-shirt. The legs were very tan and muscular, and she was wearing slim leather sandals with turquoise embellishments. She appeared to be looking at the menu for the Mexican food booth, but there was something about the way her head was cocked; Peri got the distinct impression this woman was eavesdropping.

"That's interesting," Peri said, and began to walk toward a beautiful '65 Mustang, candy-apple red with white interior, its hood up, displaying its sparkling 289-V8 engine. "I love this car."

"Maybe Skip can buy you one."

"Does he have a Swiss bank account I don't know about?"

Daniels laughed. "Nah, I'm just trying to get him deep in debt and hope you dump him."

She smiled and looked at Blanche, who had joined them. "Well, I don't think I'd be a very good P.I. if I tried to follow people in a flashy car like that."

"You aren't going to be a private eye forever, right?"

"Maybe not, but I'm not quitting any time soon." She looked past him to see the straw-hat woman turn from them toward a '57 Chevy convertible. Peri still could not see her face, but caught a glimpse of black hair. She lowered her voice. "Look, I just want to go home. The sooner I can go back to my normal life, the better."

He patted her shoulder, giving it a little extra rub. "I think I can talk the chief into an extra patrol, if you want to go home."

"Thanks, Craig." Peri saw the mystery woman still by the Chevy, acting like she was inspecting the engine. One of the owners walked toward her, flexing his biceps underneath the fitted t-shirt with an airbrushed rendering of his classic car. His hair was blond and slicked into a retro pompadour.

She must be pretty, Peri thought, *because he's smiling.*

The woman turned to walk away from them, allowing Peri to get a look at her. Sleek black hair in a bob, large black sunglasses on her elfin face, and bright red lipstick, made her easy to remember and describe. She moved back down to the coffee cart.

"Thanks, Craig. I'm really missing my stuff." Peri pointed toward the craft booths. "Beebs, why don't we check out the jewelry?"

Blanche nodded and they left the detective and passed the vehicles to get to the back side of the festival, the sweet smell of grass rising from their shoes as they walked. Peri leaned toward her friend. "I think there's a woman following either me or Daniels."

"Where?" Blanche started to look over her shoulder, but Peri elbowed her.

"Don't look." She kept her voice low. "Why do people always look? She's a little chick, black hair, red lips, straw hat."

"Why do you think she was following you?"

"She was just always where Craig and I were, standing really still, kind of looking at things without looking at them." Peri curved around to the first booth and picked up a pair of crystal earrings. She held them up and looked past them. The straw-hat was making her way toward the craft booths.

Taking her sunglasses off to see the jewelry better, she turned to Blanche, "These are cute, aren't they?" As she did, she met her friend's eyes and directed them toward the path.

Blanche looked past the earrings and nodded. "Darling."

Peri replaced the earrings and moved down the booth. She and Blanche sorted through necklaces, bracelets and more, in different patterns and colors of crystals, picking them up, talking, laughing, always with an awareness of the mystery woman on the other side of the table.

They moved to the next vendor, who sold handmade t-shirts. Blanche held up a pink tie-dyed V-neck.

"What do you think?"

"Remember that thing you said about buying high-end clothing to keep looking good?"

Blanche looked at the shirt. "You're right." She put it back on the rack.

They continued to paw through the merchandize, noticing the straw-hat woman joined them after a minute or so. They spent another few minutes in the clothing booth, and then moved on.

Over the course of the afternoon, Peri figured out the woman's pattern. No matter which vendor she and Blanche visited, she would stay at the old booth until they crossed to the opposite side of the new booth, at which she would approach the new booth.

The two friends continued their normal conversation, picking up items, making comments, enjoying the day. At the electronic scrapbooking display, a tune began playing in Blanche's purse. She reached for her cell phone and pressed a button.

"It's a text from Dani, wanting to know where I am. Looks like she's at the park already."

The mention of Dani gave Peri an idea. She leaned into Blanche, her voice low. "I think I may have a job for your daughter."

CHAPTER 26

Peri picked up a scrapbook brochure and handed it to her. "You could use one of these, Beebs, to make memory books for your family." She stared at Blanche and smiled, rolling her eyes slightly toward the vendor.

Blanche nodded, and waved the brochure. "Could you show me how this works?"

While the salesperson, a petite Chinese woman, demonstrated the features of the wonderful world of e-scrapping, Peri pulled out her cell phone and sent a text to Blanche's daughter, Danielle.

DANI, WHERE R U?

A few seconds later, she received a response.

HI AUNT PERI I'M @ THE PARK W/MY BFFs.

Happy, Peri sent the next text.

GOT A JOB 4 U. WANNA PLAY SPY?

Dani's response made her smile.

COOL!

The rest of the texting outlined her plan. When Peri put her phone away, she waited until Dani was in sight, then touched Blanche's arm.

"Thanks for the information," Blanche told the vendor. "I'm not certain if my computer has enough memory for this. I have to check with my husband, but I've got your card."

Peri and Blanche moved out of the booth, trying to keep a conversation going and act like they didn't recognize the trio of girls strolling toward them. Dani Debussy, Blanche's daughter, held the center of the pack, a tiny tan dynamo with sleek dark hair, pulled into a ponytail high on her head. Her friends were exotic-looking girls, taller than Dani by several inches, with sturdy legs and agile bodies. They wore similar outfits in the latest teenage uniform of short shorts peeking from sleek layers of tops in muted colors, and sandals so spare they barely counted as footwear. Giggling, joking, they commandeered a path through the crowd, in the full bloom of insolent teenaged flower.

As they passed, Peri caught Dani's attention long enough to roll her eyes back toward the booth. The young girl looked away from Peri and pushed at one of her friends, who pushed back and laughed. Peri and Blanche continued to walk back toward the classic cars. By the last craft booth, Peri glanced over her shoulder, to see if Dani had created the chaos she requested.

She'd been successful beyond Peri's wildest dreams. The straw-hat woman was surrounded by the three young girls, who all fussed over her outfit, which had been stained with the large drink Dani had been carrying. The woman's head was down, so Peri grabbed Blanche and headed behind the tented backside of the jewelry booth.

She peeked from the canvas to see the rest of the scene. The woman leaned down and handed something to Dani, who kept gesturing in wild, overwrought apology. It was hard for Peri to keep track of the action, but she managed to catch Dani place something in her bag as the straw-hat woman rushed toward the cars.

Blanche grabbed her arm. "What are we doing?"

"Trying to get behind that woman," Peri told her. "If I can follow her, she might lead me to someone or something."

They watched the woman walk past the booth, making certain they stayed out of her sight. When she had gone down the path toward the food, Peri followed at some distance, Blanche right behind her. At the Mexican food stall, Peri stopped and slipped to the side.

"Beebs, I think I need to finish this alone. She'll spot us both before she spots just one of us."

"Oh, no, I'm not leaving you alone."

"I won't be alone. Stay in the park. Find Daniels and tell him what's going on. Maybe he can help." She pushed her friend toward the path. "Besides, if straw-hat woman sees you, she may follow you, hoping you'll lead her to me."

"Against my better judgment, Periwinkle, but I'll do it." The petite brunette turned and walked down the pathway. Peri watched her try to stroll, look nonchalant and yet search for the detective.

The straw-hat woman had returned to the classic cars, still searching for Peri. As Peri suspected, the woman caught a glimpse of Blanche, looked around to see if Peri was nearby, then turned and picked up Blanche's trail toward the crafts. This made it easier for Peri to follow. The park was filling with people, so she could hang back in crowds and watch the mystery woman chase her friend.

At the t-shirt booth, Blanche caught up with Detective Daniels. Straw-hat woman apparently recognized him as police, and Peri had to find quick cover as she turned and left the craft area.

The woman marched toward the parking lot at a quick but not rapid pace. Peri slipped through the clumps of people to see her get into a silver Mercedes Benz, just like the one at the country club when Peri was following Nikki. Digging a pen from her tote, she wrote the license plate number on her hand, then turned back to find her friend.

Blanche and Craig Daniels were pushing their way through the masses when Peri looked up the path. She joined up with them in front of the coffee stand, which was now selling iced frappes in the warm October sun.

"Peri, what happened?" Daniels wiped a drop of sweat from his temple.

"I need you to look up a license plate." She told him the whole story, including the similarity between the Mercedes Benz at the country club and the one the straw-hat woman drove.

Dani and her girlfriends trotted up, breathless. "How did I do, Aunt Peri?"

"You did great, kiddo. Did you get it?"

"Did I get it?" Dani reached into her bag and pulled out a small coin purse, carefully holding it by the top. She handed it to Peri, who also carefully handed it to Daniels.

"I think we got her fingerprints."

The girls all crowded around Peri and Blanche. "Mom, that was so cool," Dani said.

Her friend with the thick black ringlets gushed in latent excitement. "Ohmygod, Mrs. Debussy, we were so scared we thought we might not pull it off and then Dani stepped into her just right—"

"You should've seen it," the other friend completed the story, her hands pantomiming the action. "Her frappuccino went kersploosh all over ohmygod it was so great."

Dani gave Peri a hug. "Aunt Peri, can I work for you?"

"No," Blanche said. "You've got that little college thing to do first, remember?"

"Oh, Mom, I was only thinking of part-time work."

Peri jumped in to save a working mother-daughter relationship. "I'm grateful for the offer, Dani, but I really need you to get that degree first." She winked at Blanche. "Then we'll talk."

"I'll have Jason run this for prints." The detective turned to Dani. "Did you touch this purse anywhere besides the top?"

She shook her head. "Aunt Peri told me not to. But even if I did, my fingerprints are in the system."

Blanche's head whipped around. "What?"

"Don't you remember, Mom? You had me fingerprinted for that child safety thing."

Peri laughed as she watched her friend relax. "Thought you were raising a career criminal?"

"All I can say is, kids and their surprises," Blanche said. "Not always a good thing."

Peri pointed to the coin purse. "Don't suppose you got a hair with that print? Just in case."

"No." Dani adjusted her own ponytail. "But it wouldn't have mattered. She was wearing a wig."

Daniels turned to her. "How do you know?"

"Oh, that's easy," Dani's curly-haired friend replied. "When Dani spilled her drink and they were all, like, having a big hissy and the lady was trying to clean her shirt and all, her hair kind of, like, shifted. Like it wasn't attached or something."

"I may have to hire all you girls," Peri said. "You're very observant."

Blanche cleared her throat, so she added, "When you get out of college, of course."

A round of "aws" signaled the trio's disappointment. Exchanging hugs and kisses with Blanche and Peri, they sauntered back into the park. Peri watched them disappear.

"Ah, to be young again and own the world," she said.

Blanche patted her shoulder. "Nah, they just rent it for awhile."

Peri continued to look at the crowd, where the girls had been. She was thinking about a group of friends, about their weekly lunch dates at the country club, about a woman in disguise, and the unknown meaning of 'Bettys'.

"Dani's been friends with those girls for a long time."

Blanche nodded. "Amazingly, since grade school."

"Beebs, what would you do to help a friend?"

"You know what they say. A friend will help you move. A good friend will help you move a body."

CHAPTER 27

"When's the last time you were out on the links, Carlton?"

Skip and his boss, Chief Dale Fletcher, stood at their first tee, waiting for the rest of their party.

"I haven't had much time to play since summer league ended." Skip pressed his fingers into his golf glove, smoothing it into his hand. "But I still hit a bucket of balls once a week."

"Well it's more than I've gotten to do, so I'll try not to embarrass us."

"I'm guessing our partners will save us with their scores."

The two men stood for a moment in the cool morning air. The lack of coastal fog made the golf course look crisp in the sunlight.

Skip took a driver from his bag and loosened his shoulders with a few swings. "Did you get playoff tickets?"

"Yeah, my wife managed to get two for Game 3. Looks like it'll be the Angels facing the Red Sox." He nudged Skip's shoulder. "Make sure we don't get any D.B.s that night, okay?"

"I'll get right on that." Skip looked past Fletcher and nodded. "Here comes the rest of our party."

Fletcher turned and the two men watched a golf cart careen down the path toward them, carrying their country club partners. Skip recognized Don Keller at once. Craig Daniels interviewed him as part of Peri's case, and Keller had preferred to come to the police station rather than have anyone interview him in his office. The man with him looked like walking money. Even from a distance, Skip noted his perfect tan and the soft cashmere sheen of his green striped polo shirt.

They stopped the cart and got out. Keller extended his hand to Chief Fletcher first. "Chief Fletcher? Don Keller, Keller and Patterson Development."

His partner was next in line. "Clinton Silvan," he said, shaking Fletcher's hand. "CFO, Keller and Patterson."

Skip watched them court his boss before turning his way. *So, that's the way it is*, he thought. *No wonder I hate these things.*

"And you are?" Silvan offered Skip his hand.

"Skip Carlton, PPD." He could have said he was a detective. Hell, he could have listed all the medals he'd won, if they wanted to play that game. Instead he took the man's hand and gave it a pump. The return handshake was firm; he noticed the way Silvan maneuvered just enough to roll his hand on top of Skip's.

Keller's handshake was similar. Skip wondered if they ever shook hands. He guessed it would evolve into arm wrestling within thirty seconds.

"Gentlemen," Keller said, glancing at his watch. "Let's get this scramble started."

He selected a club from his bag, took out a ball and stepped up to the tee. Skip noted the expensive driver, a Callaway customized to fit Don Keller, which included him being left-handed. He watched him take a few practice swings before driving the ball a couple hundred yards down the fairway.

"Good shot, Don." Silvan passed him on his way to the tee.

Skip glanced at Chief Fletcher, wondering if he felt as low on the totem pole. Fletcher looked back at Skip, the right corner of his mouth curling. *Yeah, he felt it, too.*

Clinton Silvan's ball was to the right of Don Keller's, not quite as far. "Guess we'll go with your shot."

"Mind if we get in on the action?" Chief Fletcher walked toward the tee, driver in hand.

Keller laughed. "Sorry, gentlemen, Clinton and I are so used to coming out here on Saturday mornings, we forget when we've got a foursome."

Fletcher's ball ended up several yards short of the longest shot, nestled against the long grass. He turned to Skip and winked. "Go for it."

Skip took a ball and his driver to the tee. He looked down the fairway, which curved slightly right. A center shot now might make the next shot more difficult, but keeping it left would give a straighter line. He swung the club a few times to loosen his shoulders before squaring up to the tee. After a brief glance at where he hoped to place the ball, he looked down and took the shot.

"You've got an interesting style, Carlton," Keller told him as they all watched the ball sail down the course. It bounced, then rolled to a stop, past his ball by a few yards to the left.

"Looks like we play the detective's ball," Silvan said.

Skip smiled. "Lucky shot."

The men got into their carts and drove to the next shot. Skip's luck didn't hold out, so Keller's position was the next to be played. The rest of the hole ping-ponged between the four players, allowing them to amass par.

"Didn't know detectives had so much free time to practice their golf game," Silvan said as they walked toward the next tee.

"They don't," Chief Fletcher told him. "Skip's just a perfectionist."

"Probably not a lot of crime in Placentia to persue." Don Keller said this in a casual tone, but Skip saw the back of his neck flush pink.

"You'd be surprised." He watched the pink on Keller's neck turn fluorescent. Looking over at Silvan, he saw no response.

This time, it was Silvan's ball they played from first, then shared spots as they finished the hole for one over par. The remainder of the round was more of the same. Everyone had a great shot, then everyone had a miserable shot, typical of golf.

At the last hole, Keller added up the scores and gave the card to Silvan to verify his math. Skip felt the chief's elbow brush his ribcage, pointing out they weren't asked to do anything as important as addition. He kept his eyes forward on Keller, but he smiled in acknowledgment.

"Good job, guys," Keller told them. "We almost made par."

Silvan patted the chief on the back. "Will you be at the dinner tonight?"

"Yes, I'll be there, as well as my detectives."

"Whoa," Silvan laughed. "Hope they're not on duty."

"Our every intent is to have a good time," Skip told him, his deep voice solemn. "But, of course, if anything comes up, we'll protect and serve."

"Will your wives be attending?" Keller again sounded innocent, but Skip detected a higher level of interest.

"Irene can't wait. She's a lot more excited about getting dressed up in a fancy outfit than I am about putting on a tux." Chief Fletcher turned to Skip. "How about you? Bringing Peri?"

Skip looked at him and nodded, but watched Keller and Silvan in his peripheral vision, knowing sometimes it's the things that don't mean anything that mean everything. Silvan's expression was relaxed. His eyes were on the chief, and his head tilted upward a little as he listened. Keller's face stayed blank, but rigid, as if it took effort to keep his emotions away.

Remind me to play poker with you sometime, Skip thought. He turned to the two men. "Peri's excited about it, too. I'm sure she'll have a great time meeting everyone. She loves to schmooze."

Again, he saw Keller's face stiffen. "That'll be great," the developer said. "We can't wait to meet her."

Skip stared at Don Keller and smiled. He held Keller's gaze until he saw the developer's eyes soften in knowledge. "I'm sure she can't wait to meet you, either."

"Gentlemen." Clinton Silvan interrupted their exchange. "Why don't we catch up with you at the bar? Don and I will turn in the score card."

Skip and the chief strolled toward the clubhouse.

"Think he's involved with what happened to Peri?" Chief Fletcher waited until they were out of range.

"I don't know, maybe he just gets nervous about hiring Peri to spy on his wife, but he sure acted like he wanted to talk about something without talking about it."

They sat down at the bar and ordered beers. The bartender, an older black man with skin like tanned leather and clouds of gray hair, gave them the bill with their order. Chief Fletcher picked up the tab and read it.

"Sure can't afford to get drunk in this place," he told Skip.

"Got that right," the bartender said as he walked past.

Skip smiled and took a sip of light beer, thinking about Peri's snooping and their fight. "Daniels hasn't been keeping me in the loop with Peri's case, but from Jason's reports it looks like we're not finding anything."

"Pretty much dead ends in every corner."

"Trace evidence?"

"A little, but nothing to compare it with. The bullet in her laptop is the only thing we can even call a crime. She might have just taken a hit from a stray golf ball on the course, and a dead bird on the doorstep, even headless, might have been left by the neighborhood cat." Fletcher drank deeply from the frosted glass of dark ale. "It's frustrating."

"Tell me about it. Peri wants to go home, and we can't tell her yes or no." He removed his gray PPD ball cap, rubbed his scalp, and replaced the hat.

"She's having all kinds of trouble with that new career, isn't she?"

"You have no idea." Skip shook his head, still angry about having his files read, and hoping the chief never found out. "I'd like to talk her into retiring, but she resists."

"Like I tried to talk Irene out of skydiving on her fiftieth birthday?" Fletcher laughed. "Nah, I get the feeling she does what she wants. Otherwise, you two would be married, right?"

"Yep." Skip looked toward the bartender and saw the TV over the bar. A baseball game was in progress, the last batter of the inning attempting a hit. The pitcher coiled his body and released the ball, over the plate in the blink of an eye. The batter was denied his goal and the TV station went to commercial while the teams exchanged places.

An ad for the Sunday movie came on, Ocean's Eleven. Skip watched the clips of George Clooney and a cast of thousands, each with a different part of the process, of stealing from Andy Garcia. His first thought, in these movies, was always how to catch the criminals. He'd have trace evidence from eleven people; how would he connect them?

"Chief, ever think that Peri's case may be a team effort?"

"A team?"

Skip nodded toward the TV screen. "Like Ocean's Eleven. Everyone takes a turn doing something. You may have fingerprints, trace, from each piece of the crime, but they're all different and no way to put them together."

Chief Fletcher scratched his head. "Let me talk to Daniels. It's an idea."

The bartender walked over and pointed to their empty glasses. "Another round?"

Skip looked to the chief, who nodded. "My treat."

"You work here often?" Skip watched the bartender pour two drafts.

"I never go home, Buddy." He held his hand out. "Name's Alvin."

"Hey, Alvin, I'm Skip Carlton and this is Dale Fletcher."

"Beat cops or detectives?"

"I'm the detective." Skip smiled and gestured left. "He's the chief."

Alvin shook the chief's hand. "Dad was a beat cop. I nearly joined, but ended up in the Marines instead. Made a career out of it."

Chief Fletcher nodded. "What put you behind a bar?"

He shrugged. "Wife died two years ago. This gets me out of the house."

"Bet you see a lot around here."

"Goddamned Peyton Place sometimes," Alvin told him. "The older people are good folks, always a smile and a generous tip, but some of the younger ones are still making their mistakes. Wife X is seeing Husband Y, you know. Then there are the folks who pull up in their spanking new Mercedes but haven't paid their bar tab in six months."

Skip laughed. "Have a lot of women in here?"

"Oh, yeah, Tuesdays is Ladies Day. We got 'em pouring in here for lunch." He leaned forward. "The longtime members come in for their iced tea and sandwiches, talk about their grandkids, books they've read, sick friends they need to visit. The young 'uns talk about calories while they order one more martini. Between you and me, some of them pour themselves into their cars for the trip home. A DUI checkpoint would rake 'em in around two, three o'clock."

"Aren't you supposed to be cutting them off, Alvin?" Chief Fletcher looked solemn.

Alvin stood up, his hands in the air. "I do, but women are funny. They look fine after a couple of drinks, then suddenly they get up to use the powder room and can't walk the floor in a straight line. Too late for cuttin' anything off by then."

Skip motioned for him to come closer again. "Alvin, do you know Nikki Keller?"

"Oh, yeah." He leaned on the bar, looking left to right. "She's in every Tuesday with her three buddies. Thick as thieves, I tell ya."

"Ever see anything, hear anything that sounds unusual?"

"What doesn't sound wacky from those gals? They're always talking some kind of code, playing games."

Chief Fletcher leaned in. "Like what?"

“First thing they do is put four slips in a wine glass, then pass the glass around and everybody takes a slip. They all count to three and open the slips at the same time, then laugh like hyenas.”

“Anything else?”

“Yes sir,” Alvin told the chief. “Last thing they do before they go home is raise their glasses and say, ‘betties rule’, or ‘petties rule’, or something like that.”

“Hmm,” Skip said. “Almost like a team cheer.”

Alvin nodded. “Yes sir, just like that.”

Skip turned to the chief. “I don’t want to step on Daniels’ toes with this—and I don’t want to jeopardize a case because of my relationship with Peri.”

“Don’t worry,” Fletcher told him. “I’ll give the information to him.”

The bartender looked up. “Did you say ‘perry’?”

“Yeah.” Skip looked up. “Why, what did you hear?”

“I remember the other day, the little dark-haired gal excusing herself and saying something about getting rid of a ‘perry site’. Maybe she was just talkin’ about a bug, but the way she pronounced it didn’t sound right. Caught my attention.” Alvin looked over his shoulder to a group of men motioning him over. “If you’ll excuse me—”

“Thanks, Alvin.” Chief Daniels stuffed a twenty in his tip cup. “You’ve been very helpful.”

The two men finished their beers in silence. Skip spoke first.

“Parasite, huh?”

“Daniels will handle this, Skip. It may not be much, but it’s more than he’s working with right now.” He rose from his bar stool. “Come on, we’ve got time to brief him before we have to get the monkey suits on.”

They walked outside and Chief Fletcher pulled out his cell phone. “Hey, Daniels, you still at the park... I think we’ve got another lead on the Peri case… “

As Skip listened to the one-sided conversation, he couldn't help laughing about 'the Peri case'. Even his boss couldn't pronounce her last name. After a few moments, Chief Fletcher got off the phone.

"Seems like we're suddenly leaping forward," he told Skip. "Peri was followed through the park today by a strange woman, but got her fingerprints and a license plate number. Daniels is going to see where it leads."

Skip removed his cap and rubbed his forehead. "For ten years now she's worried about my safety. I just can't get used to worrying about hers."

Chief Fletcher smiled and patted his shoulder. "Go get ready. I'll see you back at the bar at six."

Skip got in his SUV and drove out of the parking lot, toward his house. He spent the entire drive thinking about his conversation with the chief about Peri. They'd had fights in the past, but this was a big one. She'd read his emails. He loved her, they shared everything, but he always assumed there were boundaries neither of them crossed. She had snooped where she shouldn't have. The anger rose and subsided as his sympathy for her situation grew and waned.

He wished she'd go back to housecleaning, or find a less dangerous career. If she'd just marry him, she wouldn't have to work at anything. Peri wasn't an extravagant gal. He could support both of them on his salary, even when he retired.

I love her, he thought, *but when does this get too hard for us?*

CHAPTER 28

Peri glanced down at her dress, smoothing the blue chiffon and then touched the dangling rhinestones at her ears. She watched the reflection as she and Skip walked toward the glass door of the clubhouse. Two people moving alone, together. They hadn't repeated their fight of the day before, but they hadn't resolved anything, either.

Skip held the door, and then leaned toward her as she entered. Her heart fluttered, hoping he'd kiss her and break the wall between them. "Now, no business talk tonight, right?"

"What do you mean?"

"I mean, we'll be mingling with the Kellers and their friends. No fishing for information. Craig Daniels will be there. No talking about any new evidence." He held up his hand, unfolding each finger as he spoke. "Nice, safe subjects."

"Like what?"

"I don't know. The weather, sports, shopping. Actually, in your case, religion and politics are safer than anything you want to talk about." He moved away from her, without a kiss, or even taking her hand.

Peri put her hopes back on the shelf. "Don't worry, I'll try to behave."

They walked into all the opulence Placentia could buy. The foyer of the club had been decorated for the evening in gold and crimson sashes across entrances, large floral arrangements on the tables, and low, twinkling lights. The effects made Peri feel like she was walking into an enormous tapestry.

Several people milled around the room, drinks in hand. The men all looked like a herd of penguins in their tuxes. Tall, small, thin, fat flightless birds. Most of the women wore short, black dresses, although a few wore bright colors. Peri felt a little conspicuous in her vibrant blue, but didn't see many heads turn in their direction, so she relaxed and hunted around for familiar faces.

"Skip, Peri."

They looked up to see Chief Fletcher motioning to them. Peri hung back for one second to allow Skip to shake his boss' hand, before offering her own.

"Good to see you, Chief," she said.

"You're looking great," he told her. "Irene should be here any minute. She had to work late at the hospital, so she ran home to change."

"Poor Irene, how long has she worked ICU?"

"Twelve years. She loves it, but her hours can be as unpredictable as mine sometimes." He looked at his empty beer glass. "Care to check out the bar?"

"I think it's time," Peri told him.

The three walked over to the corner of the room, where a no-host bar had been set up. A friendly face was pouring wine.

"Good evening, Alvin," Skip said. "I'll take a light beer, get the boss whatever he wants, and, Peri?"

"I'll have the usual."

Skip turned to Alvin. "Grey Goose dirty martini, four olives."

"You got it," Alvin said.

Skip introduced her to the bartender.

"Perry?" Alvin's eyes widened. "As in the perry-site?"

"What?" Peri looked at Skip for explanation.

He picked up his drink, without looking at her. "We'll talk later."

"How much later?"

Chief Fletcher leaned toward her. "Much later."

She turned to Alvin, who handed her a delicate glass of cloudy liquid, a skewer of green olives floating on top. “Thank you.”

“Alvin looks pretty busy,” Skip said. “We should let him get his work done.”

Chief Fletcher motioned toward the dining room. “Looks like they’re ready for us.”

A rush of black jersey caught Peri’s attention. “Here comes Irene.”

They all greeted the chief’s wife and joined the others walking in to the dining room. At the door, they spied Craig Daniels at a table. Skip waved to him as they approached, but their path was interrupted by a slight young man in a fitted suit tuxedo.

“Pardon me, are you one of our law enforcement invitees?”

“Skip Carlton, PPD.” Skip extended his hand.

Peri watched the man slide his diminutive hand in and out of Skip’s paw so quickly it could barely be called a handshake.

“We’ve made arrangements for each member of the police department to be seated with a table of their sponsors.” He looked at a card and then scanned the room. “Ah, yes, you and your guest are seated at the Patterson table.”

Peri smiled and followed the young man to a table near the floor-to-ceiling windows. Three couples were already seated. The men rose as Skip and Peri approached.

“Well, Detective— “ The beefy man with the ruddy face held his hand out while he fumbled for Skip’s name.

“Carlton. Skip Carlton. Nice to see you.” He turned to Peri. “This is Peri Minneopa. Peri, this is John Patterson.”

“Peri, this is my wife, Kim.” The stunning brunette at his side nodded as handshakes were exchanged across the table.

“Skip, nice to see you again,” Clinton Silvan said, reaching for a handshake. “This is my wife, Lisa.”

A pixie-ish woman with short, ash blonde hair, smiled at the couple. To her right, an older man smiled and extended his hand.

"Phil Nickles." His voice was low and full of gravel. "My wife, Nancy," he added, gesturing to his side.

A small, silver-haired woman with large blue eyes smiled and nodded from her seated position. "Nice to meet you, Detective, Peri."

"Please, call me Skip," the detective said as he held Peri's chair, and then sat next to her.

"Clinton tells me you held your own at the tournament today," John said. "Wish I could've been there, but this knee has to heal first."

Peri smoothed her napkin on her lap and tried to sound interested. "Injury?"

"Nope, it just gave out and I had to have it replaced. Probably too many tackles when I played football at Ball State."

She glanced at the others' faces for whether to take this as a joke or not. Everyone seemed serious, so she nodded and changed the subject. "Kim, did you play in the tournament today?"

Kim's smile was enigmatic. "No, we had a few appointments to get ready for tonight, didn't we, Lisa?"

The other woman laughed, so Peri turned toward her. Lisa Silvan was an elfin creature with large green eyes. Peri noted the acorn-shape of her face, her full lips. Looking at these women without dark glasses and surveillance equipment made her feel exposed, but she tried to look relaxed.

"Well, it was worth it, wasn't it, Gentlemen?" John chuckled.

"Absolutely," Clinton said.

Silence hung over the table, surrounded by uncomfortable smiles. As if to break the surface tension, the server arrived with plates of salad, followed by another young man with bottles of red and white wine.

Peri picked up the bowl of ranch dressing from the table and ladled a small stream onto her greens before passing it to Skip. She looked up to observe Kim squeeze a lemon wedge onto her salad, while Lisa poured a small puddle of Italian dressing on her bread plate, where she proceeded to anoint each leaf before eating it.

If we were on the Titanic, these women would soon be kicking themselves, Peri thought. She looked over at Nancy, who had joined her in a spoonful or two of dressing.

"I just love ranch on my salad, don't you?"

Peri agreed, smiling. "So, did anyone see the parade this morning?"

"I had to go to the office," John said.

Lisa shook her head. "Spa."

"I went for a run." Kim gave Peri a slight grin.

"It was a lot of fun," Peri said, thinking, *strike one for innocuous banter*. "All of the high school bands performed."

"We saw it," Nancy said. "Our grandson was in the El Dorado band. We've watched the parade for years now."

Silence descended again until the salads were removed and the chicken was delivered. It was, to the best of Peri's reckoning, breaded and panfried, with a lemon-caper sauce, served with roasted fall vegetables, and a rice pilaf. Typical banquet and wedding reception fare.

Nancy looked up from cutting her chicken. "Peri, do you have children?"

"Me? No, I can't even keep a goldfish alive, although, I am fostering a cat."

Phil laughed. "How's that going?"

"Not as hard as I thought. Of course, I haven't been home for awhile."

This seemed to pique Kim's interest. "Really? On vacation?"

"No, I—well, I've been staying at a friend's house." *Think, idiot*. "She just had surgery so I helped out. I'll probably go home tomorrow."

"What a nice friend you are," Lisa said.

"Friends are the most important things in life." Kim's voice gave her opinion a strangely ominous tone.

Peri felt Skip's leg press into hers, so she turned to him. "How's your chicken?"

"Fine." He smiled a little, but she could see the tension underneath.

"Well, I think my cats at home will get most of mine," Kim said, peeling the breading off a slice before eating a small bite of it.

Now Peri was interested. "You have cats? Would you like one more? He's pretty well behaved, as well as being pretty."

She could have sworn she saw Kim's nose curl in disdain. Her husband laughed.

"Kim raises champion Abyssinians. She wouldn't be interested in some old orange cat."

Peri's eyes narrowed. *How do you know what kind of cat I'm fostering*, was on the edge of her lips. All she got out was the "H—" before she felt Skip's shoe knock against her ankle.

"H-owch." She winced and then looked up. "Sorry, I accidentally hit my ankle bone on the chair. Abyssinians—how interesting. Well, if you know of someone looking to adopt a cat, let me know."

"We might want a cat," Phil said. "How old is he?"

"Well, I don't really know," Peri replied. "He was owned by my neighbors, they both died recently, so he's kind of an orphan."

Nancy gasped a little. "Oh, I'm so sorry."

"It was kind of a shock," Peri said. "They were an older couple, but neither of them seemed to be in particularly ill health." She wasn't sure whether she should mention the unnatural cause of their demise, but another warning tap from Skip's foot told her to keep her mouth shut.

"It's pretty common for elderly couples to go a few days or weeks apart," John Patterson said.

Nancy looked dismayed at his remark, and Phil's cheeks flushed.

"Well, what I mean is, couples who've been together a long time tend to…to…that is, people who've spent their lives together want to…to…well, um…" The stumbling went on while John tried to dig his way out of his gaffe.

Peri was enjoying the show, when she heard Skip come to his rescue. "Peri, why don't you exchange phone numbers with the Nickles? Maybe they can come and meet Mr. Mustard."

"That would be wonderful," Phil said.

The conversation again stalled, so Peri ate her meal and looked around the room. She noticed the Fletchers had been seated with Nikki and Don Keller. Craig Daniels was at Susan Leske's table. Peri smiled. Even though Susan had a date, Peri thought she'd be right up Craig's flirtatious alley.

"Peri, I understand you're a private investigator." Kim was again doing that inscrutable smile thing Peri hated. "You have to work with some pretty low types, don't you?"

"I don't think of them as 'types'. I have clients, from all walks of life."

"But, don't you find yourself sinking to the lowest common denominator?"

I've been such a good girl tonight, Peri thought. *I don't deserve to be baited by this rich witch.* She wanted to be snarky, but decided to be obtuse. "I don't understand. Sinking how?"

"You know, like, hanging out with the wrong people, getting tattoos, or piercing your eyebrows."

Peri stared at her a moment while she allowed the quiet to grab everyone's chest and squeeze them. She caught Alvin's eye and lifted an empty wine glass. He nodded and smiled.

"Well, Kim," she said at last. "The only people I hang out with are my friends in the Placentia police department, and my friends in the Orange County Sheriff's office. Which group should I drop?"

Kim's husband laughed, in forced huffs. "I wouldn't mess with either."

Peri decided to put the topic to bed with a bold fabrication. “And as far as the tattoos and piercings, I’m Jewish. Those things are against my religion.”

Alvin brought two bottles to the table. Peri pointed to the cabernet and he poured her a glass before looking around. “Would anyone else like wine?”

Everyone selected, red or white, and he started back toward his post. On his way, Peri saw him stop at Chief Fletcher’s table and whisper in his ear, looking at her the entire time.

Dessert and coffee were served. Although she was usually a dessert queen, Peri’s plate did not excite her. A thin slice of white cake with red filling, white icing, and raspberries as garnish, it was not her idea of a good time. She felt compelled to eat it just so she didn’t look like the two wraiths at the table, who had picked at their dinner like anorexic birds.

She pushed the cake around on her plate. “When does the dancing start?”

“Soon, I hope,” Lisa said. “Clint and I hardly ever get to dance.”

“They usually start after the Mayor does his spiel,” John said. “Should be any time now—he’s over there in the corner with his assistant.”

Peri looked back to see Mayor Scott going over notes with the young man who had seated them. The two men moved from the corner and meandered to the front of the room. The smaller man pulled a podium out from behind one of the silk ficus trees, knocking a few of the twinkling lights down in the process. Mayor Scott put the papers on the podium and looked around the room. A few people had been watching the setup, and began to applaud. The noise got the attention of the rest of the people, who joined the merriment. Soon, everyone was clapping and the mayor was smiling and pushing his palms down to make it stop, which made everyone keep going.

At last, the game ended and the mayor made his speech. He congratulated the organization on raising money for Placentia, he thanked the police for their daily diligence to protect and serve, and he promised to make the city proud by his efforts as mayor. It was lovely and heartfelt, but more importantly, it was over.

"It's a pity you're in a cast, John," Peri said. "Your lovely wife is going to miss the dancing."

Kim stared at Peri. "Don't worry about me. I can make my way around the floor." She rose and turned to Skip. "Detective, could I have this dance?"

He paused for a moment, and then replied, "Certainly." He stood up and took her offered hand. Peri watched them glide out onto the dance floor. While it wasn't an especially romantic song, it was a slow tempo and required the couple to be fairly close, Skip's hand around Kim's waist. Lisa and Clinton, and Phil and Nancy, joined them.

"My wife loves to dance," John said. "She was a little miffed that I had this surgery before October, but I was hurting."

"Well, Skip loves to oblige," Peri told him. She watched him move the lithe brunette across the parquet tiles. Skip was looking at Kim and saying a word here and there. Kim seemed to be responding. As they neared the table, Peri saw Kim look past Skip at her; her face looked as content as a cat. She reminded Peri of Mr. Mustard, right after he had broken the blue vase.

The song at last ended and everyone came back to the table.

Peri rose from her chair. "I think I'll freshen up before I hit the dance floor."

"Sounds like a great idea," Lisa said. "Kim, you want to come along?"

"Women," John said. "Why do you have to go to the ladies room in a clump?"

"To talk about you," Peri replied.

She could hear nervous laughter as she walked away.

The ladies room at the country club was small but luxurious. The club's décor had been extended to the wallpaper and the seat cushion of the bench in front of the vanity mirror. There was already a line to use the four stalls; one of the stalls was reserved for handicapped people. Peri hoped it would not open up when she was next in line. She felt it was wrong to use a handicapped stall when she had no disability, but sometimes Nature overruled her desire to be morally upright with her need to pee.

Kim and Lisa were in the restroom, but not in line. They were at the vanity, adjusting their already perfect makeup. Nikki Keller ran in and greeted them, along with Susan. They were all in cocktail dresses of high quality understatement, providing the perfect background for their tanned, toned bodies and expensive jewelry.

There was a lot of hushed giggling and admiring of dresses and jewels. Peri watched them, bored with their conversation. Her eyes drifted to their feet. All wore strappy, sexy sandals, with narrow heels of three inches or more. They each also had a small tattoo on their ankle. Peri couldn't quite make out the object. It looked like some kind of flower, but each woman's was in a different color. These were serious friends.

She noticed Kim's focus coming back to her from her reflection. Suddenly, the brunette turned to face Peri.

"Nikki, Susan, I'd like to introduce you to Peri. She's here with one of our fine detectives."

"Good to meet you," Peri told them, glad she wasn't hooked up to a lie detector.

A regular stall opened up and she rushed in, did what she needed to do, and made certain her clothes were in their rightful place before she walked out. The foursome were still at the mirror when she emerged. She washed her hands and paused to find her own corner of the vanity area, fluffing her blonde curls, and reapplying lip gloss.

"I hear you've been away from your house for awhile, Peri," Nikki said. "Sick friend?"

Peri kept her eyes on her own reflection, running her fingernail under her lower lip to smooth her lipstick. She decided to play a hunch. "That's the official story," she told them. "The truth is, I had to have my house sprayed. ***Perry**-sites*, you know."

She turned toward the door, but not before she heard a small gasp, and saw two astonished faces looking at her in the mirror. Nikki and Kim did not look surprised. They looked angry enough to kill.

CHAPTER 29

"This is nice." Peri looked at Skip as they moved to the cool stylings of Luther Vandross. She wished Skip would hold her a little closer, like he usually did, but at least he was dancing with her.

She felt his arm stiffen around her waist. "Mmm, Hmm."

They shuffled in a general pattern, staying in a tight square on the busy dance floor while their bodies swayed in rhythm, slowly rotating for a panoramic view of the room.

"By the way," he said, "since when are you Jewish?"

"She started it."

"You don't need to finish it."

"How do you know?" She wanted to lay her head against his neck, but he was too far away.

The click-click-click of heels out of rhythm made her look up. Nikki Keller stood at the doorway, looking around the room.

Peri watched Nikki at the doorway. "Wonder who she's looking for?"

"Don't know. Don't care."

"Wonder where Don is." She perused the crowd over his shoulder. "I don't see him anywhere."

"Probably at the bar."

"Doesn't look like he's there."

"Okay, then the men's room." Skip turned her away from the doorway, toward the wall. "I thought you wanted to dance."

The song ended and a more upbeat disco number ramped up. Peri became aware of a burst of unexpected activity on her edge of the dance floor. Mr. Nickles was at Skip's side, tugging his sleeve and gesturing, his grey hair frizzed and wild from the sweat across his brow. She couldn't quite hear what he was saying to Skip, except that it contained the words hurry and dead.

Skip dropped her hand and ran off with the older gentleman, so Peri had no option but to follow. They rushed to the building's entrance and took a hard right turn. Mr. Nickles stopped and pointed.

"I just came out for a smoke," the older man said. "I came out for a smoke and there he was."

The decorative lighting on the side of the building was so low it barely cast shadows, but visible in the moonlight was a body sprawled in the flowerbed. Peri took a step beyond Skip to get a better look and wished she hadn't.

It was a man, in a tuxedo, with his head smashed. His forehead was concave in the middle, with a deep, torn gash running down toward his nose, which had been flattened. Blood was everywhere, dark and shining. The accent light of the flowerbed streaked across his face. His eyes stared, empty, at the sky. They were light, but not blue, and his teeth glowed white. Even with his head disfigured, Peri guessed who it was.

"Tyler Garvey," she told Skip in a breathless whisper. "I think it's the golf pro."

Stepping back, she touched her fingers to her forehead and noticed their trembling. Her head felt light, and she could not get enough air into her lungs. The night-blooming jasmine smelled too sweet and the dead body too sour. Just before her legs collapsed, she was aware of strong hands guiding her away, to a stone bench nearby.

"You okay?" Skip's deep voice reached into her consciousness and she nodded.

"Sorry." She rested her head on her hands and closed her eyes. After a few deep breaths, she looked up at him. "I'll be fine. Go do your job."

News of the discovery spread through the dance, enticing everyone to come out and see for themselves, just to turn away in horror. Chief Fletcher swam through the crowd to Skip, who was trying to keep the curious from damaging the crime scene. Getting them to calm down and return to the clubhouse for questioning was difficult. Some people wanted to leave immediately. Others wanted a closer look. One young waiter tried to videotape the chaos, but Skip caught him, midarm, and asked him, politely, to rethink that decision.

Peri, seeing the two men try to take charge of 200 people, watched Skip pull his cell phone out, say a few words, and then put his phone back.

All the patrol cars in Placentia should be here soon, she thought.

She watched a figure trying to herd everyone back inside and recognized Craig Daniels. Mayor Scott jumped in, with the other city officials, to restore order. Three black-and-whites screamed up the driveway, lights blinking. Chief Fletcher issued directions for all. Two uniforms would tape off the area and guard the body. The rest would come inside and help take names and phone numbers. Jason Bonham ran up from the street, where he'd parked, his kit slapping against his leg.

Skip walked over to Peri. "Chief Fletcher's going to take your statement. I'll be here for awhile, so you may have to get a ride back to my place."

She stood up. "Maybe I should just go home, Skip. Craig said he can assign a patrol to drive by my address. You need time to process… to sort out… you'll be busy."

He looked at the ground. "No, go ahead and stay at my house. We'll talk about everything when I get home."

Peri returned to the dining room, which had been completely cleared of all remnants of dinner, except for the tables and chairs. Everyone milled about, discussing the tragedy. Only Skip had heard Peri's guess about the victim's identity, so there was conjecture everywhere as to whose body was in the flower bed. Officer Chou worked Peri's side of the room, so she walked over and gave him her name and contact information.

"There you are, Miss Peri. Chief wants to see you," he told her, and motioned toward the foyer.

She walked to the next officer, who directed her to the bar area. As she approached Chief Fletcher, she saw the journal-style notebook the chief was writing in. He motioned to the chair across from him, so she sat down.

"I heard you gave Skip a name," he said. "Would you like to share?"

"I'm pretty sure that's Tyler Garvey out there, the golf pro."

"His face is awfully demolished for that kind of quick ID."

Peri looked down, remembering. "I can't be one hundred percent, but those look like his eyes. His teeth, too. His teeth were that straight and white."

"How well do you know him?"

"I met him once, here, on the course. I was doing some surveillance work."

Chief Fletcher kept writing. "Was he involved in your case?"

"You could say that. He was having an affair with my client's wife."

The chief put his pencil down. "I don't suppose you have to cooperate, except that Detective Daniels has been giving me steady reports on your case, so I already know all the players. These questions are just for the record."

"Of course." Peri smoothed the chiffon overlay of her skirt. "I'm sorry, Chief. I don't mean to be petulant. I'm just a little overwhelmed."

"I understand." He picked up the pencil and turned the page in his notebook. "Now, what were you doing after dinner tonight?"

"I danced with Skip." She rubbed her hands together, massaging her palms as she remembered. "At the beginning of the third song, Mr. Nickles came and got him. Oh, wait – just before that, I saw Nikki Keller in the doorway, looking around for someone."

"Do you know who she was looking for?"

"No, but I know who wasn't in the room. Her husband."

The chief smiled. "And you know this, because?"

"Because when I saw her looking around, I looked around, too. He wasn't there."

The chief was silent for a moment. "Had you made Mr. Keller aware of his wife's relationship with Garvey?"

"No. I gathered the data, wrote the report and offered to send it, but he declined. Said he changed his mind and didn't want to know."

"Did you believe him?"

She shook her head. "Of course not. Everybody lies."

"I know I told Skip to keep you out of the station, but I'm beginning to think I should hire you instead."

"Thanks, but I'm no policeman. I'm just naturally nosy. When I get old, I'll be that woman at the curtains, spying on the neighbors."

They laughed.

"Is there anything else you can think of," he asked her.

"Not really, unless you'd like to tell me what the bartender whispered to you at dinner."

Chief Fletcher's eyes widened. "What do you mean?"

"I mean, after he poured our wine, I saw him pass three tables to get to yours, where he leaned in to whisper something in your ear. When I add that up with his comment about 'Perry site', I've got to think he was telling you something about our table."

The chief smiled. "I think we're done. Do you have anyone who can pick you up?"

"Oh, come on, Chief Fletcher. Don't I deserve to know what's happening?"

He motioned to the officer at the door. "Miss M—Peri is free to go," he told him, and then turned back to her. "I know you were planning on going home soon, but if you can stay with someone, I think it would be best."

"Thanks." She added *for nothing* under her breath, and left the bar.

She saw Skip in the foyer. He was kneeling beside Mr. and Mrs. Nickles, speaking in low tones with them. Nancy was dabbing at her eyes, and Phil slumped as though he had aged a few years in just a few minutes. Peri joined them, patting Nancy's shoulder in sympathy.

"Excuse me," Skip told the couple. "I'll be right back."

He stood and motioned Peri to follow him toward the front door. "You okay?"

"A little shell-shocked, but I won't faint on you. The chief took my statement and is sending me home."

"I may be here late. I don't think you should go back to my place alone. How about Blanche's place?"

"Blanche is on call tonight, so she'll be here shortly. Paul's out of town, Dani's moved out, Nick may or may not be home, so her house is mostly empty." Peri rubbed her arms. "Frankly, her house is so large, it'd give me the creeps to stay there alone."

"Then there's only one thing to do. Call Benny."

"Oh, Skip—"

"He can hang out with you until I get home."

"But you may work all night."

"So put him up in the spare bedroom."

"Do you know what you're saying? I mean, I like Dean Martin, but this will be a Dino marathon. Movies, TV shows, music, all narrated by Benny. Every piece of trivia will be trotted out for my education." She rubbed the back of her neck. "If I wasn't sick when I saw the body, I'll be sick by the time you get home."

"Lock yourself in the bedroom and let him have the family room. He can watch Dino in high def on the flat screen. Make the call."

Thirty minutes later, Benny's black Caddy rolled into the country club entrance. Peri watched him hesitate at the sight of patrol cars, then make a U-turn and pull alongside the curb at the exit. He got out and waited by the car.

The streetlight washed down on the little man, dapper in a tuxedo. His white shirt glowed against the black suit, and Peri's eyes were drawn to the red slash of a pocket square across his chest.

"Did I drag you away from a party, Ben?"

He looked perplexed. "Miss Peri, you told me this was the country club dinner. I couldn't show up in casual wear to pick you up."

She smiled. "Good thinking. You look very nice."

Skip came out of the clubhouse and joined them, to give Benny instructions. "I want you to take her back to my place. I may not be home for awhile, but you need to stay until either I get home or I send a patrolman. Do you understand?"

Benny's head bobbed up and down in vigorous assent.

"If it gets too late, go ahead and sack out in the spare room."

"Overnight? At your house?" Benny appeared stricken.

"Skip's got a nice TV, Ben. Home theater, surround sound. You can watch your Dean Martin movies all night."

He brightened. "That sounds like fun."

True to form, he hopped in his Caddy and waited for Peri to get in, a feat made harder by the fact he had parked so close to the edge, she had to totter along the edge of the curb in her high heels, pushing ornamental shrubbery out of her way to open the car door.

"Watch the paint job," Benny said. "You're gonna scratch it."

"Don't park in the bushes and I won't."

They drove away, out to Alta Vista and toward Kraemer Boulevard.

Peri removed her earrings and rubbed her earlobes. "How's Mr. Mustard?"

"Who?"

"The cat, Benny. You are still feeding him, right?"

He laughed. "Oh, him. Oh, sure, Miss Peri, I feed him every day, twice. But I don't call him Mr. Mustard." He snorted. "What a stupid name."

"What do you call him?"

"Matt Helm, of course."

"Of course." She sighed. "Well, I may have a home for him. I met a couple tonight who are interested in adopting him."

"Adopting? Really?"

"He's a nice cat, but I don't want to keep him. Why, do you want him?"

He was silent.

"I'm sorry, Ben, I thought you didn't want him. Did you change your mind?"

"No. Yes. I don't know. I'm afraid he'll make a big mess out of my house. But he's kind of interesting. He stares at me all the time, and plays fetch with stuff. Couldn't you keep him so I can visit?"

"Uh, no. Maybe you can visit him at the Nickles' house." She watched the streetlights pass in the darkness, wishing they were already at Skip's. Fatigue washed through her bones and she longed for comfortable clothes and a cup of tea. She tried not to think of the fact that Skip hadn't kissed her, or even squeezed her hand, before he sent her off with Benny for the night.

"How's my house?"

It took him a few seconds to answer. "Good. Your house is good. Um, were you very attached to the blue glass moose on your shelves? You see, Matt was playing, and—"

Peri scowled. "I was fond of that moose, Ben. I mean, how attached are you to your Dino ashtrays?"

She was sorry the moment she said it. The color drained from Benny's face. He pulled the car over to the curb. "Maybe I should go home now and check on my things. What if one of them broke? Oh, dear, I really need to go home."

"No, Benny, I'm sure your ashtrays are okay." Now she had to do damage control. "I'm positive. After all, you don't have a cat, right?"

He sat for a moment, apparently in thought. "No, I don't have a cat. You're right, Miss Peri. My stuff should be fine. I don't need to check it."

"Skip really needs to you to get me back to his place."

"That's right. I better do what Detective Skip says." He nodded and drove away from the curb, continuing toward the detective's house.

Benny finally guided the Cadillac into Skip's driveway and they entered the house, turning off the security system and turning on all the lights. Peri changed into her sweats and then fixed her herbal tea while a constant replay of the body kept looping through her mind. She looked over the counter at Benny, who was fiddling with the surround sound controls to ensure proper modulation of Dino's voice.

"Want anything, Ben?"

"Thanks, Miss Peri, I'll take some tea. Do you have Lipton?"

"I don't know, let me check."

"Cause Lipton's all I drink. And honey, do you have honey?"

Peri rearranged the pantry, searching for the proper ingredients. "Yes, looks like we have both."

She had just poured hot water over the teabag when Benny added, "I need cream, too. Real cream, not milk or half-and-half."

This is why no one invites you to their slumber parties, Peri thought. "No cream, Ben. Two percent or nothing." She set the mug and condiments on the counter. "Help yourself."

A trumpet's blare heralded the opening credits of a movie.

"Turn it down a little," she said. "We do have neighbors."

Benny scowled but obeyed. He moved backward toward his tea, his focus glued to the screen. Peri leaned over the counter to see what engrossed him so fully. Dotted numbers crawled around while an orchestra blasted a song. After a few moments, she saw it was Ocean's Eleven.

"This looks a lot different from the one with George Clooney," she said.

"Pfft, that hacked-up remake? Half the film this one is. Not even worth the name."

She smiled and tested her tea. It felt like a warm blanket, comforting her. "Maybe, but this one certainly seems less action packed."

"People nowadays expect explosions out of the gate. This movie develops. It gives you time to get to know the characters. Shh—here he is."

Dean Martin walked out of an airport gate and began a conversation with what turned out to be an old Army buddy. Peri moved to the couch and folded herself into the corner, letting the movie wash over her, happy for the distraction from her memory of that smashed-in skull. The tea continued to soothe; she gripped the mug and held it close, even after she had emptied it.

Halfway through the film, her eyelids lowered in a twilight of sleep. The actors moved about casinos, signaling each other and running metal objects around doors. She had missed some of the plot, but she recognized the teamwork. In her dreamlike state, Frank Sinatra became Nikki Keller, and Dean Martin was Kim Patterson. Peri thought about the bonds of friendship, and the recent events.

What wouldn't she do to help Blanche?

"Benny, I'm going to do some work in the bedroom. You okay out here?"

He raised a hand to indicate he heard, but kept his eyes on the movie. "This TV is so good. It's like Dino is in the room with me – do you think Detective Skip would let me come and watch movies all the time?"

"You'll need to ask him. Hopefully, he'll be home soon."

Peri picked up her tote and headed to the master bedroom, where she sprawled out on the bed with her laptop and her notes.

CHAPTER 30

Skip felt a hand on his shoulder and turned to see Craig Daniels.

"So, James Bond, bet you didn't think we'd be investigating a murder in tuxedos, did you?"

"Just be careful, Pal. It's rented."

The detective laughed. "What've we got?"

Skip filled him in. "Offhand I'd say blunt force trauma, although I guess he could have been dead before someone smashed his head in. Coroner's on the way. Driver's license found in the pocket, says his name's Tyler Garvey, 26, resident golf pro."

"Tyler Garvey? Isn't he—"

"Yep, he's the guy Nikki Keller was fooling around with. Jason found a bloody golf club in the dumpster. He'll process it for prints, but it's a high-end, left-handed Callaway driver. Guess who owns a set of left-handed Callaways?"

"Nikki's husband." Daniels rubbed his chin in thought. "And I'm guessing Peri was here when this happened."

"It's like playing Six Degrees of my girlfriend," Skip said. "Chief wants to make certain there's no conflict of interest. You're doing the interviews. I'm allowed to watch."

He pointed at the clubhouse, and they both strode toward the door.

Chief Fletcher was still in the bar, taking names and addresses, and asking the perfunctory, "Where were you" questions. An older woman sat at the table, looking distressed. He looked up, smiled and thanked the woman, and then walked over to his detectives.

"So far, everyone was inside, dining and dancing," he told them. "What have you got?"

When Skip told him about the solid identification, and the golf club, he nodded. "That gives us a suspect with a motive. Let's move carefully with this guy. I'm guessing he's the kind who'll lawyer up at the drop of a hat. I'd rather he didn't invoke before we get a little more information." He picked up his notepad. "You guys take the bar. I'll set up in the office down the hall and we'll try to knock these interviews out."

Skip and Craig took seats at the table and nodded to the officers, who disappeared for a moment, and reappeared with a petite blonde.

"Good evening, ma'am, I'm Detective Craig Daniels. May I have your name?"

"Nikki Keller. Missus."

Craig motioned for her to sit down. "Mrs. Keller, we're just asking everyone to retrace their steps this evening. Sometimes people see things and don't realize they're important."

He opened his notepad and wrote a few lines. "So why don't we start at the beginning. What time did you arrive?"

"Around seven." Her expression was relaxed, although her foot tapped a staccato beat. "I was running a little late. Is this going to take long?"

"I hope not. Were you alone?"

"No, I came with my husband."

"What did you do when you got here?"

Nikki looked at the detective, twirling the diamond and ruby tennis bracelet on her wrist. "Everyone was in the dining room, so we found our table. We sat with Chief Fletcher and his wife, the Hanlons, and the Parkinsons."

Skip looked at the notes Chief Fletcher had left. The others at their table had been interviewed, so he skimmed their accounts to see if they matched with Nikki's.

Craig resumed his questioning. “Were you in the room for the entire dinner?”

“Yes – well, no, I did go to the ladies room once.”

“Do you remember who was there?”

Nikki ticked them off on her fingers. “My friends – Lisa Silvan, Kim Patterson, Susan. Mrs. Nickles was there.”

Skip caught Craig’s attention and nodded, so Craig pressed further. “Anyone else?”

“Oh, yes.” She smiled. “Mr. Carlton’s friend, Peri, was in the ladies room.”

“What did you do after dinner?”

“I chatted with some friends, danced.”

“Danced with who?”

“My husband, Clinton Silvan, Mayor Scott.”

“Then what?”

“I don’t know… I had another glass of wine. I went to the ladies room again.”

Skip remembered Peri’s comments about Nikki looking for someone. He leaned over and passed the information on to Craig. Craig eased back into his chair and wrote. The room was quiet, except for the constant hum of the bar’s refrigeration unit.

Craig spoke at last. “Where did you go when you came out of the ladies room?”

Nikki glanced at Skip, her eyes narrow and hard. “I went back to the dance and looked around for Don.”

“Where was he?”

“Well, I didn’t find him at first, but we caught up with each other when the rumor started around about the dead body.”

Craig nodded, his expression neutral. “Thank you, Mrs. Keller. We may have some followup questions. Can you verify your contact information with the officer at the door?”

She stood. Her short red dress didn’t quite stand with her, remaining stuck to her tanned, muscular thighs. “Of course, Detective. Are Don and I free to go?”

Skip noted that her hands didn't even flutter near her skirt to adjust it. He watched her smile in their direction, and turn toward the exit. She marched out of the door, perfectly balanced on four-inch heels.

He saw that Craig also paid attention to her as she left, her firm body, packaged sleekly in that minidress, tight around the hips with a loose, plunging back that displayed soft flesh with undulating muscle underneath. She had a small pink clover stamped onto her left ankle. He pried his focus loose and turned to Skip, smiling.

"Nice view, huh?"

Skip looked at him, surprised. "Eh, I was just thinking about how cool she acted."

"Yeah, she's got it all under control."

"No, I mean, everyone else here tonight has been either distressed or animated, upset at the murder or spreading gossip and rumor. She didn't even ask you about the body." He shook his head. "And if she knew it was Tyler, wouldn't she show some emotion?"

"You'd think so." Craig picked up his pen. "One more note to jot down."

Don Keller came in next. He had removed his tuxedo jacket and his tie, and loosened his shirt. Without hesitation, he walked into the room, offered his hand to both detectives, and sat down. "At last, detectives, I was wondering when I could go home."

Craig went through his list, asking him to backtrack his evening, while Skip tried to look for bloodstains on his clothes without staring. Nothing unusual was on his shirt, and the light in the bar was too dim to see any stains on his pants or shoes.

"So after dinner what did you do?"

Keller looked up at the ceiling. "Danced with Nikki, then Kim."

"Just two dances, one with each?"

He nodded.

"Where were you when you found out about the body outside?"

"I had just gotten back from the head. Walked toward the room and everyone was leaving. Clinton Silvan told me what had happened, so I went out and joined the gawkers."

While Craig was writing, Skip had an idea. "Mr. Keller, you play pretty regularly here, don't you? Do the members typically bring their clubs each time, or do you store them here?"

"Depends. We have lockers, but I don't quite trust them. My clubs are expensive and custom-made to my grip and balance. I'm not sticking them in a closet with a two-dollar lock on it. Why?"

"Just curious. We don't get many calls about theft here."

"The lockers may be safe, but it never hurts to practice caution." Keller laughed. "Of course, I'm taking a chance right now that my car doesn't get broken into. My clubs are still in the trunk."

"I think they're safe tonight," Craig told him. "I'm not sure what kind of idiot would cross the police tape to break into your car."

They all laughed and stood and thanked each other for their time and cooperation. Skip felt a little oily when he had to do this, but knew it was part of the job. *You don't show your hand until you've got all the aces.*

He was disappointed that Keller's clubs were in his car. They could've searched the lockers with the golf course's permission, but there wasn't enough probable cause to open a citizen's trunk. It was possible that the club didn't belong to Keller. Not very probable, but possible.

Interviewing the rest of the group took another hour and a half, even with the chief's help. Kim Patterson was the last on Craig's list. Skip was a little surprised she didn't fuss about being kept until the end, but she waltzed into the bar and took a seat, her pearl satin sheath accentuating her lithe, tanned arms and legs. Like

Nikki, she also sported a clover tattoo on her left ankle, except hers was blue. She looked fresh, as if she'd just arrived at the party.

Brushing her long, dark hair from her shoulders, she eased into the bar chair and folded her hands into her lap, her legs demurely crossed at the ankles.

"Mrs. Patterson, thanks for your patience." Craig tried to begin on a good note.

She answered with an enigmatic smile. "I'm not on a schedule."

"Could you tell me about your evening?"

As with the others, Kim told him about her arrival, her dinner, and her dancing. She described her activities in a slow, languid voice, as if teaching a class on yoga, or Lamaze.

"Where was Mr. Patterson while you were dancing?"

"At the table." She studied her pale blue gladiator sandals. "Then the bar."

"When did you join up with him again?"

"I still haven't. I assume he went with everybody else to see the body."

Craig looked up from his notes. "Didn't you go?"

"No. I went to the ladies room. It was a lot less crowded."

"Just as well you didn't," Skip said. "It was pretty gruesome. Upset Peri."

She smiled a little and stared at Skip. "I like to avoid unpleasantness."

"Thank you again, Mrs. Patterson," Craig said. "I think that's all for now."

Kim stood and smoothed her dress. "You're welcome, Detective Daniels." She nodded at Skip. "You, too, Detective Carlton. You know, it's a shame I can't adopt your girlfriend's cat. I have a houseful of Abyssinians."

"I'm sure she'll find a home for it."

"I wish her luck. Cats can be very hard on the furniture." She smiled again, as if something amused her. "And wood floors."

Skip watched her turn and leave, her smile remaining in his mind like the Cheshire Cat, while he considered her words. She strolled away, graceful and elegant.

Craig looked at him. “What was that about?”

“That was to let me know she was the one who left the dead bird on Peri’s doorstep,” Skip told him. “And to rub it in that we can’t prove it.”

Chief Fletcher appeared in the doorway. “We done here?”

“Yep.” Craig stood, stretched, and looked at his watch. “We’re finished.”

“And yet we’ve just begun,” Skip said.

As they walked outside, Jason Bonham approached them. “I’m almost done processing the scene. Found a worker’s uniform in the dumpster with blood on it.”

“Thanks,” Chief Fletcher told him, and then turned to his detectives and other officers. “You guys go on home, I’ll wrap things up. Let’s meet tomorrow at eight to compare notes and see where we need to go from here.”

Skip walked to his car, his mind leafing through the information they’d gathered while his internal cop radar did its job of surveillance along the route. He had just reached for the handle of his SUV when he felt the buzz of a phone call on his belt. It was probably Peri, begging to send Benny home.

An unknown number lit up the screen, so he answered it.

“Skip, I hate to bother you, but could you come over?” It was Ella Mason. “Jorge’s out of control. I don’t know what to do—I’m sorry—I’ve called everyone else.” Her teary voice dropped off.

His radar prickled for a moment. He was trying to help a little with her son, but certainly she had other friends, on and off the force, to call. Little Jorge was fifteen; this couldn’t have been the first time he got out of control. Peri would advise him not to go. She would remind him of appearances and getting too involved with a lower-ranking officer.

Still, all things considered, someone was asking for his help. And Peri wasn't exactly on his advisory council at the moment.

"I'll be right there, Ella."

CHAPTER 31

Nestled in the warmth of Skip's king-sized bed, Peri spread her notes carefully over the navy comforter and logged into her email. Craig Daniels had followed through with his promise, and sent her the information about the killing, the one using the same gun that killed her office landlord. She printed the report, then retrieved it from the wireless printer in Skip's office.

The data was pretty dry; William Quigley, 54, from San Diego, discovered off of the 5 Freeway north of town, near the Del Mar racetrack. Last known job was as assistant manager for the Crowne Plaza Hotel on San Diego's Hotel Circle. Shot once in the stomach. Peri grimaced. It must have taken him a long time to die.

Turning back to the computer, she Googled his name. There was a news item about the murder, a nice obituary link to the funeral home, and nothing else. She hunted around a little more for businesses or properties he owned, and found a few parcels still in his name between Orange County and San Diego.

"I wonder if he and Michael shared any interests," she asked herself. Googling Michael Steuben proved fruitless. Michael was just the manager of her building, not the owner. She couldn't find any property owned by her late landlord.

She stretched up and curled her frame around her papers, her head propped and right hand on the mousepad, tapping. "I won't even be able to guess until I know more about Quigley. I may have to take a road trip."

I wonder how Benny likes freeways, she thought as her head lowered and her eyes closed.

An hour later, Peri awoke to a stiff neck and numb arm from lying in such a contorted position. She rubbed her eyes and sat up, straining to see the clock on the night stand. It was after two. She stretched her legs onto the floor and tiptoed down the hall. Benny was in the family room, sacked out on the couch. He had managed to find a station on Skip's satellite TV that played Rat Pack tunes and was snoring to the strains of Frank Sinatra. Peri couldn't help but think of her grandmother's Pekingese as she listened to his soft wheezing.

Skip's car wasn't in the garage. He said he'd be late, but they'd talk when he got there. Peri decided to call and see how much longer he'd be at the scene. She went back to the bedroom and looked for her cell phone within the folds of the plush comforter. While she hunted for the phone, she cleared the papers and laptop off the bed. At last she found it and pressed Skip's number.

It rang twice before Peri heard the sounds of music being played.

"Hello?" It was a woman's voice.

Peri knew that Skip went undercover sometimes, but she couldn't imagine him in drag. She knew enough, however, to proceed cautiously.

"Hi, I think I have the wrong number." Her voice was a little higher than usual, although she didn't know why. "Um, is Skip there?"

"He can't come to the phone now. He's changing."

Into what? A werewolf? "Oh, well, I'll call back later. Thanks." Peri sat and stared at her cell phone. *What the hell just happened? And why did I thank her?*

A number of scenarios went through her mind, none of them enjoyable. Skip could be at the office, changing out of his tux, although Peri didn't usually hear music at the precinct. He could still be at the country club, changing into a hazmat suit for some reason. Or perhaps he's in some kind of trouble.

Perhaps gangsters have him and one of their molls answered the phone.

After flitting around these ideas, her brain lit at last on the one she dreaded: he's with another woman.

I'd rather he was with the gangsters, she thought, then felt a pinch of guilt.

Peri padded into the kitchen and lifted a small snifter out of the cabinet. She then picked up a half-full bottle of Mount Palomar sherry and shuffled back to her room while Benny still slept. A couple of sips of the smooth, nutty warmth stopped her muscles from twitching to take action. After all, what was she going to do, hunt him down?

Instead, she turned on the TV. The classic movie channel was showing *All About Eve*. Bette Davis was just announcing that it was going to be a bumpy night.

"You said it, sistah." Peri lifted her glass.

The next hour sauntered by with such long spaces between the ticks, she put a pillow over the clock to keep from counting. Characters came and went on the screen, all delivering important and interesting lines, but she couldn't hear them. All she heard were the tires of the occasional car passing down the street. With each car, she listened for the tires to turn into the driveway, for the garage door to open, for Skip to walk into the room.

Several times, Peri picked up her cell and selected Blanche's number, before pressing End and putting the phone down. Blanche's calm, no-nonsense voice might have put everything into perspective, but at three in the morning, her best friend might not be so calm, or have any perspective beyond her own need for sleep. She spent the next three hours squeezing her eyes shut in a parody of sleep, checking the clock, listening for the garage door opener and ignoring that burning anvil in the pit of her stomach.

At six o'clock, she couldn't stand it anymore, and got up. Padding softly into the kitchen, she saw Benny asleep on the leather couch. The Rat Pack was still on the satellite radio station, singing Las Vegas lullabies, just for him.

She poured a glass of milk, hoping it would soothe her stomach, and retreated to the bedroom. The TV was still on, showing “The Letter”. They were already at the party scene. In a very short time, Bette Davis would be dead, stabbed by the widow of the lover she had slain.

I wonder if I could use it as an excuse for why I stuffed Ella Mason into a chipper, she thought. *Wait, no. I don’t mean it. Probably.*

The milk helped, somewhat, as well as three pain relievers and a hormone pill. She watched Bette crumple to the ground, then got up and showered. As the hot water sprayed across her shoulders, the full weight of the night hit her.

Skip didn’t come home.

This was it, then, the rift that couldn’t be mended. Peri cried a few tears in the streaming water, before pulling herself together. First, she thought, she’d get her life back. Then she’d grieve losing a big part of it.

By seven, she was dressed and fidgeting. Blanche had to be up by now. Peri picked up her cell phone and dialed. When her friend answered, she froze.

“Peri? Hello? Peri?” Blanche’s voice was even huskier in the mornings. “Did you butt dial me again?”

“Beebs.”

Best friends know in an instant when the world has fallen apart. “What’s wrong?”

“Skip didn’t come home last night.”

“Oh, Girlfriend, he’s worked an all-nighter before. Did you try calling him?”

Peri found her voice choking in tears. “At two. A woman answered.”

“Oh, Peri.”

“I think I’ve done it, Beebs. I’ve pushed him away for good.”

"I just can't believe he'll never forgive you. I mean, I know it's emails and oh-so-sacred, but come on. And I sure can't believe he'd go have a one-nighter after one fight, I don't care how big it is."

"He'll forgive me." Peri's tears were subsiding. "But I think he's decided we can't be together as long as I'm a private eye. My new career is the breaking point for us."

"What are you going to do?"

She sighed. "I don't know. I'm going to finish this case, then figure out what to do with the rest of my life."

"In the meantime, what can I do to help?"

"Just hang by the phone, Beebs. I'm going to San Diego today to get some information."

"By yourself?"

"No, Benny's taking me. He just doesn't know it yet."

"Well, be careful," Blanche told her. "Love you."

"Love you, too, Beebs."

Ending the call, Peri wandered back into the family room. Benny was up, still in his tuxedo, fiddling with Skip's stereo system. Dean Martin was singing, his voice getting louder and softer, deeper and brassier, as Benny turned the knobs.

"Good morning, Ben. Do you have any plans for today?"

"Just feeding the cat. And going home. I'd like to go home."

She took out some bread to make toast. "Well, why don't you go home and change, stop by my place, then swing back around here. We need to go on a road trip."

Benny looked troubled. "A road trip? How long of a road trip?"

"Only down to San Diego. I'll pay for the gas."

"But Miss Peri, I don't go on the freeway."

"Since when?"

"I don't like it. It's too stressful."

"But you go to Vegas every year for Dean Martin's birthday. Don't you drive?"

"Yes, but that's different," he told her. "That's for Dino."

Peri rubbed her sherry-soaked temples. "Well, then, I'll drive and you can ride shotgun."

"Your car is so small." His voice began to take on a petulant quality that made Peri want to make him sit in the corner until he could act like an adult.

She pointed toward the front door, her voice clipped and stern. "You are going to go home, run past my house and feed the cat, then return here. Somehow, we are getting to San Diego, Benny. Don't make me pull the whole Parole Violation threat out again."

The effect this had on Benny went unnoticed by her, as she turned and strode down the hall to the bedroom. Peri finished putting on her makeup and pulled her hair into a ponytail. There was nothing to do but wait and see if he'd return.

Return he did, an hour later, smiling and perky.

"Miss Peri, thank you for the road trip. I completely forgot about that song, 'Thirty More Miles to San Diego.' I think maybe Dino played golf down there. When are we leaving?"

"Right now, if you'd like, Benny. Am I driving, or you?"

"Oh, I'll drive. Your car is too small."

Peri grabbed her tote, stuck her notes and her cell phone inside and slipped into the black Cadillac. She couldn't help but notice, as Benny pulled out of the driveway and down the street, the Caddy didn't seem to roll down the road as much as it floated. She wondered if he was truly steering it, or merely herding it along the pavement.

Once they got onto the 57 Freeway, heading south, she began to understand why Benny didn't like to take the freeways. Driving 55 miles per hour, he hugged the right shoulder to the point Peri thought they might go off-roading down the embankment. Cars whipped by them like bullets, most of them with scowling drivers, who were giving the Caddy dirty looks and middle fingers.

"Don't suppose this car goes any faster," she said. "Or any closer to the center of the lane."

"No – talking – Miss – Peri." His words were pronounced with great effort. "I. Have. To. Concentrate."

Two slow hours on the road to San Diego without conversation sounded like the most boring thing she'd done since she was stuck in a doctor's office for a half hour with last year's magazines.

"Wake me when we reach the I-8," she told him.

Peri reached into her tote and produced an iPod; she turned it to Shuffle, plugged in her ears and fell asleep. It proved to be the best use of her time; she felt very refreshed when Benny woke her two hours later.

"Take the I-8 east, then move immediately to the far right lane," she said. "It's an insanely quick offramp."

"I can't do this." Benny's voice raised an octave. "It's too hard, too hard."

She tried to reassure him. "It's okay, Ben, you're good, you're good. Just signal and move to the right. You're clear."

Benny screamed like a girl and floated the Caddy right. The traffic around him slowed to allow him to exit, probably happy to get him off the freeway.

"See, you're fine," Peri said. "Now go up here and turn left."

She continued to direct him around the Hotel Circle until at last they pulled into the Crowne Plaza Resort, one of the dozens of hotels that encircled the freeway, making visits to SeaWorld, the San Diego Zoo, and other tourist attractions easy. The Crowne Plaza had begun life as another hotel chain, one with tropical roots. The landscaping of palm trees, ferns, and birds of paradise retained an island feel, even if the hotel itself was a series of tall, blockish buildings, all very beige and stucco.

Benny looked worried. "I don't have to go in there, do I?"

"No, just pull into one of these front spaces. You can wait in the car while I talk to the manager."

Benny spent a few moments finding the right space, then pulling in and backing out until it was perfectly aligned within the white lines. Peri waited as patiently as she could, reminding herself the whole time that this was the price of napping instead of driving.

At last, she was able to hop out and walk to the lobby. The entrance was large, paved with flagstone in light neutrals. The lobby sat just beyond the length of glass wall at the bottom of three wide, shallow steps. With the tropical plants on either side, the effect was like stepping into a pool. Peri smiled and nodded to the man standing at the valet counter, and then entered the hotel.

The lobby was also in cool tones of beige and tan. A large counter ran along the entire left wall. As Peri entered, she was aware of the scent of potpourri coming from the gift shop to the right. A woman in a burgundy jacket and white blouse stood behind the counter, doing paperwork. Peri approached her and introduced herself.

"I'm doing some background work in the William Quigley murder case. Is there anyone here I could speak to about his last day, or even week, of work here?"

The young woman's eyes widened. "Oh, that was so sad. I had just started working here when it happened, but let me get the manager. She worked with Bill all the time."

She disappeared for a few minutes, then returned with a slightly older woman, slender with blue-black hair tied back at the nape, her dark eyes made larger by the glasses she wore.

"My name is Lorraine. How can I help you?"

Peri introduced herself again, and explained her visit. "I'm certain the police went over everything with you, and I know several months have passed, but I wanted to touch base with his home and business, make certain nothing was overlooked."

"I miss Bill so much," Lorraine said. "I knew him for about seven years. He was a lovely coworker, pleasant to be around, a real joy."

"Was this his fulltime job?"

"As far as employment, I think so. He was here every day, nine to five, so I can't imagine him having a second job. The only other thing he did was buy investment property."

"Investment property? Developed or undeveloped?"

"Mostly undeveloped. He liked to buy little parcels, then sell to developers. His first couple of parcels, we all chipped in to buy, then when he sold them, we all got a tidy sum. After he got enough money, he was able to invest by himself."

"If he was doing so well, why didn't he quit his job?"

Lorraine smiled. "I used to ask him that. He'd just smile and tell me how much he'd miss this place."

"And you believed that?"

"No. But I figured it was his way of saying it was none of my business."

"Did Bill have any visitors the last week?"

"No, but he had an appointment. I gave his calendar to the police, but he had an entry on Thursday to meet a Mrs. Keaton for lunch. Friday he didn't come to work. He was – discovered, the following Friday."

Peri looked up from her notebook. "You're sure it said Mrs. Keaton?"

Lorraine looked at the counter, shaking her head. "I can't forget it. For weeks, the police circled around that name, convinced if they could find Mrs. Keaton, they could solve the case."

"And?"

"They never found her. We'll never know who killed Bill, or why."

Peri's soft heart melted, and she frowned. "Don't give up hope, Lorraine. There may be new evidence, or a new way of looking at old evidence. As long as one person still cares, we can still push forward."

She thanked the manager for her time and returned to the Caddy.

"Let's go to Riverside, Ben. I need to see the County Clerk."

He looked at her. "Riverside? You didn't tell me we were going to Riverside."

"I know, I didn't know we were going. But I have a hunch."

She directed him back to the freeway and they made their way north on the I-5. Once again, she told him to wake her at a particular point before hooking up her iPod and falling asleep.

"Miss Peri, we're almost to the 55." Two hours later, Benny's wake up voice sounded stressed. "What do I do?"

"You take the 55 north to the 91 east," she told him, her voice slow and crackling with sleep. She dozed a little more, until they had managed to get to the Riverside Freeway.

After a few miles on the 91, Peri was able to direct him to Lemon Street, and a large, official-looking building. The mid-afternoon sun was searing, even in October. Peri left Benny in the car while she walked up the stone steps to the large brass and glass doors.

Once inside, she verified the Clerk's office number on the directory, then walked down the shiny tiled floor toward the address. She found a small door that led to a large room, separated by a counter. A large black woman with an open, friendly face awaited her.

"How can I help you today?"

"I need to look at some real estate records," Peri told her. "I'm looking for a history of ownership for a particular piece of land."

"Certainly. Do you have the address?"

"No, but I have the parcel number."

The woman smiled. "That's even better."

Peri handed her a slip of paper with numbers written down. The clerk took them and came back with a large book, heavy enough to thump when she placed it on the counter.

"You can't take this book away," she told Peri. "You must keep it on this counter."

"No problem. Thank you."

Peri opened the tome and leafed through the pages, looking for her parcel number. She found it about a third of the way through the book. After whipping her notebook from her bag, she wrote names and information from the parcel's previous owners.

"Thank you very much," she said, before closing the book and striding out of the office.

Benny was engrossed in his new Dino anthology when she got back to the car.

"Okay, now it's time for the Placentia Police Department," she told him.

"Miss Peri, I'm exhausted."

"I know you are, Ben. This is my last stop, I swear. Maybe I can get someone to take me home, okay?"

"Okay." His voice sounded sullen.

The thirty minute ride took fifty minutes, due to Benny's driving, but they finally arrived at the police station.

"Just wait here," Peri told him. "I'll find out if you can go home, and I'll come out and tell you."

Craig was in his office, but Skip was not.

"Hey, Craig," Peri said, trying to sound casual. "Is Skip here?"

"No, he's out investigating the dead guy's life."

She relaxed a little. "Oh. Listen, Benny's been driving me around all day and I think we've both had enough of each other. Is there anyone who could take me back to Skip's after I fill you in?"

The detective smiled. "Why, I'd be happy to."

Peri ran out to the car and told Benny to go home, then returned to Craig's office.

"Okay, here's what I've learned." She told him about her conversation with the hotel manager, and then gave him the information about a parcel of land in Riverside County.

"This is the parcel that Bob and Dottie Peters owned. There are four previous owners of record – a lady name Victoria Hagen, then Oscar Mendoza, Philip Hughes, and William Quigley."

"Did you find any connection between Quigley and Michael Steuben?"

"No. But at least two owners of that parcel of land have been murdered."

"Maybe more than two. Skip's been investigating the rest. Seems Keller and Patterson have been trying to buy that land for years, but keep missing out on the deal. Each new owner buys it from the estate of the previous one."

"Wow. How did the others die?"

"He's still investigating that." Craig smiled. "Doesn't your boyfriend keep you up to date?"

Peri smiled back, a little too quickly, to mask her pain. "We've been on different topics lately."

"Let me add to the puzzle," Craig said. "The fingerprints on the coin purse from the park, and the fingerprint found in the upstairs office in your building are a match, although we don't have them on file. But, the license plate number you gave me from the park belongs to Lisa Silvan."

She gasped. "Lisa Silvan. I knew her face looked familiar at the country club. That little pointy chin and high cheekbones. It was her in the park, wearing a black wig. But shooting at me? I would have guessed Kim."

"Why her?"

Peri told him about the conversation Blanche overheard in the restroom and what she had gleaned from her recording. "My theory is, Nikki's friends are all very protective of her. Who knows? Maybe they'd kill to keep each other safe from scandal or poverty."

Craig leaned back, looking thoughtful. "I guess Lisa could have done the shooting, then Kim broke in and stole the photo with the memory card."

"Maybe."

Craig nodded. "Wish their prints were in the system. None of her little clique is in any database."

"Damn. They're so young, you'd have thought they'd be in that children's file."

"Well, they might be there, but their prints would have aged."

"The patterns would be the same, though, right?"

"Yes, we'd just have to request their specific prints and have Jason 'grow them up'. It would take time."

Peri sat down and looked at the board. "Okay, why would Lisa Silvan, or any of these women, kill a bunch of people and follow me around?"

"Damned if I know." Craig eased back into his chair, his hands on top of his head. "We know that Patterson and Keller wanted that parcel of land, and Clinton Silvan works at their firm."

"But what do I have to do with a parcel of land?"

"Nothing."

"Damn." She stretched up in the chair. "All my troubles began when I started following Nikki Keller. She and her buddies were onto me from day one. The flat tire, the dead bird, everything was supposed to back me off, and for what? Because she had a boy-toy?"

"Maybe there's another reason," Craig said.

She nodded. "That's what I'm thinking. There's something else out there they don't want me to know about."

Craig looked at his watch. "I'm almost off duty. You ready to go for that drink?"

"What drink?"

"Well, I just figured, if I was going to take you home, maybe we could stop off somewhere and have a beer."

Peri fussed with her tote. In her current state, she was just vulnerable enough to have a drink with him. He was a shameless flirt, and a boost to a girl's ego. But she had a list of things to do. One, get her life back. Two, work things out with Skip.

"Yeah, probably not, Craig. I've got a pretty full plate right now."

CHAPTER 32

Skip headed down Alta Vista Street toward the Archstone Apartments. Although Tyler had a roommate, the manager was expecting him, in case no one was home. Large blocks of beige stucco greeted him on Jefferson Street, square arches jutting out at angles, supposedly to earn the name of "Archstone." He found a parking spot and went to the office.

A Pakistani man greeted him, slight of build, with terra cotta skin and a warm smile.

"Good afternoon, Detective. I will show you to the apartment. Has Mr. Garvey done something wrong? He has always been a good tenant, very good tenant. Pays the rent on time, always, no noise or parties. Considerate young man." He kept talking as they kept walking, without much encouragement from Skip.

"He has lived here for nearly two years – I checked his lease agreement. I hope he is not in trouble. His roommate is another young man, a student, Mr. Lawrence. He is also very nice. I asked them once, why young men are not giving me more headaches, and Mr. Lawrence says, 'I am too busy getting my doctorate. I have headaches of my own.'" The manager laughed at this, and then stopped at a door. "Ah, here we are."

Skip knocked, but there was no answer.

"Allow me, allow me," said the manager, and pulled out a key.

The living area of the apartment was an open space that could be completely viewed from the door. It was barren, except for a few necessary pieces of furniture. There was a couch, a chair, and a dining room table. No pictures hung on the walls, no extraneous tables, lamps, or tchotchkes littered the space. The taupe carpet looked like it had been vacuumed recently.

Skip walked over to the kitchen alcove and opened a few cabinets, the dishwasher and the refrigerator. There was nothing very interesting in any of them.

He walked back into the two bedrooms. The largest room was obviously the roommate's. Textbooks were stacked around a computer, and pictures of what appeared to be family members were tacked to a cork board. From the pictures, Skip surmised the roommate was African American.

He stepped into the other bedroom. A bit smaller, it had a queen-sized bed, a nightstand, and a desk, but it was the décor that made it more fascinating. Pictures of Nikki Keller were everywhere. There was a framed photo by the bed. Candid shots were on the wall above the desk. Everywhere Tyler looked in this room, he'd see Nikki, except possibly the ceiling. Skip looked up, just in case, but that area was untouched.

Just short of creepy, he thought.

He opened the nightstand and rifled through the papers. He also looked through the closet. Most of the clothes were polo shirts and khaki slacks, a golfer's wardrobe. He left the bedroom and closed the door. Hearing voices in the living area, he walked in to find the manager talking with a young black man.

"Are you Mr. Lawrence?"

"Yes, I'm Gary Lawrence. Have you found Tyler? He was supposed to go out for a jog with me this morning, but he didn't come home last night."

Skip took a breath and delivered the bad news. "I'm sorry to have to tell you both this, but Tyler Garvey was murdered last night."

The two men gasped. Gary sat down, his hands cradling his forehead. "How did this happen?"

"We're still investigating," Skip said. "I was hoping to gain a little insight into his life by coming here today."

"Like I said, very nice young man. No troubles, ever," the manager told him.

"Tyler was a great guy." Gary's low voice had softened. "We did a few things together, though I was usually busy with my schooling."

"Any other friends?"

"I guess so." Gary shrugged. "Every once in awhile he'd go have drinks with some of his high school buds. He went to Villa Park, and some of the guys still live around here."

"How about girls?"

Gary nodded toward his room. "You saw the pictures." He shook his head. "That was Tyler's one weak spot. I kept telling him she was not only married, but married to a rich guy, but he loved that woman. Loved her bad."

"Did he ever bring her here?"

"Once or twice, but you could tell this was not her thing. Even if she loved him, the thought of giving up her million-dollar home for this teeny place must've been a real turnoff." He turned to the manager. "No offense, Mr. Patel."

"None taken. It is understandable."

Skip looked up from his notes. "Do you think Tyler would have ever tried to pressure her to leave her husband?"

Gary laughed. "According to him, it's all they ever fought about." His face grew somber again. "I can't believe he's gone, man. This is just so… so wrong. Do his parents know?"

"We called them. They're on their way back from Hawaii now."

"Detective, would it be wrong if I removed all those pictures in his room? I hate to think of them coming back and finding out what a fool their son was."

"Believe me, I understand how you feel," Skip told him. "But I'd like our crime scene analyst to come over first and process the room. He'll collect the pictures as part of the evidence chain. His parents won't be able to see the room until that's done."

Skip called Jason, gave him the details, and then turned back to the two men. "Okay, well, thank you both. I'm going to wait here for our CSU to arrive. If you have things to do, please go ahead."

Skip sat down on the couch and made notes while he waited for Jason. The manager left, but Gary went out to their mini-patio and sat in a lounge chair. Skip thought he saw him wiping his eyes now and then. Thirty minutes later, there was a knock at the door.

"Hey, Detective." Jason walked in. "Right after you called, I got a hit on the prints on the golf club. Don Keller. They sent a car to bring him in. Still want me to process this place?"

"Um, yeah, process the small bedroom, just in case. Don Keller, huh?" Skip stuck his head out of the sliding glass door. "Gary, our CSU is here. I'm going to need you to leave for awhile so he can process everything. Before you go, it would be a good idea to get your prints, so we know which ones to ignore. Jason will lock up when he leaves."

Gary nodded and headed back into the apartment. He sat down at the table and Jason got out his fingerprint kit.

"Call me when you have any results," Skip told him.

Returning to his car, Skip got in and sat, looking at his notes and thinking. He wasn't surprised to find out the golf club belonged to Keller. It was possible Keller knew about Nikki and Tyler, confronted him, killed him in a fit of rage. It made sense.

He thought about Keller's demeanor when he was being questioned in the bar. If it was a rage killing, Don Keller didn't show any sign of being a murderer as he answered Daniels' questions. Usually, Skip could count on a killer's behavior as anything from anxious about being caught, to shell shock that they've actually killed someone. Keller was slightly annoyed at being kept so long, but otherwise relaxed.

Skip had seen Keller try to keep a straight face, and fail, during their round of golf. He couldn't imagine the man being questioned about murder and not breaking.

Don Keller as the murderer made sense in theory, except that it didn't make enough sense in practice.

Tyler wanted Nikki. Nikki used him for fun. First, her husband was mad and wanted the scoop on them. Then, he forgave her and didn't want to know about Tyler. Who had the best motive for wanting Tyler to disappear?

He started the engine and turned the car back toward Alta Vista.

CHAPTER 33

Skip pulled up in front of the Keller home, ready to ask Nikki Keller a few questions. He approached the large, ornate doors of leaded glass, holding a portfolio, which contained, among other things, the photos Peri had taken of Nikki and Tyler.

The first time he rang the bell, a yappy bark whispered from the recesses of the house, growing louder until he could see beige fluff running at the door. The beveled glass distorted the image, but there was a small dog leaping and barking as he rang a second time.

At last a shadow descended the steps, followed by a petite shape. Nikki Keller strolled to the door, reached down to pick up the beige fluff, and then greeted Skip.

"Detective, how nice to see you." Her voice had no life in it. The little dog in her arms growled and wriggled while she attempted to wipe the tears from her cheeks.

"Mrs. Keller, I need to talk to you about last night's murder."

"Certainly. Let's go out to the backyard." She escorted Skip into the house and led him to their private oasis, stopping to put the dog in its crate and lock the door.

They went out to the patio, a custom-designed retreat with a full kitchen, bar, and living room. Skip noted that the outdoor furniture looked more expensive than the stuff in his house.

Nikki curled up in one of the chairs, her legs tucked into her aqua sundress. "Please sit down," she said, gesturing.

"Mrs. Keller, I assume you know we've identified the body."

Nikki's hand flinched as it came up toward her mouth, then lowered. "They think Don—" She collapsed in a fetal position, weeping.

"I know. But I'm not certain Don did this. Maybe you could help me."

She looked up.

"Now then, tell me what you can about Tyler Garvey."

"He was a nice boy. He was just a nice, simple boy." She rose and went to the cabinet to pull out a box of tissues. "I had no idea it was him out there on the lawn. And Don would never, never do anything like—oh, god, this is awful."

"Was Tyler into any dangerous activities, like drugs or gambling?"

"Not that I knew. Truly, I didn't know him well. He was a summer playmate, that's all."

"Did you know any of his friends?"

She shook her head. "No. I met his roommate once, but that's it. And I didn't know of any enemies. He was the golf pro, the pretty boy for the women to flirt with."

"Except you. You flirted more than anyone."

"He was just a summer fling. And now he's dead and my husband is accused. None of this was supposed to happen."

"I'm sure it wasn't, although I'm not sure how you thought you'd keep your relationship secret. You didn't hide it very well."

Nikki looked up at him, her red-rimmed eyes wide. "How do you know this?"

"Because I've seen the evidence gathered by the P.I. your husband hired." He patted the folder in his hand.

"I don't understand. Why would you have seen it?"

"Because the P.I. came to us when you and your friends started harassing her. As soon as we have the evidence together, arrests will be made."

She lowered her head. “This has gotten so out of control. We just wanted to scare her. We didn’t want her dead. We didn’t want anyone dead.”

“Who is ‘we’?”

“I can’t tell you.”

“Yes, you can, unless you want to take the fall for everyone.”

“Then I’ll take the fall. It’s my fault, anyway.” She collapsed back into her chair, weeping.

Skip sat down on the ottoman, facing her. He placed his hand on her arm. It was time to play the Empathetic Cop. “Nikki, you can’t take this all on yourself. The others may have been protecting you, but it was their choice to murder.”

“She said as much force as necessary. She always said as much force as necessary. It just never took much force before.” She looked up, her eyes swollen. “Why wouldn’t that stupid woman scare?”

“Who was trying to scare Peri?”

Nikki shook her head.

“Mrs. Keller, we can do this here or we can do it at the station, but I’m going to find out. Who was trying to scare Peri?”

She was crying. “We didn’t want to hurt her.”

“How is whacking her in the head supposed to be not hurting her?” Skip fought to keep his anger from rising.

“I didn’t hit her that hard.”

“Nikki, tell me who else is in this. You aren’t betraying them. The police will find them, hunt them down, embarrass them in front of their families. Do you want that?”

“No.”

Skip stood up. “We’re gathering more evidence every day. We already know about Lisa Silvan’s involvement. If you give us a statement, tell us what happened, we can bring them in quietly, without any fanfare or publicity.”

With a heavy sigh and a tremendous shudder, she began.

“Kim and I have known each other since grade school. We’ve always been best friends, closer than blood. I was kind of pudgy, glasses, you know, real ugly duckling. Kim always stood up for me, kept the bullies at bay. When we hit high school, we made friends with Lisa and Susan. They just kind of—clicked with us. The rest of them were already pretty, but I had lost the baby fat and gotten contacts. By our senior year, we ruled the school.” She smiled at the memory.

“Then Eddie Peralta asked me to winter formal. Kim didn’t care for him. She said he was too cocky, disrespectful. I thought he was cute. I mean, it was just a dance, right?

“Except, not only did he sneak a bottle of vodka into the gym that night, he managed to drink almost all of it. I didn’t realize it until he followed me into the restroom.” She began to cry again. “He was sloppy drunk, and horny. I pushed him away, I hit him, I kicked…” Her hands and legs twitched as she described it.

“He was too drunk to get it up, but not too drunk to tear my dress and grope me in a million ways. It was horrible. When I finally got away from him and out of the bathroom, I found Kim and told her what happened. She got Lisa and Susan, and they helped me get home. I was a mess, but Kim was cool. ‘Eddie needs a lesson in manners,’ she said.”

Nikki stopped and wiped her face with the tissue.

“What happened to Eddie?” Skip had taken out his notebook and was writing.

“I passed a note to him on Monday morning. I told him he was so much fun, my girlfriends were jealous. He was too drunk to remember any of it. I told him we all wanted to have a ‘date’ with him. How could he resist?

“Kim’s grandma had a piece of property out in Palm Desert. It had a trailer on it, so it seemed like a great place to party. He met us there. Once we got to the trailer, he brought out a bottle. Kim got out glasses and poured—only she added some of her grandma’s sleeping pills to his glass. He practically chugged his down. We just pretended to be drinking. Lisa and Susan started to undress him, kiss him, get him all excited. I was supposed to help, but the thought of touching him nauseated me. Kim understood. She snuck up behind him with a rope, dropped it around his neck and –" She pantomimed a strangling motion.

"It was harder than I thought. Even drunk and drugged, he tried to fight back. Susan and Lisa held his arms down. I ended up having to take one end of the rope to apply enough pressure – he was a football player, so his neck was kind of thick."

Nikki looked down at her hands. "I was so angry, but after he was dead, I felt awful. I ran outside and threw up. Susan and Lisa came out after me. We were all crying, afraid, didn't know what to do, but then Kim joined us. She was so calm. She told us we just had to hide the body and keep our mouths shut." Nikki raised her head and stared at Skip. "That's when Kim told us. Eddie had raped her. We didn't feel as bad about killing him after that. I know it sounds bad, but we were teenagers."

Skip nodded. "What did you do with the body?"

"Oh, Kim said she'd take care of it. His truck, too." She sighed again, as if signaling the end, then buried her face in her husband's shoulder. "Oh, God, what have I done?"

Skip looked up from his notes. "Does your husband know any of this?"

"Not all of it. Only that I had a secret that would never be revealed. She'd do anything to protect me, protect our group, even if it meant throwing our husbands under the bus."

"Your husband suddenly dropped the investigation. Do you think Kim threatened him?"

Nikki reached into the pocket of her sundress and withdrew a piece of paper. "I found this before you came. I was looking for our attorney's number."

Skip took it and read it. The block lettering, although done by hand, showed no obvious stylistic quirks.

FIRE THE P.I. OR ELSE. WE WILL PROTECT NIKKI AT ALL COSTS, WITH AS MUCH FORCE AS NECESSARY.

Skip turned to Nikki. “Who does that sound like?”

“Kim.” She began to weep harder. “I’m so sorry, I’m so sorry.”

Skip stepped away and placed a phone call, then returned to the petite blonde. “Mrs. Keller, uniformed officers will be escorting you downtown to take your statement.”

He remained at their house until the patrol car arrived. Nikki was taken away and Skip walked to his car. The next step would be to issue arrest warrants for Susan, Lisa and Kim, something he dreaded, only because the rich get so indignant when they’re handcuffed.

He drove back to the station and went into his office. He could fill out warrants for the other three women, but there were a lot of little problems gnawing at his brain.

The first was, he had no evidence against any of these women. Only Nikki’s confession implicated any of them, and only for a fifteen-year old murder and threatening a private investigator. There was nothing to link them to the other murders. If he hauled them in and the meager forensics they had didn’t match any of the women, he was screwed.

He picked his folder on Bob and Dottie’s murders, and started skimming through the material.

Craig Daniels strolled into his office. “Anything interesting?”

“Not really, but it’s a good time killer while I figure out what to do.” He told Craig of his interview with Nikki.

“Wow. I’ll see your interview and raise you an interesting fact.” Craig told him of the bullet match between Michael Steuben and the previous owner of the property.

“Keller and Patterson were trying to purchase that parcel from the Peters, although John Patterson told me they weren’t pushing very hard.”

“Did you believe him?”

"Not after I got this from his secretary." He held up the notes about the previous bids.

Craig read the report. "Why do you think they want it so badly?"

Skip shrugged. "Beats me. Think I'll Google Earth it and see what it looks like."

"Can you really find it by parcel number?"

"I don't know, but I can at least look at the area."

The specific parcel couldn't be located, but the satellite image showed barren landscape in the general area. Mottled beige dots looked like bugs on vellum. There were no structures, nor even roads.

Skip studied the map. "Is this an updated satellite image?"

"I don't know."

"Patterson indicated that an outdoor mall was being built, but I don't see any construction." He logged off his computer. "We may need to take a little trip tomorrow."

"Can we pack our clubs and get in a few rounds?"

Skip chuckled. "Sounds good to me."

"I'm already beat." Craig yawned. "How about you? Done for the day?"

"Almost."

"Well, don't work too hard. That girlfriend of yours is home, waiting for you."

CHAPTER 34

Once Peri had reassured Detective Daniels five times that she really did not want to go out for a drink, he dropped her off at Skip's house.

"I'll send a patrol car to wander by several times until Skip gets home," he told her.

Peri fixed herself a glass of iced tea and retreated to the bedroom to do more research. Gathering her laptop, she climbed onto the bed and turned the classic movie channel on, as background noise. She began with the names of the property owners. Victoria Hagen had a lovely memorial on her son's website. She had passed away quickly, due to an aggressive brain tumor. The whole family missed her.

Oscar Mendoza was missed, too. Literally. The news item on him said he had gone missing four years ago. He was a landscaper, and one of his workers had been convicted of his murder, despite the fact they couldn't locate his body. There was, it seemed, enough evidence to convince a jury. Oscar left a brother, who had sold the property to Philip Hughes.

Hughes was an electrical engineer from Fullerton. Peri dug around the archives in the Orange County Register and found that he had committed suicide. The news item on him said he had left a letter announcing his intention. Interestingly, his body also was never found. His parents sold the parcel to William Quigley.

Unlike the others, Bill was dead and dumped, where someone could find him. Was this on purpose? Or did something keep the killer from hiding the body?

And then there were the Peters. Poisoned coffee, probably given to them as a gift, with no actual timeline for their deaths. Sooner or later, they'd make a pot and drink it. Sooner or later, they'd die. Did the killer think both of them would die together? Even at their ages, that would send up a red flag to police.

And all of them, coincidentally, owners of a small parcel of land in the desert. Either this was the most cursed property in southern California, or the most valuable to someone, who wouldn't stop killing until they possessed it.

Craig said Keller and Patterson wanted that land, but Peri couldn't believe they'd murder to get it. Development companies usually just offer you more money. If they want the land badly enough they'll even offer you more than it's worth. She leaned back into the pillows. Skip probably had details about that parcel in his notebook. He might know how much the firm offered each time it came up for sale.

She wanted to ask him, but that door was closed.

Thinking about what other dead ends she could review, she looked back at Nikki's Facebook page. She had changed her profile picture to include her husband. Her status said "Chillin' with my hunny." Peri reviewed all of her status messages for the week. One entry piqued her interest. "Getting too hot for the Bettys. May have to cool down," was written yesterday.

Whatever or whoever the Bettys were, it sounded like they were laying low.

Peri looked out the window and saw the late afternoon settling in. Skip's backyard grass deepened its green in the shadows. She rubbed her temples, wanting to keep working on the mystery, but exhausted from all the little strings that refused to tie into nice knots.

Her tote began playing "Popular", so she reached in for her cell phone and answered it.

"Where you been, Girl?" Blanche's husky voice sounded lighter than usual.

"Ugh, everywhere, Beebs. I'm so glad you called."

"You aren't going to ask me to get you information you're not supposed to have, are you?"

Peri laughed. "Not this time."

"Good. And don't be asking me to break in anywhere with you."

"Geez, Thelma, you're no fun. What's up?'

"Well, I finished my work on last night's body, so I wanted to know how San Diego went."

Peri filled her in on what she had discovered. "I'm so frustrated. I feel like there's one piece of information that would make everything fall into place."

"Well, of course there is. Talk me through all the fragments, maybe I can help."

"There seem to be four women at the center of it all – Nikki Keller, Kim Patterson, Lisa Silvan, and Susan Leske. I don't know what role they all play, but my gut tells me they've all been involved in harassing me. Who knows? Maybe they killed Tyler, or Michael, or the Peters."

"I heard they arrested Nikki's husband for killing the golf pro. His prints were on the club."

"Wow, I didn't know."

"Haven't talked to Skip yet, huh?"

"No, and I don't want to talk about it. At least, not without a drink in my hand. I guess it's possible Keller would have enough rage to lash out."

"Death was definitely from the beating. His head was smashed to pieces."

"So, I've got these four women who I can't tie to anything, but I feel are in it up to their pampered necks. I'm starting to wonder if the infidelity was the least of Nikki's crimes, and my investigation made her worry that I'd find the bigger sin."

"Like what?"

"I don't know. Drug running. Blackmail. Prostitution. What else can a group of rich women do for fun, once they've played a round of golf? Did you know the gun used to kill Michael Steuben was used in another killing, down in San Diego? What if they're assassins?"

Blanche's throaty laughter made Peri pull the phone away from her ear. "Assassinations R Us? I can see it now – a flip of the hair before pulling the trigger. Then, 'Oh, darn, I chipped a nail.' God, Peri, that's rich."

"Oh, stop. You said for me to talk it out, that it might give me an idea."

"You're right, you're right. No idea is stupid when you're brainstorming. I learned that in my sensitivity training seminar last year. So, let's go with these brain storms. What would support the argument for a group of assassins."

"Well, the fingerprint in the upstairs office matched the one Dani got for us at the park. The license plate on the car the mystery woman drove away is registered to Lisa Silvan. We don't have Lisa's fingerprints on file, but if Lisa was driving her own car, then those were her fingerprints."

"And what proves that she actually aimed a gun out of the upstairs office and shot at you?"

"Because her fingerprint was on the window pane."

"But no evidence of a gun."

"No, but…" Peri was silent for a moment. "Okay, maybe you're right. No assassins."

"You're right, Peri. You have a lot of trails that don't lead anywhere unless and until you can get fingerprint and DNA samples from those women, not to mention a weapon or two. Sorry."

"Yeah, I can't see that happening any time soon. Beebs, would you consider doing a little recon work?"

"I am not breaking into their homes to steal their hairbrushes."

"Are you trying to help me or not?"

“I am trying to help you – stay out of jail.”

“Thanks, you’ve done a great job.”

Blanche laughed. “Serving you proudly since high school.”

“I thought I was keeping you out of trouble in high school.”

“Let’s call it even. Hey – is it possible your four gals went to high school together? Maybe there’s some gossip to be had on one of those reunion websites.”

Peri considered this. “I’m pretty sure they all went to USC, but high school—that’s a possibility I hadn’t thought of. Let me peruse the great and powerful Internet and see what dirt I can dig up.”

“Okay, I’ll let you go. We on for dinner tomorrow?”

“You bet. Love ya mean it.”

She ended her call with Blanche and turned to her computer. Nikki was on Classmates, so she started there. Orange Lutheran High School was listed as her alma mater. Peri pulled up the Orange Lutheran class list for her year. As Blanche had suggested, all four women were friends in high school. Most did not enter much information in the profile, or post messages, except for Susan Leske.

Susan had filled out all of her information, including a long story of her life as an artist, a homemaker, and finally, a divorcee. Peri clicked on her bulletin board to find she had dozens of entries about where she was going to be, from vacations to events, including the Placentia Heritage Dinner and Dance.

“Wow, Susan, you really want me to find you easily, don’t you?” Peri said to the screen.

One of the bulletins talked about an upcoming high school reunion. “The Bettys will all be there,” Susan had written.

So it went back to high school, Peri thought.

She searched around the reunion site. People were RSVPing, asking if so-and-so was going to be there and posting pictures. There was a special box for students who had passed away, in memoriam. Peri noticed a boy’s name, Eddie Peralta, who was missing. She read a little further and saw that he had disappeared just prior to graduating and people were posting rumors about what had happened.

Realizing that she was off-task, Peri went through the photos that had been posted. Susan had uploaded pictures of them in high school. A quartet of girls posed on a lawn, mugging for the camera. Peri recognized the younger versions of everyone. Nikki and Lisa wore their cheerio uniforms and were in some kind of "Go Team" configuration. Susan was poured into tight jeans and an oversized tee, applauding her friends. Kim stood in the background, in shorts and a tank top, her expression blank.

The caption below said, "Nikki Simms, Lisa Scharf, Susie Keaton and Kim Hagen – Total Bettys, just ask Cher!"

The sudden meaning hit her like a Beverly Hills BMW.

"Clueless," she said aloud. "Good God."

The movie Clueless, released when these women were still in high school, popularized a lot of slang, one of the terms being 'betty', a term for a hot girl. Peri sat back and rubbed her temple. She felt depressed, to have chased this lead only to find out it meant nothing. They thought they were hot. End of story.

Two of the maiden names sounded familiar. She looked up her notes and saw the Peters' land was originally owned by Victoria Hagen, possibly a relative of Kim. Just as interesting, both Michael Steuben and William Quigley had appointments with a Mrs. Keaton on the day they were murdered. Could it have been Susan Leske using her maiden name?

She called Craig, though, just to give him one more piece and hope they could get this thing resolved.

"Hi, you've reached Detective Craig Daniels. Please leave a message."

Peri waited dutifully for the beep. As she did, she heard the garage door open. Her heart leapt in anticipation. She hadn't seen Skip since the dinner last night. She was brimming with things to say to him.

"Hey Craig, it's Peri. Listen, I found out what Bettys means. It was our group of women in high school—" She looked up as the door opened, expecting to see Skip.

It wasn't him.

"Um, Kim…" Peri's hand drifted to the bed, taking the cell phone with her. "What are you doing here?"

Kim's face was as smooth and placid as ever. She appeared calm, even serene, as she pointed a gun toward Peri.

"Put down the phone. You've meddled enough in my friends' lives," she said. "I think you need to go away now."

"I wasn't trying to meddle, Kim. I was hired for a job, which would have been neatly tied up and over with if you hadn't started messing with me."

"You shouldn't have taken the case. People deserve their privacy."

Peri was increasingly aware, by Kim's lack of emotion, that she was not the most stable woman in the room. Or possibly even the planet.

"Um, you're probably right, Kim. People deserve their privacy. I'll remember that next time."

Kim's lips curled in a tiny smile. "You won't need to remember it next time. Where we're going, you won't need anything at all."

She motioned with the gun. "Get up, Peri. You're going to be my chauffeur."

Peri rose from the bed, then tripped and fell forward onto her keyboard.

"Sorry," she said, pushing herself from the laptop, hoping that she was typing KIM as she did. The phone had fallen into the folds of the sheet, she tried to palm it as she got up. She hadn't ended her call with Craig, and she was hoping his voicemail was recording as much of her abduction as possible.

"Get up." Kim's voice was hard. "And give me the phone."

Peri handed it to her, then watched her throw it on the floor and step on it.

"Ah, man, I just got that phone."

"Don't worry. You don't need it anymore." She gestured for Peri to leave the room.

"Where are we going?"

Kim smiled again, with as little enthusiasm as before. She held out her car keys. "It's a Range Rover. I think you'll like it. You'll have to move the seat back."

The advice on what to do in this situation ran through Peri's mind while she tried to figure out a course of action. Getting into the car was high on the list of things not to do, but she wasn't certain how to accomplish that, given Kim's gun pointed at her, and the fact that the woman was nutty as a fruitcake.

Perhaps Kim was not as murderous as she seemed. Peri tested this idea. "That's a nice gun, Kim. Had it long?"

"Awhile."

Peri saw her look down at the weapon and stroke it with her left hand. *Not a good sign.*

"Take it out to the range much?"

She smiled fully, her eyes shining, showing a row of blindingly white teeth. "I get plenty of practice. You'll find I've never had any complaints on my work."

They walked outside toward the black Range Rover in the driveway, Peri in the lead. Kim shut the door, keeping the weapon hidden from plain sight, while Peri looked around for a way to use that to her advantage. The street was as silent as the grave; no neighbors were out to form a distraction. At last, there was no option except to get into the car or be shot.

Peri had been shot before, but not at close range and not so very alone. Kim could kill her and drive off, leaving no evidence and no witnesses.

She sunk into the driver's seat, Kim getting into the seat behind her. A hard, round object jabbed at the back of her head. She felt Kim's breath on her ear.

"If you're thinking about making any movements that would alert the police or throw me off guard, my little friend here will be pointed at the base of your skull for the entire drive. Did you know that's the one place you can be shot that will kill you instantly? You will be dead mid-breath."

"Aren't you afraid of dying when the car crashes?"

"I'm guessing your fear of death trumps my fear of accidents." The object moved away from Peri's head, although she still felt a residual ache. "Oh, and fasten your seatbelt, Dear. I wouldn't want to be pulled over for such a minor offense."

Peri started the engine, her body shaking so violently, she almost couldn't put the car into gear. She managed to back it down the driveway. As they passed Skip's house, she was glad to notice the door ajar. Kim hadn't shut it hard enough. Maybe someone would notice something was wrong.

"Where to?"

"Let's get to the 57, shall we? I think today's a good day to see the desert."

CHAPTER 35

The first thing Skip noticed as he pulled into the driveway was that his front door was slightly open. He got out and walked up the steps. The door gave when he pushed at it with his foot. Removing his gun from its holster, he slipped inside.

The living areas were empty, so he tiptoed down the hall toward the bedroom. He noticed a pile of debris on the floor. Picking it up, he recognized what it used to be – Peri's phone.

He fought the panic down and looked around the room. There was no blood, and no sign of a struggle, so she hadn't been able to fight. Her laptop was on the bed, along with her notes. Skip looked at the computer and saw KKIMMMNN on the screen, just as his phone began to vibrate.

"Skip, it's Craig. I just got a message from Peri. I think something's wrong. She cut off in the middle of her message, then I heard mumbling sounds, like two voices, then a crunch and silence. I think I heard her say 'Kim'."

"I'm at the house. She's not here and her phone has been smashed. Put out a BOLO on Kim Patterson. I'm going to see Patterson try to figure out where they're going."

Fortunately, the offices of Keller and Patterson were not far from his house, although it wouldn't have mattered anyway. Between the flashing light and the siren, Skip bullied his way at breakneck speed to reach State College Boulevard. He didn't park so much as he slid his car sideways to a stop in front of the building and ran up three flights of stairs to the development company's office.

"Where's Patterson?"

"In a meeting," the secretary said as Skip pushed through the doors.

John Patterson was seated at his desk, with Clinton Silvan on the other side. Clinton got up from his chair. "Detective, we're in a conference call with Tokyo."

Skip stepped to the desk and slammed his hand on the phone, disconnecting the call. "And I'm a detective whose girlfriend has been kidnapped by Kim Patterson."

"Kidnapped?" Clinton sounded stunned, but Skip noticed John's red-faced silence.

He turned to John. "Where would she take her?"

"How would I know?"

"You'd know because you know your wife, Patterson. Where would she dump a body?" As soon as the words came out of his mouth, Skip felt sick inside.

John gurgled like a drowning cartoon, but Clinton sat down again, and nodded his head. "The Palm Desert land. The parcel that the Peters owned."

"Why? What's so special about that parcel?"

"I don't know," Clinton replied, shooting a look at the senior partner. "I only know that John was intent on buying it. He said it was a present for Kim."

"He told me it was part of a shopping center your firm was developing."

"No, no that's not true."

Skip looked to John Patterson for an answer, but the beefy man had yet to form a word, much less an explanation. In his fear and impatience, the detective pushed Patterson's chair against the wall and grabbed his shirt. "Why does Kim need that land?"

John opened his mouth several times before squeaking an answer. "Family land. It was in the family."

In an instant, Skip knew why she needed it. "I need specific instructions to that parcel of land. Now."

Clinton jumped up and ran to the door. “Tanya, I need the file on the Peters property, as soon as possible.”

A few moments later, Tanya rushed into the office, followed by Craig Daniels.

Skip looked over the file. “Looks like this place is off Frank Sinatra and Bob Hope Drive.”

“Let’s roll,” Craig said

CHAPTER 36

The late afternoon sun was behind them as Peri made her way from the 57 Freeway to the I-10 toward the desert.

"I'm guessing you were the one who did all the killings." Peri thought a little light conversation might keep her mind off things.

Kim was apparently not in the mood. "You're driving awfully slow."

"I'm doing the speed limit. I'm not used to this car." Peri eased her foot on the gas and inched up toward seventy. "Why did you kill Michael?"

"Michael who?"

"My office landlord." Peri looked at her rearview mirror. She could see Kim, who now had a dour expression.

"That wasn't me. That was Susan."

"But I'm guessing she used your gun." She saw Kim hold her gun up and stroke it again.

"Hers was in the cleaners." Kim smiled at her own joke.

"But why? Because he could identify her?" Peri shook her head. "As if anyone would believe a country club gal would be involved in a shooting."

Kim pounded the door with her left fist. "He should have left it alone. Susan didn't want to kill him, but he wouldn't keep his mouth shut."

"And Susan shot my window out."

"You think you're so smart. Susan didn't shoot the window. Lisa did."

"Then who broke into my office and stole the memory card?"

Kim was silent for a few moments. "Susan."

"Did you kill Tyler?"

"He was ruining everything. Even when Nikki wanted to leave him, he kept pursuing her."

"Clever setup of Don Keller, using his golf club."

Peri looked at Kim again in the rearview mirror. This time, she smiled. "Yes. I figured we could kill Tyler and frame Don, which would get both of them out of the way."

A driver crossed over the lanes at the last minute, causing Peri to brake hard. For a moment, she feared Kim would shoot her, either accidentally or on purpose. Her body tightened against the possible pain and she heard herself put out a quick "save me Jesus" distress prayer. After she resumed cruising speed, Peri heard laughter in the back seat.

"You thought I was going to kill you."

"It was a possibility."

"And yet you kept driving. Why don't you scare?"

"I was scared, Kim. I still am. Someone paid me to do a job. For me, finishing the job is the honorable thing to do." She looked at Kim again, who seemed lost in thought.

"Yes, the honorable thing."

"You care about your friends, don't you, Kim?"

"Very much."

"You'd do anything for them."

"Of course."

"Their safety and happiness is all you want."

Kim's reverie seemed to have left. "It's all there is," she said, her voice raised.

Peri felt the muzzle of the gun against her head again.

"Now shut up and drive."

They drove past Banning and the last true vestige of civilization. Peri felt her stomach tighten with every mile as they passed through the San Bernadino and San Jacinto Mountains, the dry brush whipping by them. As the windmill farm in the San

Gorgonio Pass came into view, she thought she might have to pull over and throw up. No one would know where to look for her. She wasn't even sure if she managed to type Kim's name on the computer.

No body, no witness, no weapon.

She now officially regretted getting her P.I. license.

A few miles off the I-10 and Ramon Road was a barren piece of land, in the middle of other barren pieces of land. Small stakes with red flags were the only markers to tell one parcel from another. There were no other distinguishing characteristics. As she got closer, Peri saw a small mobile home on the back of the property, its color so faded it blended in with the scenery.

"Pull over here," Kim said.

Peri started shaking again.

"Get out." Kim's voice was flat and hard again, and Peri wondered if she'd be able to walk on legs that felt like noodles.

Even in early October, the heat was overwhelming, sucking Peri's breath out as soon as she stepped from the car. She wobbled, nearly fell, but held herself upright at last.

"I don't understand what you hope to accomplish by killing me," she said. "I ended the investigation, Don paid me, I didn't deliver the evidence, it's over."

"Yes, but you know. You know what Nikki was doing."

"But why would I tell anyone? The only person who cared was Don."

Kim seemed to be finished with the subject. "Walk."

Peri walked forward, glancing back at her captor. "Are you going to kill the entire Placentia Police force too?"

Kim stopped. "Why would I kill them?"

"You've done your homework on me." Peri turned and faced her. "You know I date a detective. When I started being threatened, I went to the police. I gave them every piece of evidence I had gathered about Nikki Keller."

The look on Kim's face was one of confused anger. While she processed the information, Peri did the only thing she could.

She jumped on Kim.

A gunshot exploded next to her ear, but she kept pinning Kim to the ground, despite the little brunette's attempt to wiggle away from her. Peri grabbed her wrists and held them tightly. Kim rewarded her by reaching up and biting her shoulder. Words, curses, and guttural noises came from Peri's mouth without her knowledge.

"Ow, you whore." She pulled away from Kim's teeth and punched her, hard.

Kim moaned and went limp. Peri looked around for the gun; it was about two feet from her left hand. Just as she reached for it, her opponent awoke and tried to kick her. She managed to nail Peri's right shin multiple times until Peri was able to step on her ankles and stop the motion. Kim thrashed wildly, screaming, so Peri headbutted her, as hard as she could.

Brilliant pain and stars immediately entered Peri's head. She groaned and tried to regain her vision and stay conscious. While Kim was still dazed, Peri rolled off and grabbed the gun, then scooted away from her and stood up, wobbling. She trained the gun on Kim while she rubbed her forehead with her left hand.

"Oh my god, that hurt." She watched Kim push herself to a sitting position. "You little crazy people are strong."

Kim held her head and looked at Peri, her expression a childish pout. "Now what are you going to do? I'm not helping you get out of here. You'll have to shoot me to get me in the car."

"You're mean, too." Peri glanced around, trying to think of how to motivate her prisoner. "Why did you take me out here? I'm assuming this is the Peters property. Is this where the rest of the bodies are buried?"

"It's not their property. It's my property." She gave Peri a satisfied smile. "My family shouldn't have sold it. Grandma wanted me to have it."

"I'm assuming you hid Mendoza and Hughes on the property. But why not Quigley and the Peters?"

"Quigley was an idiot. I didn't get a clean shot, and he ran. I wasn't going to ruin my new Manolos chasing him." Kim yawned, as if this was tiresome for her. "And I didn't kill the Peters."

Peri believed her. "Are there more bodies?"

"A few. People shouldn't be so mean."

"To your friends?"

"Your friends are all you have." Kim's voice returned to its natural indolence.

Peri heard sirens. She wasn't much of a praying woman, but she prayed they'd come closer. Her prayers were answered.

She watched two Riverside County Sheriff's cars, Craig's sedan and Skip's SUV grind to a stop. There was a lot of shouting that sounded like, "Drop the weapon" and "Put your hands in the air" and then she watched Skip waving his hands before she realized she was the one they were shouting at. She held her hands in the air, gun pointed upward.

"No, it's okay, she's the hostage," Skip said as an officer reached up and took the weapon from her.

She thought about trying to explain, but decided she'd better wait until everyone had calmed down. There was a momentary bit of confusion as Skip and Craig Daniels straightened it all out with the deputies. At last, everyone's roles were clear and Kim Patterson was handcuffed.

Skip turned and embraced Peri. Feeling his arms around her was the most delicious sensation she had ever known. Her head still swam from knocking it against Kim's, and she rocked against him.

"Are you okay?"

She looked up at him. "I guess I shouldn't have headbutted her."

"Peri, I'm so glad you're all right."

"It was all about friendship. When the group found out I was tailing Nikki, they tried to frighten me off. When Michael recognized Susan as the woman who was looking at the second-story offices, Susan shot him. Kim killed Tyler Garvey, but that was pure rage."

Skip nodded. "Tyler wanted Nikki to leave her husband. Kim knew it would ruin her."

"Someone needs to look into this parcel." Peri gestured toward the vacant lot. "I'm pretty sure there's more than one body buried here."

A blue sedan pulled up, kicking a swirl of dust. John Patterson pulled himself out of the car and limped up toward the group.

"So that's what this parcel was all about," Craig said. "It was their dumping ground. I guess murdering the owners was just part of the job."

"But she didn't kill Bob and Dottie." Peri looked at John Patterson. "Did she, John?"

Everyone turned to look at him.

"You were the one who tried to purchase the parcel from the Peters. How else would you know about their big orange cat? When they declined your offer, you brought them a present. Fancy schmancy coffee." Peri was aware of tears on her cheeks. "They may not have been young, but they deserved to live to the end of their days."

Patterson was crying, too. "I didn't mean to kill them. I thought Bob would have a heart attack. Dottie doesn't even drink coffee. Bob was supposed to have a heart attack, a small one, and then they wouldn't be able to get out to the desert and I could offer them enough money to get the land back for her. She's my wife. I love her. I'd do anything for her."

The deputies took another pair of cuffs and put him in a patrol car.

Peri looked around and saw them loading Kim into the other car. She remembered the Classmates reunion page. "Kim – will we find Eddie Peralta here?"

A hardness like concrete crossed Kim's face. "He shouldn't have done that to me."

The squad cars drove away with their passengers to be processed.

"Nikki told me what happened," Skip said, putting his arm around Peri's waist. "Eddie raped Kim, attacked her. The girls lured him out here and killed him. I think it was the start of a cycle for the four women. If one of them was threatened, the rest of them took care of the problem."

"Yeah, I'll bet this whole property is covered in 'problems' they buried," Craig Daniels said. He patted Skip on the shoulder while he squeezed Peri's hand. "Peri, so glad you're safe. Why don't you get her back home? I'll wait for Jason."

Peri watched Craig walk back to his sedan, talking on his cell phone as he went. She turned to face Skip. "Oh, Skipper, I've been so miserable." Tears formed and fell as she spoke. "I'm so sorry about the snooping. I'm sorry I've lost your trust. I'm sorry if, if you can't do this anymore, if you can't love a P.I. the way you loved a housecleaner. I love you so fiercely it's breaking my heart—"

"Shut up, just shut up." Skip wrapped his arms around her and kissed her. "I'm glad you're safe."

"If I hadn't heard Kim on the tape threatening me, I wouldn't have snooped, but I needed to know how to stop her and no one was telling me anything."

"Oh, Doll, why didn't you tell me about the threats?"

"Because I thought we'd just fight about my safety."

"We would." He kissed her head. "But I still want you to tell me. I love you. I worry. I have to learn to be okay with that. Now I have to – we have to – find a way to respect each other's boundaries when it comes to work information."

They walked back to his SUV, Peri leaning on him for support. He helped her into the car and then got in and started the drive home.

Peri relaxed into the seat. “When you didn’t come home last night, I didn’t know what to think.”

“Yeah, funny thing happened. I was finished with the scene when I got a phone call from Ella. Jorge’s run off and out of control, and she doesn’t know where to turn. So I go over to help, and it seems she was lying. Jorge’s just out with his friends. Ella told him she and I had a date tonight and to go ahead and stay out late. By the time the hoopla was over, I just went back to my office and sacked out on the couch.”

“Oh, Skipper.” Peri shook her head. “Ella’s a nice woman, who’s tired of being alone. You’re Placentia’s Most Eligible Bachelor, at least according to the newspaper. She would like to date you, maybe even marry you.” She smiled. “Give you that son you’ve always wanted.”

“But she knows I’m with you.”

“For a lot of women, a girlfriend isn’t as important as a wife, territory-wise. If he doesn’t have a ring on him, he’s fair game.”

“But I never gave her any encouragement.”

Peri started laughing. “I’m sorry, I can’t help it. You are such a good read with people, but you’re blind as a bat when it comes to yourself. All you had to do was stand still and it encouraged her.”

The sun burned the last of its rays, red and sinking, into the horizon. Skip turned on the headlights and eased the black SUZ down the I-10, back toward Placentia.

“Doll, when you say I’m blind about myself, does that include when we met?”

Peri thought about their first meeting. Her first housecleaning job was with an organization who contracted with businesses, and city buildings. She’d been scheduled to clean the Placentia Police Station, along with the adjoining City Hall, for a couple of weeks. But when she saw Skip Carlton, broad-shouldered and beautiful, she pulled every string possible to remain on that duty as long as she could.

There was just enough office chatter to inform her about the young police officer. He had been divorced for a year, worked constantly, and was trying to get his Detective's Shield. She didn't cross the line to stalker territory, but she knew his work shift and made certain she cleaned the office on those nights.

Every evening, she got to walk into his office and empty his trash. Every evening allowed her one or two words of the "How are you" variety. Those words branched into a few more about the weather, the latest news, the upcoming weekend or holiday.

One day, she reached for his waste basket and saw him look at her. His dark brown eyes were mostly unreadable, but they were a little wider than normal, and a smile hovered around his lips.

"This might be my last week here," she told him.

He frowned. "Why?"

"Because you might find it awkward to ask the housecleaning crew out for a cup of coffee." She smiled.

"No, I wouldn't." He turned back to his paperwork, then added. "Want to go out for a cup of coffee?"

She looked at him and smiled. "No, Skipper, we met by complete accident."

CHAPTER 37

"Walking into this place is like going to heaven," Peri said as she entered her front door. "Look, there's my furniture." She pointed as she walked. "And there's my moose collection."

The rest of the house got the same kind of introduction. "Look there's my TV", "look there's my bookshelves", "look there's my refrigerator."

Skip got a kiss in every room, so he didn't complain.

"I'm just so happy to be back."

Soft feet tapped across her wood floor. Mr. Mustard greeted her in the manner of all cats who feel like they've been snubbed. He waltzed into the room, turned his tail to her and waltzed out.

"Oh, Mr. Mustard, I'm even glad to see you. I think I have a nice new home for you."

She went into the laundry room to see if he had food and got a surprise. Mr. Mustard's bowls sat on a placemat, with a framed picture of Dean Martin to the right. She started laughing.

"What's so funny?" Benny's voice startled her.

"Hey, Ben. I just didn't know that Mr. Mustard liked company when he ate."

"Matt Helm. His name is Matt Helm."

"Well, who knows what his name will be when the Phil and Nancy pick him up."

Benny pouted, so she added, "Maybe they'll let you come over and play."

Skip stuck his head in the doorway. "Want to go to dinner?"

"Sure," Benny said.

Peri smiled. “I would, too. I’ll call Blanche and see if any of the Debussy’s can make it.”

Thirty minutes later they were sitting down at a large table in Buca di Beppo. Their waiter was a slight young man who spoke very quickly.

“CanIgetyousomethingfromthebar?”

“Bar?” Peri replied. “Yes, I’ll have a Grey Goose dirty martini, four olives.”

Skip and Benny gave their orders and the waiter disappeared.

“Thank you, Benny,” Peri said. “For watching my place while I had to be away. And for chauffeuring me around when I needed it. I appreciate it.”

Benny smiled. “It was hard work, but you need more Dean Martin music.”

“I’ll consider that.”

Skip nodded to his right. “Look who’s here.”

Peri looked towards Skip’s nod. At a table in the next room, Phil and Nancy Nickles were having dinner.

“I’ll be right back,” she said.

Phil saw her approaching the table. “Peri, how nice to see you.”

“I saw you two over here and just had to say hello. How are you, Nancy?”

“Fine, thank you. Phil and I were just talking about that cat of yours. Is he still available?”

“Oh, yes, very available, but I have an odd request. I have a friend, that is, I have an acquaintance, I mean, there’s a man who’s been taking care of the cat and he can’t keep him in his home, but he’d like to be able to visit the cat from time to time. It’s not a deal breaker, but would that be a problem?”

“Oh, no, not at all,” Phil said.

“He’s over there, having dinner with us. Would you like to meet him?”

“Certainly,” Nancy replied.

Peri motioned Benny over. He shuffled to the table, slightly blushing. “Benny, this is Phil and Nancy Nickles. They’re going to give Mr. Mustard a nice new home, but they said you could visit.”

“Matt Helm, Miss Peri. His name is Matt Helm.”

She smiled at the couple. “In my absence, Benny rechristened the cat after a favorite Dean Martin character.”

“You like Dean Martin? So do we.” Phil sounded delighted.

Benny brightened. “You do? I’ve seen all his movies. And I have some of his stuff. I’ve got the ashtray he used in Some Came Running.”

“Wow. We’re planning a trip to Steubenville next June.”

The little man gasped. “Steubenville. I’ve only dreamed of going.”

“Let me know when you’re ready for him, and I’ll drop Mr. – Matt Helm at your house,” Peri told them.

She returned to Skip, while Benny talked with his new friends about all things Dino.

“I think our little Benny has found a new home with his own kind,” she told him. “Dean Martin fans.”

“So, Doll, now that the kids are out of the house, should we have that talk about your line of work?”

The waiter presented them with their drinks, so Peri took a nice big, time-stalling sip of hers.

“Okay, I was never so scared in my life as when I was walking across that dirt with Kim’s gun at my back. That woman’s certifiable. I might have, for a brief instant, regretted my career change.”

“But?”

“But seriously, Skip, most private investigators live dull, normal lives. I mean, how many times do you run into a whack-job who protects her friends by killing their enemies? I’ve done a couple dozen surveillance jobs now without any brouhaha.”

"I understand statistically, but percentages don't mean a thing when I'm trying to chase down that whack-job and praying she hasn't already killed you."

Peri took Skip's hand. "I love you, Skipper."

"Get a room," Blanche said as she arrived at the table.

Paul was behind her, so Skip and Peri rose and exchanged hugs with the couple. They all sat down and studied the menus. Skip looked over at Benny, who was still chatting with the Nickles.

"What do you think Benny wants?"

"Anything with marinara sauce," Peri said.

The restaurant served family style portions, so they ordered dishes to share, including a bowl of spaghetti and meatballs for Ben.

"So, I hear you had some excitement," Paul said.

"You could say that," Peri replied.

"Geez, getting your window shot out like that, must've been scary."

Skip looked at Peri, who looked at Blanche.

"That's right, you haven't heard the latest," Skip said.

Peri tried to spin her day toward a G-rating. "So, right after I talked to you, Kim Patterson came to see me. Who knew she was a psycho killer? We took a little trip to Palm Desert, where she usually buries her bodies, but I tackled her and took her gun away, and then Skip and the Riverside Sheriff Department showed up." She took another sip of her drink. "No biggie."

"Wow," Paul said. "That is exciting."

Blanche was a little more vocal. "Dear God, Peri, get out of this business. Skip, talk to her."

"Preaching to the choir, Beebs," he told her.

"Oh, please," Peri told them. "When I'm not being chased by angry spouses and whack-jobs, I make good money for relatively little effort. And, really, how many times do I have to deal with crazy people?"

Benny rushed up to the table. "Miss Peri, the Nickles want to take me to Steubenville next June. Can you watch Matt Helm while we're gone?"

She looked at the three people looking back at her.

"Okay, not counting that."

THE END

Acknowledgments

The author would like to acknowledge how much more frightened she is of releasing her second mystery than she ever was of publishing her first. All she can think about is Christopher Cross and the sophomore jinx.

That being said, there are a couple of people who must be thanked for ironing out the kinks in this story. They're friends of mine from the Southern California Writers Conference, and they are the best beta readers I could have asked for.

Rick Ochocki is one of the nicest, most positive writers I've ever met. His critique of my manuscript gave me great feedback about what was wrong, but in such a gentle and constructive way, it was like being smacked with a fluffy mitten.

Jennifer Carlevatti's mitten was not as soft as Rick's but her notes were equally good and different, without being contradictory. Not only did she read my manuscript and offer her opinion, she printed it out and did line edits.

Between these two friends, I couldn't have asked for more.

I'd also like to thank the city of Placentia, if that can be done. Although my characters and events are pure fiction, and even some places have been "tweaked" a little to fit the story, the heart of my mysteries is that little town in north Orange County where I've lived since 1984.

Of course, I must finally thank my husband for his unending patience with a wife who often spends too much time in her fictional world and not enough time cooking dinner. Love you, Honey.

About the Author

Gayle Carline is a typical Californian, meaning that she was born somewhere else. She moved to Orange County from Illinois in 1978, and landed in Placentia a few years later.

Her husband, Dale, bought her a laptop for Christmas in 1999 because she wanted to write. A year after that, he gave her horseback riding lessons. When she bought her first horse, she finally started writing.

Gayle soon became a regular contributor to Riding Magazine, and in March, 2005, she began writing a humor column for her local newspaper, the Placentia News-Times. Every week, she entertains readers with stories of her life with Dale and their son, Marcus.

Believing that she should experience reincarnation while she is still alive, Gayle has been a software engineer, a dancer, and even a flying angel for the Crystal Cathedral's Glory of Christmas.

In her spare time, Gayle likes to sit down with friends and laugh over a glass of wine. And maybe plan a little murder and mayhem.

For more merriment, visit her at **http://www.gaylecarline.com**.

www.ingramcontent.com/pod-product-compliance
Lightning Source LLC
Chambersburg PA
CBHW030518310726
48979CB00010B/1722/J

* 9 7 8 1 9 4 3 6 5 4 1 9 2 *